LEPIDUS THE CENTURION

This is a volume in the Arno Press collection

LOST RACE
AND
ADULT FANTASY FICTION

Advisory Editors
R. Reginald
Douglas Menville

See last pages of this volume for a complete list of titles.

LEPIDUS
THE
CENTURION

EDWIN LESTER ARNOLD

ARNO PRESS
A New York Times Company
New York • 1978

Editorial Supervision: MARIE STARECK

Reprint Edition 1978 by Arno Press Inc.

Reprinted from a copy in The Library of
    the University of California, Riverside

LOST RACE AND ADULT FANTASY FICTION
ISBN for complete set: 0-405-10950-4
See last pages of this volume for titles.

Manufactured in the United States of America

Library of Congress Cataloging in Publication Data

Arnold, Edwin Lester Linden, d. 1935.
    Lepidus the centurion.

    (Lost race and adult fantasy fiction)
    Reprint of the 1901 ed. published by T. Y Crowell,
New York.
    I. Title. II. Series.
PZ3.A753Le 1978 [PR6001.B775]   823'.8   77-84196
ISBN 0-405-10954-7

LEPIDUS
THE
CENTURION

"STOP, STOP, I COMMAND YOU!"—Page 276.

LEPIDUS
THE
CENTURION

A Roman of To-day

By

EDWIN LESTER ARNOLD

Author of "Phra the Phœnician," etc.

New York
THOMAS Y. CROWELL & CO.
PUBLISHERS

Copyright, 1901, by
THOMAS Y. CROWELL & CO.

CONTENTS

CHAPTER	PAGE
I. I EXHUME MYSELF	1
II. THE SLEEPER AWAKENED	15
III. —AND REHABILITATED	31
IV. SOME DINNER AND AN ALARM	41
V. THE CENTURION PLAYS CENTAUR	57
VI. AN INTERRUPTED EXPLANATION	76
VII. THE ROMAN REFLECTS	87
VIII. SHE COMES	113
IX. THE OLD LOVE AND THE NEW	128
X. A CHAPTER OF ACCIDENTS	136
XI. A STRANGE DISCOVERY	150
XII. WE PICNIC WITH OUR ANCESTORS	165
XIII. LOVE, THE IMMORTAL	177
XIV. THE HERO TURNS CYNIC	197
XV. LEPIDUS PHILOSOPHISES	224
XVI. SOME REPROACHES AND A PROPOSAL	240
XVII. SO AS BY FIRE	250
XVIII. THE LAST RESORT	266
XIX. "SPOILS TO THE VICTOR; DEATH TO THE VANQUISHED"	281

Lepidus *the* Centurion

CHAPTER I

I EXHUME MYSELF

THERE could be no doubt about it: I, Louis Allanby, Squire and J.P., young, healthy, in full possession of all those faculties with which it had pleased Providence to bless me at my birth, and in the enjoyment of a rent roll exceeding even in these hard times three thousand per annum, was unequivocally bored!

I was bored to death of sleek sufficiency that afternoon on which this narrative begins. I was sick of the good fellowship of those laughing men and women who drank my wine, and rode my horses back yonder at the Manor House; there was no pride in my wide acres, no pleasure in the stream that ran speckled with summer sunshine through the park; my rods were idle, I hated my guns—if I had only been a little more vicious there might have been fun in life for me, and if I had been virtuous there might have been contentment. But I was a blank, a cipher, a healthy living nonentity, and in gloomy knowledge of the fact I had strolled out into the pine woods to sulk over my good fortune that pleasant summer afternoon.

Had I been a fool, life might have been pleasanter, for an empty head and heart are easily filled, but I was not absolutely that. At school "young Allanby" was branded as the cleverest—and laziest—fellow in his class. At college he broke the hearts of two well-meaning tutors, and then astounded friends and enemies alike by plunging red-hot one day from a rat hunt into the sacred quiet of the examination hall and emerging with a creditable degree!

And thus it had been with me always; wasting my opportunities so assiduously, that my well wishers could but thank Providence my stomach would never have to rely on my head for sustenance; and even my dear widowed mother sighed as she put away in lavender all the womanly ambitions she had had for me, and tried to console herself with the vague reflection that if I failed in everything else, at least I might make a creditable country bumpkin.

Amongst my studies at college, classics had always interested me. In my dullest moments the rhetoric of those fine old Romans who wrote for a young world with the ardour of youth rarely failed somehow to stir a current in my stagnant blood, and thus it was that on the afternoon in question, being especially dull, I had wandered through the dusty library at the Manor, and brought out the topmost volume of a pile someone had thrown out from the shelves in a hasty quest. It was not much of a book to look at, but as it was quite certain to bore me as efficiently as any other of its fellow thousands, I strolled away with it; down over the tennis-courts, where the peach-cheeked girls were playing tennis; down where, at the garden bottom, the stream widened out into a lake, dotted with water-lilies and shadowed by fringing trees, and thence sauntering along its rim, through meadow-sweet and yellow water flags, till the reedy mere narrowed again, and crossing the neck by a rustic bridge, I turned up into the firs on the hillside.

Here was comparative peace. The ridiculous laughter of those strawberry-sucking jades was lost in the distance; the glitter of the pool came up only here and there in gold spangles into this welcome gloom, the brown pine needles were soft under foot, the sigh of the wind in the resinous boughs overhead sounded to me like the monotonous pulse of my life, and with a growl of discontent at all things and all men, I pulled that book from my pocket and dipped into its crabbed pages.

Bah! it was the stupidest stuff in a hundred stupid books I had sampled that week. The classic fool, where I opened on him, was declaring life to be splendid and extensive, passing on and on while each continuous soul, broadening and brightening some distant goal, wore out as it went through the ages many bodies—the giddiest rubbish that was ever handed down by time to prove that some day, as the circles of existence were completed, those who lived when that classic dreamer penned his nonsense in ancient Rome would be ripe again—would be due each ancient spirit to inhabit once more a human form and tread this earth anew—what nonsense! I did not even try to understand the writer closely, I dimly gathered what he meant by a glance at his first half-dozen headings, then, for comment, shut his ancient leather covers with a snap, and flung him into a bush for stoats and weasels to study at their leisure.

And yet there was a certain dreamy pleasantness in the idea. One must believe something, I idly speculated as I leant against a rock and stared at the freckled sunshine through the leaves—and why not this? Such a scheme would give a man a chance to amend his misdeeds in new lives, pay his debts and collect his rents, moral and spiritual. Even if that mildewed old heathen in the gorse bush at my feet had not lighted on the absolute truth, yet he might have been on the trail of it. Even I myself had often thought I felt at times something of that which I had never experienced in fact, and had knowledge somewhere in my remotest nature of things of which I had not had experience; why should not all this be the dim evidence of some such scheme as that ancient writer had concocted?

I brooded over it for an hour or so, not in truth making much of the fancy, and then sauntered on again, hands in pockets, whistling to my idleness, until, half way round the steep forest knoll overlooking the valley, and deep in shadowy pine and juniper, a sprightly little squirrel caught my eye, and then another. They were love making, poor beasts, and I smiled to see their ardour. The little lady in russet was dodging round and round a tree stem, now head up, now tail, and the gentleman after her, his bead eyes glittering with excitement. Round and round, to and fro, in splendid merriment and fun, up and down, round and round the branches, till at last the breathless pursued was fairly " cornered "—driven in a careless moment to the end of a broken limb, and retreat cut off behind! Surely he had her now. I heard him squeak with exultation, and a ripple of joy seemed to run up his bushy tail, but in a twinkling the lady had thrown herself off into the air, had lit safely on the moss twenty feet below, had rushed to a fallen pine tree, and spinning round and round its prostrate stem half-a-dozen times in sheer exuberance of fun and spirit, went off into the distant undergrowth with a long start, and her wooer hot in pursuit again.

But for those little beasts, this book might never have been written. I walked over to the broken pine, a fine stem fallen only a night or two before, and you know how such a one lies? The green head, crushed by its descent, rested, a confused mass, in the shadow of the nearest trees; the red bole, straight as an arrow, gleamed in the slanting sunshine coming through the gap above left by its fall, and beyond, the great shield of root-tangled turf and gravel stood upright over the broad scar of earth it had left exposed. Going round behind that ragged buttress I kicked the loose new rubble idly with my foot, and as I did so, noticed a squared corner of stone amongst the rest. The angles were clear and sharp, and my first idea was to stoop and pick it up, but it would not come. I cleared a little more sand and rubbish away with a boot tip, thinking nothing of the find as yet, and then saw it was not a broken brick or such like lying before me, but the corner of an earth-fast flag stone.

This began to be interesting, and I stood still a minute or two, half amused and half surprised. There certainly had been an ancient settlement hereabouts, I told myself, though never as far as we knew upon this hill, and in the Manor hall were two glass cases of red Roman pottery dug up from a field half-a-mile down the stream. But this hill had always been unexplored and silent—sacred to shadows and sleep; how could this well-trimmed flagstone, newly laid bare, have come here, and were there more like it? I set to work diligently, with a flat bit of stone for spade, and, as the rubble was all loose, and the slab lay flat and shallow, soon defined its shape, and, what was more, to my increasing wonder discovered a bronze ring at the further edge, green with age, but sound and perfect still. It was like the cover of a well, and when I had given my find a final brush down with a wisp of bracken leaves, I stood perspiring and staring at it with silent interest—yes, the first genuine interest that had stirred my stagnant pulses for many weeks.

Then it goes without saying, I wanted to see what was below; but though, taking off my coat, I tugged at that bronze ring until my muscles ached, it would not move. So strategy had to come to the aid of main strength, and fetching a stout fir branch from the neighbouring heap, one end was pushed in under the flag-stone, and leaning all my weight upon the lever, after a breathless moment or two, with a strange thrill of delight and fascination, I saw the soil gape, a black crack start and fly round the dusty square of the block, and directly afterwards the loosened stone rose on its rear as I worked at it—up until it was perpendicular, and then a final push sent it floundering over on its bronze-ringed back in a cloud of dust, and left me master of whatever lay hidden down underneath.

A square, deep hole, black as midnight, lay before me, whence rose the quaintest, the most antique of smells, as I stood gaping over it. I have often thought there is more in the philosophy of scents than we yet recognise—that maybe the way to our souls through our derided noses is as short as any other—but, anyhow, that quaint aroma coming up from the black void fascinated me. It was not wicked, nor unpleasant, yet somehow that impalpable taint, that breath of long silence and suspension sent my blood to my head, and the courage out of my knees for a moment, as though a voice had spoken, or I had seen some sight of terror down in that black patch before me. Fortunately no one witnessed my momentary weakness; the repose of the afternoon woods was all around, the curtain of the shadows hid that little arena from all outsiders, and the now drooping sun began to pour his rays right across the mouth of the hollow.

I looked again, and by the yellow gleam saw the hole was not so deep as had seemed at first—it was scarcely deeper than my own six feet of height, with a broad step at the bottom, and a show of sandy floor beyond—why, if that was all, there was nothing so dreadful about the matter; and the smell, too, had all but passed away. Probing the bottom with my fir pole, and finding it as it looked, firm and substantial, I hesitated a minute, then boldly dropped through the opening on to the smooth floor below.

Black darkness again for a minute or two to my unaccustomed eyes, with an awe-inspiring silence! Then, as I came to see better, slowly four narrow walls built themselves up out of the shadows, walls of rough strange masonry with courses of red tiles showing dimly round them, plain, unsmoothed, rising from a clean-swept sandy base, and across that floor, right in the mid of the little underground chamber, there rose to my strengthening vision from the gloom an oblong block of masonry, island-like in the shadows, and my heart beat a trifle faster again as I noticed there was something grey, indefinite and mysterious stretched out upon it! I stood for a moment flat against the entrance wall, a white butterfly hovering, I remember, daintily in the golden gleam just overhead, then slowly and stealthily sidled into the chamber with a tumultuous rush of feelings in my heart out of all proportion to the necessities of the case.

By the great Jove, there *was* something on that central bier, something human and long, its shape only dimly shown by sad sage-coloured wrappings that seemed to be falling to pieces, so old they were, even as I looked. It was a man for certain, perfect in outline, now that I could see his geography, and stepping over to the pile, I picked up a corner of the dusty cloth covering his face, and drew it gently off. It was not, as might have been expected, only the bare framework of extinct humanity lying there so still beneath it, but the head and shoulders of a being marvellously preserved, singularly and extraordinarily life-like. I gazed with amazement at the dim outline of those features for a space, then, urged I know not by what, pulled down the dusty rags again wherewith he was covered, inch by inch, until he was unshrouded to his knees—a well-built supple fellow in ancient clothes, about my height and make—it was marvellous to see him lie there so still

I EXHUME MYSELF

and perfect, and I eyed him over while a cool, resinous, refreshing breath from the pine trees outside came down into our den, and a square patch of sunlight crept up the bier lying in a pool of brightness upon his feet—I looked him up and down, and the third time could almost have sworn that one of his skyward pointing toes twitched under its dusty coverings. An absurd idea! It was, of course, but the wavering reflection of a pine branch against the blue sky, or a freak of my excited fancy, and to give my nerves time to cool, I fell to exploring the crypt as well as might be in the uncertain light.

The place was absolutely bare and void of interest, except on the wall farthest from the entrance. There, directly in a line with the recumbent figure's head was a tablet, and on it, to my delight, an inscription. Most lovingly those faded letters were dusted with a handkerchief, and fingered over until they came out with something of their pristine freshness.

"Marcus Lepidus, the Centurion," I translated to myself, "is Asleep; Tread Lightly!"

Asleep! I should think so, but how long had he slept? There was no date, not the slightest other sign or clue. Still it was something to know yonder old fellow was a Roman, and this a Roman-British tomb into which I had blundered so strangely.

What a good paper it would make for an antiquarian journal, and how those beflannelled tennis players would stare when the story was told to them at dinner-time!

I went over to my friend Lepidus again and gazed at him with folded arms and silent awe. It is not every day you come on such a page as this from the book of the Old World, and my classic reading was still fresh upon me. What a strange unkempt England it must have been to which this olive-skinned exile came! Was it the galleys that brought him?—two weeks of sour black bread and water as the peaked prow of the trireme plunged slowly through the black waters of Armorica. Or was it overland, over the green flats beyond Albi, round under the knees of the Southern sloping Alps, and so to Gaul and the British seas? There were no refreshment rooms at Anderida when *this* traveller landed you may take it for certain, and walled Camulodunum fringed with marshes, Deva on the Northern estuary, Eboracum itself, and all those other city-keeps where the Roman eagle lorded it over interminable barbarian wastes—oh, for an hour's remembrance of the things those tight-shut eyes had seen! Poor Lepidus—I laid my hand across his face sympathetically, then snatched it away again, for I could have sworn the lid my finger touched had winked.

I EXHUME MYSELF

It was too foolish, he was dead—dead for certain; and yet as I bent over him a vague unreasonable dread rose within me. I stared and frowned at that dim, handsome, dusty face, then calling my pride to aid—and, thank God, that at least has never yet failed me—put a hand again lightly upon his chest. Poor heart, it was still enough, not a flutter now to tell how it must have pulsed and jumped once on a time. Think how it ran riot in its first battle, think how it jumped when the peach-cheeked Amymone, the proud, the unbending, on her way to the baths one day slipped a flower and her own warm fingers for a second into the Centurion's hand! It was still enough now, still as still could be, ah!——

Was I mad? was the warm, stagnant air of the place turning my brain? Wondering and smiling to myself like that, I had kept a hand upon the Roman bosom where it was impossible, incredible that a spark of life could be after all this lapse of time, and yet either all my faculties were false or something *did* move within there. Down in that hollow chest where the soldier's heart had once been, under the very palm of my hand, as I speculated on his remote emotions there came a thrill, a swift rapid pulse for a moment, then a pause; and then clear, unmistakable, below my fingers a throb or two!

It would have turned anyone's head. It turned

mine. Away to the wall I sprang, then sidled to the shaft, copper coloured now with the last rays of the setting sun: put my toe into a crevice, and vaulted fairly out again into the fresh clean air as though invisible springs had sent me aloft. The big flagstone I had coolness enough to replace—it did not fit so well this time; there was an air space all the way round—and then set off, dusty, bewildered, and —must I say it?—fairly frightened out of my philosophy, down the hill, across the meadows, and so home just as the dressing bell was ringing for dinner, and the odour of the soup was steaming hallwards from the kitchens.

CHAPTER II

THE SLEEPER AWAKENED

THE evening meal was interminably long that night. I was barely civil to our guests, who set my strung nerves jarring with their chatter, their interminable small talk, their village gossip, their recounting of scores at tennis—how could I take them into my confidence, or tell them the wonderful story that was seething in my mind? My dear good mother saw my absent-mindedness and pallor, and as I never have grown or shall grow out of boyhood to her, she came into my room in her dressing-gown after I was in bed, and administered two pills to me—bless her kindly heart!—two of those pungent family pills whereof she alone knows the prescription, though I and her friends understand the efficacy. It was not medicine I wanted, but sympathy. I sat up with my chin between my knees, wondering, while she gently lectured me on the laws of digestion and sociability, whether I could trust her with my secret. But though all the sympathy was there, how could I expect that dear prosaic lady to rise to a tale of wild imagination, a narrative which I, in the full fever of it, could scarcely believe? No, I kept my lips shut, and meekly promising to be more careful of my diet, and not to smoke quite so much in future, took my pills in silence, and let her turn out the lights without an idea she had not solved my malady.

For an hour I tossed to and fro, while every shadow in the room shaped itself into the likeness of a gaunt, dusty Roman face, and when I eventually dropped off to sleep it was with the firm determination of having that vault hermetically sealed up on the morrow, and the biggest sapling fir on the estate planted on top of it.

And when I woke up the next morning, I found myself equally resolved that when breakfast was over I would go and see that wonderful thing again. Yesterday I was out of sorts. The dear mother was right, I had been bilious and silly; my own irregular pulses had filled me with ridiculous imaginings, but now, what with the broad seven o'clock sunshine streaming into my room, and those blessed pills—either it was they or the confidence of another day which made me feel physically limp but morally courageous—clearing mind and body simultaneously—yes, I would certainly go and see the Centurion again—smoke a cigar over that poor brown

THE SLEEPER AWAKENED

husk of withered humanity, and once for all put the silly fancies of yesterday to flight.

So, the morning meal over, I slipped away with one of those excuses only too familiar of late, and making sure no one saw me, went off boldly to the fir-covered knoll. The nearer it came, however, the slower I went, till by the time the fir-trees were waving like black flags, and the steep needle-strewn path twisted up into the shadows just ahead, I was going very slowly indeed. What would there be in the crypt now? All yesterday's awe came back to me, and I was by no means so sure as I had been before breakfast that the throbbings of that long dead heart were all fancy. I could feel them again. What if this was the verge of a story-book romance, and those throbs had indeed been a faint flicker of real life miraculously preserved? Suppose it had increased, suppose the soldier had returned to existence, and, pushing back the slab that alone held him down, was stalking about the gloomy knoll in his rags? But this was sheer folly and cowardice. I straightened myself up and boldly marched into the clearing where the prone pine tree lay. All was still, nothing had altered, the silver dew was thick upon the ground—not a footstep had brushed it, while on a branch beyond, a blue wood-pigeon was pruning her wing feathers in the morning sunshine.

Whereat, plucking up heart of grace, I went over to the slab, and getting my fingers into the crack, pulled it up. All was well so far, a little rattle of gravel falling down the shaft perhaps, but not another sound.

Peeping and peering, I got down into the abyss, and at a glance satisfied myself the Centurion lay as he did before. This was just what a sane man would have expected, and it proved that yesterday I was a fool. A little angry with myself, I went over to the Roman, and stood by him, while my eyes got accustomed to the light. Yes, he was just as ever, a trifle rounder in outline I might have said had that not been impossible, a little fuller in chest and waist under the dingy rags somehow, but the same—just as he had been yesterday; and greatly relieved, I pulled down the coverlet from his face, then started back with a thrill of amazement.

The same, did I say? Why, he was as different as could be. The face was the same as before, and yet utterly, unmistakably different. Yesterday it had been dry and void, no more life in it than in a dead leaf. It had been perfect and uninjured in every respect, but a mere mask, a shred without a trace of the roundness of life in it. And now—I cannot express the extraordinary change that had taken place. It was still as silent, as grey as ever under its piled-up

THE SLEEPER AWAKENED

dust, but it was the face of a *sleeper,* of one immersed in profound and easy slumber, rather than the features of a mummy! There could be no mistake about it! I rubbed my eyes and stared, and rubbed and stared again. There was no illusion, and a grim, desperate resolve to see this mystery out took possession of me. I shut my mouth resolutely, and peeled the stranger of his coverlet. It came off in cobwebbed tatters that fell in shreds from my fingers as I held them up, and underneath it there he lay at last, in his ragged Roman finery, plump, yes, certainly plumper than he had been, full, perfect, well proportioned, dirty with the harmless dirt of ages, but above all and everything, a *sleeper,* and not that other thing I had thought him.

Then a sort of frenzy seized me. I do not quite know for certain how it was, or what I did the next few minutes, but I know I vowed, there in that dismal place, that Lepidus should live again though I gave him half my life, and rushing to him, forgetting everything, all the strangeness of it, I chafed his hands, rubbed his olive knees, and at last, throwing myself upon him, chest to chest, did as they do who rouse drowning men, working his arms and breathing into his nostrils with all the strength and tenderness in me. At last, exhausted and panting, streaked and smudged with the Roman's dust, I stepped back a space and looked intently. I had triumphed! With a gentle, regular movement his broad chest was rising and falling—you could measure its heave by the mortared cracks between the opposite stones, and there was the slightest twitching in one further toe—I shouted with unreasonable joy and rushing at him, whipped out my handkerchief (it was the Rector's black-eyed daughter Kate who had worked those initials into the corner, and Heaven only knows what soft and foolish hopes besides) and down upon my knees I went, taking the curly Roman head upon my left arm, while with my right hand wiping the dust from his cheeks as tenderly as a mother smooths out the fright from the face of her little one. "Lepidus," I whispered in his ear, "wake; I *will* have you wake; by all the gods living and dead, by all you hope or fear, wake! 'Tis I, Lepidus,—I say it, and you *shall* wake!" and I shook him till the dust rose in a grey cloud from end to end of that marvellous being.

As that fine impalpable powder, pungent and aggressive, entered the Roman nostrils, an extraordinary thing happened: I tell it nor more briefly than it came about. The whole geography of the recumbent face was contorted in an instant. An earthquake spasm shook cheek and chin, the dust of centuries fissured and cracked from side to side, the broad soldier forehead puckered itself into a portentous frown, the offended eagle-nose twitched and twitched again, and then with a mighty explosion that echoed round the crypt, the Roman gave a sneeze that sent me with an uncontrollable cry staggering back against the furthest wall.

Only cowards declare they are never frightened. Brave men often are—I am! At that particular moment, when the dusty grey figure on the block in the mid of that dim chamber showed such gross, such startling evidence of healthy life, I was as near to being scared out of my wits as I ever was. If there had been room for an ignominious flight, that course would certainly have commended itself to me. But the *thing* was between me and the narrow exit, and now as the sunshine gleamed down again between the curdling grey dust streaming upwards in long tongues through the orifice, I saw, with a thrill of wonder, Lepidus was moving; he was up, sitting there on the end of his own monument in a pool of light, kicking his heels against his own monumental slab. As for me, I spread my hands flat out upon the wall on either side and with staring eyes, invited the irresponsive stone and mortar to absorb me.

Presently our eyes met, as the strange being began to stare about him, and I felt that anything was possible in that moment of exquisite expectation. But, as so often happens at a supreme crisis, the occasion was not equal to its opportunities. Our eyes met across the intervening sand, we stared at each other grimly for a minute, and then in a husky and somewhat angry voice the wonder asked, "What on earth are you shouting at?"

I hung my head, until again the sleeper asked in a voice imperious in spite of its dustiness, "I say, what were you shouting for? Can't a gentleman lie down for an hour without being disturbed like this?" and I was constrained to reply that he had frightened me by sneezing.

"So!" he answered haughtily, "it seems I am not at liberty to sneeze save with your leave."

"No," and I had meant to add, "not while I was dusting you," but the sentence seemed so trivial it died away upon my lips.

"Ahem!" said the sleeper awakened, getting down from his pedestal and feeling his left side for his empty sword belt in a suggestive way. "I would have you know that I am the Centurion Lepidus, nephew to the Emperor Vespasianus, and Prefect for the moment of these beastly British hills of yours. It is beneath my dignity to ask who *you* are, but if you have got a sword, or can borrow one, I will show you that it is bad to try to stop me sneezing where I will, and worse to wake me when I do not want to wake."

"Lepidus," I exclaimed, falling into familiarity with singular ease, "this is worse than folly; I have no sword—nor you either," pointing to his side, "nor is there any quarrel between us. If you are indeed all you look, alive, living—not some creation of my excited fancy—come out into the sunshine," and as I pointed to the entrance he tottered over there.

Never shall I forget the marvellous figure he exhibited, standing at the bottom of the narrow shaft in a flood of light. The broad strong gleams literally seemed to drip in gold from his hundred pointed rags; they anointed his curly Roman hair with glory, and oh, the eager upturned face they shone down upon! It was unwashed to the point of pathos, the dust of centuries lay thick upon it, it was masked with grime, and yet behind all that dingy veil was life, real life, a glint of eager bright eyes looking up to the blue sky in delighted wonder; a strong Roman nose, a mouth proud and determined, though the lips were caked and grey; and what startled me most of all was that somewhere I had seen that face before, there could be no doubt of it, somewhere I had seen that countenance, yet where it was my mind was too excited to remember.

For a minute or two those upturned eyes reflected the strangest play of emotions; never had the glory of the sunlight and the splendour of this world of ours appealed to me so strongly as then, when I saw the voiceless delight of that gaunt re-visitor drinking them in. I could see his soul rehabilitating itself, as his body had done with the help of the air and the night dew, and then he heaved a manly great sigh of pleasure that split his jerkin all down the back, and turning to where I stood—

"Come on!" he shouted; "come out of the shadows there, you bat, and help me from this hole." Obediently I went over, for already he had the most singular fascination for me, and putting my back against the wall, in a trice the Roman clambered up, growling a little as he did so at the stiffness of his joints; there was the pressure of an unsteady foot for a moment upon my shoulder, then up went the Centurion into the fresh air with marvellous agility, considering all the circumstances.

Scrambling up, I joined him, and there we stood staring at each other. Could it be true, was it possible, was I dreaming? Was it conceivable I had discovered, and revived, and brought up, this extraordinary treasure trove; this quaint, ridiculous, awe-inspiring monument of rags and dust! I bit my lip, pinching myself again and again to ascertain if I were dreaming. No, the pinches were undoubtedly real, the ground was real, the trees were real; it was all wildly impossible, yet there was nothing to find fault with in the severe logic of events. As for the Roman, while I wrestled with the mental question, he was vaguely concerned with the physical. He stared about him in a way half intelligent, half sleepy, glaring at me and the black opening of the crypt. Anon he would put a shaky inquisitive hand upon his crumbling garments, and then touch a leaf with such a perplexed and childish air that my sympathy swamped all other feeling, and so, presently, taking him by a hand, I led him aside and made him sit upon the fallen pine. Then as gently as might be, I put a question or two to him about his sleep, when it had begun, and how long it had lasted. But speaking into the hollows of that long vacant mind was like talking into a sea cavern—a response came back indeed, prompt, tumultuous even, mocking each time the inflections of the speaker, but there was no sequence behind it, and when at last, abashed at my own failure, my voice dropped away into silence, the Roman's stopped too.

For a time we looked at each other's knees in awkward silence, and then an idea suddenly occurred to me—" Would he like something to eat?" I questioned with abrupt hospitality. At this the stranger, smiting his grey palms together, swore brightly it was a lordly idea—a heaven-sent inspiration if he might tack on the corollary of something to drink, not a thimbleful, he added, like a Jew's stirrup cup, but a vat of drink, a whole riverful, for by the souls of his uncle's ancestors, that strange fellow vowed, his throat felt as if it had not been moistened for a thousand years!

Delighted to have hit on a common interest, I motioned to him to sit down again, and was soon putting my best foot forward, through the pines and away over the meadows on his singular errand. Fortunately no one was about, the lawns were deserted, the terrace, blazing in scarlet and gold with its geraniums and yellow pansies, was empty, and thus I got unobserved to the garden door. Hot and dishevelled, hardly knowing whether to laugh or cry at myself, I slipped through the passages till I almost fell into the plump arms of Janet, the pantry maid, and to her I unburdened myself. "Could she get me," I asked guiltily, "a bottle of claret?" and I implied that I would go pawn if Briggs the butler ever chanced to miss it. "Why, of course, Mr. Louis," she answered, when her first surprise at seeing me there was over.

"And the cold chicken pie," I queried, "that went out last night?"

THE SLEEPER AWAKENED 27

The cold pie, too, that black-eyed hench-maiden said, was at my service, though she ventured a reminder lunch would be ready in an hour. To that I replied by saying the provender was not for myself, but for a hungry man I had lit upon; and "Mr. Louis'" eccentricities of mood being familiar to the household, the coveted provisions were soon in hand, and I was away with them, keeping as carefully to the shadows of tree or house, and avoiding even the sound of a human voice, as though I were a very felon.

The nephew of the Emperor was stalking unsteadily up and down the little clearing, deep in thought, but at sight of myself and the luncheon basket he came towards me eagerly. Never was there a better caterer he said, or one more prompt, and forthwith we sat down under a bramble bush, Marcus Lepidus getting out the half-eaten chicken pie and inhaling its aroma just as you sniff the scent of violets on a bank in springtime, while I uncorked the Château Lafitte. From that flagon he poured himself an ample tumblerful, and it was worth a whole bin of a scarce vintage to see the shine in his eyes as he handled it. For myself, I lay back upon my elbows and watched with a hundred mingled emotions of wonder and curiosity while the Roman eyed the colour of that glorious juice, smelt it lovingly as he toyed with his magnificent thirst, and then—good pagan that he was—holding the tumbler out at arm's length, spilt a few drops on the pine-needles. "To the deities of the place!" he muttered, and so drank.

Never did a freshet on the heels of summer work a greener revolution in a stony hill channel than that stuff wrought in my friend. The red drops ran down his throat at first with a rattle like rain on dusty leaves, and then as the full tide of the liquor followed them, the generous stuff passed into every corner of his long-parched anatomy; his lips caught something of its redness under their dust, his eyes brightened, his muscles twitched responsive. Higher and higher went the tumbler, until at last it was empty, and with a sigh of infinite satisfaction the Roman, setting the glass down, said: "Stranger, I grudge the gods even their libation!"

Then he took the chicken pie between his knees, and the moment was too intense for conversation. Using a knife and fork with singular adroitness after a little fumbling over the handles, that scion of ancient royalty went for the provender in a way that it would have done you good to watch. And as he ate I thought of many things.

There was the matter of his speech, for instance. It had somehow never seemed strange to me that he

THE SLEEPER AWAKENED

should speak native English until he said those few words in Latin as he made libation. Perhaps it would be better to say I had not *observed* he was speaking English till then. And on top of that was the singular fact that he was using, not only my tongue, but my idiom even. I could not fail to notice, though I may not have well expressed it to you—indeed, it only dawned on me myself much later on—that his very turns of speech, his trick and habit of expression were my own. Had I breathed into him with life the paraphernalia of life, had I not only roused his blood into existence by my exertions in the crypt, but lent to his mind also in some subtle way something of the vitality and resources of my own? I am aware it is an explanation explaining little, but what can I do? The bare facts are before you as they were before me—even more fully perhaps, for I necessarily write when all this has been subjected to the cogitation of time—whereas there in the wooded knoll astraddle of a pine log, I could but chew the stump of my Havana and roughly patch together the raw ends of speculation, while my noble Roman hunted for liver wings and sent hard-boiled egg and kissing crust hurrying down his throat in joyous indifference to my perplexities.

A right good meal he made of it. He worked

round that pie as a seaman boxes a compass; it had been intended for a dozen people, and it was scarcely enough for one. Every now and then as he finished a drumstick, or pitched a clean-picked skip-bone into the ferns, the Centurion would stick his knife, point downwards, into the earth, and help himself to a big draught of claret; it made me hungry and thirsty to look at him, and by a very human association of ideas I presently pulled out my watch, and noticed with dismay that lunch would be on the table in the Manor House in ten minutes. Here was a complication. Ideas of politeness to guests, which innumerable copy-book headings had implanted in me, and my dear mother's teachings had assiduously nourished, forbade me to stay away from the meal—I could not take Lepidus home, unannounced, unwashed, as he was, and yet would he consent to remain behind?

In renewed anxiety I glanced at him, and saw fate had come to the rescue: the chicken pie had done its work, the Château Lafitte had numbed his senses, and the curly Roman head was nodding. Another minute and Lepidus reeled in his mossy seat, his eyes dimmed with happy sleepiness, and before I could do or say anything, he had subsided peacefully amid the bracken, graceful even in negligence, and was sleeping the deep untroubled sleep of a well-fed babe.

CHAPTER III

—AND REHABILITATED

THE obvious opinion at our luncheon table that day was that I scarcely fulfilled the qualities of a courteous host. My right-hand neighbour, a very charming girl, to whom I had devoted a good deal of indolent time of late, refused my proffered lobster salad for someone else's collared tongue, though I *know* she preferred the salad, and a general tendency existed to take my sallies in the direction of remorseful civility with reserve, polite but impressive.

As for my mother, she expressed her opinions and authority while the cheese was passing round by arranging a tennis set, and allotting me to a partner without asking my opinion, or even looking in my direction. So there was nothing for it. I got into my flannels and played a hectic game, ferocious and negligent by turns, expecting all the time to see the grey figure of my Centurion stalk out of the shrubberies; and it was only when the long cedar shadows were beginning to creep across the lawns that I got away.

Lepidus was awake when we met ten minutes

afterwards, awake and vastly improved by his sleep and meal. He had filled out amazingly, his flesh had re-formed, his tightened muscles had drawn his stalwart figure into shape, while the lean, hungry look had gone in great measure from his face— where, where had I seen that countenance before? —in fact, he was twice the person he had been, and as lively as a kid.

He had obviously been using the few moments between his rest and my coming in investigating his ragged apparel, and on my approach he was twisting and turning and examining himself with an air of most comical perplexity. Finally, having minutely inspected his exceedingly scanty rags, he turned abruptly in answer to my suggestion that he should come home with me, and asked—

"Any ladies at your table, stranger?"

"Yes," I answered.

"Well," said the Centurion, "unless I sit amongst the ragged beggars in your porch, which all the gods forefend "—this with a toss of his curly head that shook out a cloud of dust—" if I do not sit amongst the slaves, I shall have to come as a naked Apollo—will they mind?"

"It would be unusual," was my answer, and then —catching the gaiety of that open-faced stranger, who from the first moment I knew him to the last, was always equally ready to smile or fight, to take the rough or the smooth of chance with the same brave front—I burst into laughter, and he laughed too, a frank, hearty laugh, until the roosting wood-pigeons left the firs overhead for a quieter neighbourhood; and somehow that mutual outpour put us in better mood with each other.

"Look here, Lepidus," I said, calling his attention by a little twitch at his vest, which promptly came away with all the sleeve up to the elbow, "sorry to spoil your underwear like this, but the fact is—well, you badly want a change of clothes and a wash and brush up; suppose you come down to the shrubbery in front of the house. I will bring you there a long ulster of mine, and afterwards smuggle you into the house;—fact is, you know, you are not quite fit for good society till you have had a wash."

Lepidus agreed to my criticisms in his large and gracious way, and just as the light was fading, the stems of the pines beginning to stand out flaming copper red in the sun's last rays now going behind a distant hill, we, after carefully covering the crypt mouth over, went off slowly down a dim, fir-scented path twisting away to where, near the foot of the hill, was a long sandy scarp beloved of rabbits, the path cutting through it between two miniature cliffs of lichened rocks.

"Hum!" said the Roman, coming to a stop as he eyed these stones, "this is funny: when I was last here the valleys seemed twice as deep, and the water ran chest-high round these crags; why, this was my favourite bathing place, and often I have taken a header from this very rock—you must have had an extremely dry season this year, comrade?" and, as though I were personally responsible for the altered geography of centuries, I hung my head and muttered that it had been dry.

Then, when we crossed the foot-bridge over the meadow stream the singular being at my elbow would have turned off sharp to the left, whereas our Manor lay to the right. "Not that way," I said, touching him on the shoulder.

"Not that way!" he answered, "nonsense, the villa's under the shadow of that hill there, or I'm a Briton," and looking where he pointed through the grey wisps of rising mist I recognised with a start that he was pointing towards those flats where, as previously mentioned, we from time to time turned up ancient pottery and bricks, the odds and ends of a civilisation which had set many a long century ago. It was no good angering him, so I replied soothingly that anyhow he, as guest to-night, was coming *my* way; and he was much too civil even in his rags to argue it. Still I am bound to say I felt uncomfortable, and as he stalked along by my side, could not help taking a nervous look now and again to see if it were possible to discern in orthodox ghost fashion the opposite bushes through his outline. But no! whoever he was, from wherever he came, he stood solid and substantial; the meadow-grass crushed under his strong feet, bats fluttered softly in his wake, for flies he unsettled, his broad outline, as like my own as could be, made a sharp-edged blot upon the russet and lavender of the evening sky. No! he was undoubtedly material by every ordinary test, so there was nothing but to wait for what would happen next.

I got him up to the shrubbery surrounding our house, and not without secret misgivings induced him to remain under cover till something decent in the way of clothes could be procured. Thereon, that eccentric person threw himself down in his tattered finery in a rustic arbour, crossed his legs, began leisurely chewing a stalk of honeysuckle, while with an easy wave of his hand he indicated that I was at liberty to depart upon my errand.

Away I went over the tennis-courts and gravelled terraces. They were just lighting up in the house as I entered; the butler was scolding the under-footman at the half open dining-room door; the housemaids, with hot-water cans and clean towels, were on the back stairs as I shamefacedly sneaked up them. Good Heavens! what would they all say to that *thing* I had back in the garden there? How would he behave? Was I wise, after all, in bringing such a waif into a civilised and decorous household? But what was the good of asking that question? I already knew enough of Lepidus to be pretty well sure that if I did not bring him here he would certainly come himself, so I reached down from my pegs a pair of trousers, a long woolly ulster, with a grey wideawake cap, and rolling them up as small as possible, started downstairs again. In the middle of the tennis lawn two white female figures came towards me with obvious agitation, and my cousin Alice, the younger of the two, broke out as soon as she was within whispering distance—

"Oh, Louis, we have had such a fright! There is a tramp down by the summer-house; do go down and drive him away."

"A tramp?" I said, with my spirit sinking within me.

"Yes, and an Italian—so ragged and dirty, and such a horrible-looking wretch."

"And so horribly impertinent!" chimed in the elder lady, who I may observe was the wife of the

Bishop of Pewchester. " He actually attempted to kiss me ! "

I groaned in an agony of spirit; it was Lepidus, of course. No one but a red-hot heathen with no fear of bell, book, or candle before him would attempt to kiss a bishop's wife at sight, and a swift vision of the horror of my mother, who venerated the Church without regard to sex, should such a sacrilegious idea ever reach her ears, flashed upon me.

" Don't say anything about it," I whispered hastily; " get indoors, and I will go and see this tramp of yours," and as they gladly disappeared down the terrace walk, I hurried on again, tumbling headlong over a croquet hoop in my agitation, and eventually finding the soldier as I left him, offensively cool and happy.

" There: get into those," was my angry remark, throwing down the garments before that noble Roman, " and if you are coming up to the house, for goodness' sake put on some decency and good manners with them."

" Oh, that reminds me," observed Lepidus lightheartedly, as he held my trousers up towards the saffron evening sky in a vain endeavour to discover for himself which was front and which back, " that reminds me—such a buxom nymph came by just now, and when I stepped out of the shadows, intent on giving her a chaste salute—you know, comrade, 'tis but what a sprightly matron looks for from a civil gentleman—she fairly screamed!"

"You are enough, Lepidus, as you stand, to freeze the coquetry in the most brazen hussy that ever lived."

"Ah, I forgot the dirt and rags; but surely they could see *me* through them?"

"Dimly," I answered; "however, never mind that now; button those braces, and stop talking nonsense, like a good fellow. There, on with the coat, and then the cap—no, stupid! not like that—right way forward, so—now take my arm and come along."

Well, at last he was presentable, a soft felt cap pulled down over his eyes, and a long ulster to his ankles; and drawing his hand through my arm, I led him over the dewy lawn towards the streaming lights of the house, conjuring him as we went to remember my admonitions and behave rationally, and though he, laughing lightly, promised, I more than doubted his ability.

Going in by the side door, as we were drying our feet on the mat, who should come running up but my baby kinswoman Flossie Burn, and her terrier. She rushed for me with a cry of welcome as usual but, ten yards away, both dog and child came to a sudden stop. They stared and stared at the stranger, whose broad back was still turned to them, then the terrier, a plucky little beast in general, clapped his tail between his legs and bolted so precipitously up the passage that he nearly spilled our second footman, who was coming from the pantry with a tray of glasses. The little maid however stood her ground, her eyes dilated and her golden curls flickering in the lamp-light. She stood her ground, staring fixedly at the uncommon-looking stranger and then the sonsie little maid of six fled sheer into my arms and nestling there, pointed a rosy finger at my friend, and burst out—

"That's not a proper man, that's not a proper man!" and glaring at him through the tangles of her hair, whispered, "where did he come from, uncle? Is he an ogre?"

"Just a friend of mine, sweetheart," I answered uneasily, unlinking her velvet hands from about my neck while gently putting her down; "just a friend of mine come to stay with us for a day or two: to-morrow you shall see for yourself, but now go to nurse like a dear, and if you can keep that little tongue of yours quiet, and not talk nonsense, perhaps I will bring you up some sweets when dinner's done." Away she went, with many backward glances, and I led my Roman to the stairs.

"Hullo! what's this," exclaimed that man accustomed to open-courted villas, "are we to perch with the pigeons on the roof?" But I assured him it was all right—my rooms were above—and after inspecting the staircase interestedly, he followed me with a shrug of his broad shoulders. At the top we met Mary, the under-housemaid, coming down, whereon the Centurion having eyed her approvingly, crowded her and the hot-water cans most outrageously—ay, and as the red and frightened girl ran downstairs my latest guest leant over the banisters, the laughing Roman eyes following her to the very basement. "What *will* the mater say to-morrow?" I thought to myself, as I led that soldier along the corridor—the mater who had brought me up so well that I dare not look even the plainest cook in the eyes. A bishop's wife half kissed in the shrubbery, a housemaid squeezed in the passage, before we have even dressed for dinner—it was awful!

CHAPTER IV

SOME DINNER AND AN ALARM

MY own rooms, a little apart from the main corridor, looked out on the front. Across the passage stood a spare-room where an occasional bachelor friend could be put up, with a bath adjoining, both being kept constantly ready, of course, and thither I led the way. Opening the guest-door we went in, and in my nervousness, not being particularly thoughtful, without any warning I turned up the little brass knob by the door, with the result that in a second, half-a-dozen electric lights, each behind its shield of soft green silk and lace, sprang into light. Lepidus fairly jumped with amazement. A dazzling flash of lightning in the open would not have scared him half so much. He blinked and winked, staring open-mouthed for a moment or two, then gasped out, " How did you work that, stranger? "—it was a little pleasantness of his that *I* was the stranger, and he the indigenous owner of the time and place—" that's marvellous! " and he went up to examine the lamps with incredulous awe on his dirty but handsome face.

Then he had to know how it was done, and in the exuberance of his delight turned the light on and off, until out of sheer giddiness, I had to beg him to desist. When I rang for the maid, and more bath towels, my Roman came over minutely to examine the electric-bell knob, and while my back was turned, rang it again and again, until our staid old housekeeper downstairs nearly had a fit, and housemaids, buttons, footmen, and bootboys came tumbling over each other up the stairs, under the impression that the house was on fire at the very least.

Pacifying them, I, unwarned by experience, sent Mary in to fill the bath, while I went across the passage to find Lepidus a suit of clothes. I had not been gone a minute when I heard the girl exclaim, and rushing headlong back, found the room in pitchy darkness, and at the next step cannoned heavily against the flying maid, who was retreating as precipitously as I was entering. We were still leaning breathlessly against the opposite sides of the door when the Centurion was graciously pleased to turn on the lights again, and to laugh gleefully at the sight of our discomfiture. I dared not trust myself to ask how he had frightened the girl, but sent her away, and with a heavy sigh, threw down the suit of evening clothes upon the bed and tried to

SOME DINNER AND AN ALARM

explain the enormity of his behaviour to the Roman, but he was much too light-hearted to be impressed. At last in despair I showed him the bath, and he was astounded to see hot and cold water flowed at a touch.

"Well," he said, "that *is* curious. I have bathed at Aquæ Tusculi, and taken a course at Ostia for the rheumatism, but this is the most convenient spring that ever came out of a rock: is it chalybeate?"

"No," I answered grimly.

"Then perhaps it is sulphurous?"

"No," again I said, "but it is what some other things are not—it is clean. Now, Lepidus, just get out of those rags, and when you have hidden them at the back of this cupboard, jump in here and scrub and rub for all you are worth. There is only twenty minutes to dinner, and a week's work before you, apparently," I observed, consulting my watch.

"What is that?" said the visitor, pointing to my fifty-guinea hunter.

"Never mind to-night, but, like a good fellow, jump in, and when you are ready, if you will call, I will lend you a hand with the clothes, for they may be a bit strange at first." Then glancing round fugitively, to see if there were any possibilities of mischief to be put out of his way, I left him and hurried off to my own room.

My dressing was interrupted only twice: once by the Roman sending in to say he wanted some wine to put in his bath, a pagan fancy which added five years to the age of our butler when he heard of it, and secondly, to ask if he could not have two "slaves" to rub him down. I returned an evasive answer to both questions, and shortly afterwards (Lepidus having refused my proffered assistance, through the door), joined my mother's guests in the inner hall.

We were a pleasant party. About a dozen men and women in all. A bishop and his wife; an Indian general; a vivacious widow, who knew as much about the world and more about India than he did, and would not have been averse, we thought, to adding a soldierly prefix to her name. Then there was a married sculptor and his wife; two bachelor students from Oxford, one of them reading for the Church; and a brace of tennis-playing damsels, whom my dear, kind, match-making mother had especially selected as being suitable to the presumptive matrimonial needs of the foresaid young men—altogether a cheerful party, if somewhat conventional in tone.

SOME DINNER AND AN ALARM 45

How would they take Lepidus? I tried to do my duty as host, and talk lightly to each in turn as we awaited the announcement of dinner, but my head was giddy with the swift sequence of the last few hours. Had I been a fool in bringing the Centurion to the house at all, and now that he was here, ought I to turn him loose, as it were, on this angelical sheepfold without adequate warning or preparation? I had told them, it is true, that a friend of mine had arrived suddenly and would join us at dinner, a relative of Italian extraction I had said, knowing very little of English ways, and had tried to hint that they must be prepared to put up with a few little eccentricities. But was this enough? To what abyss was I dragging a decorous household? Ought I not to have made a frank confession of my "find"? Still debating that knotty point in my mind, and listening inattentively to his Lordship of Pewchester, who, with his hands under his episcopal coat tails, and one foot on the marble fender was laboriously explaining the causes which had led up to his recent differences of opinion with his rural dean on the subject of benefactions, my heart sank guiltily when a footman came in and drew me aside.

"What is wrong, Brooks?" I asked.

"Oh, nothing much, sir," replied the man, looking a little nervous, " only the electric lights in No. 10, sir: they are going on and off in a way we cannot understand, and there's quite a crowd in the garden watching them."

Making hurried apologies to the Church, I rushed off after Brooks, down a passage and out into the garden, abutting on the rear of the house, by a glass door. It was true enough: there was a crowd fifty yards lower down—all the stable men, ostlers, horse boys and gardeners on the estate, with a sprinkling of female servants, their aprons over their heads, were collected there, staring up at a pair of windows that I knew were those apportioned to Lepidus. And from those opened curtained casements came every few seconds a twin blaze of light as all the electric lamps were suddenly put on at the full—a glare lighting up the laughing faces below, and flooding the leaves of the walnut trees in the courtyard with gold, and then an interval of murky darkness illuminated again by another outburst of brilliancy.

It was that off-shoot of Imperial Rome, of course, there was no one else within twenty miles fool enough to waste his time in such a way, and with rage in my heart I turned back into the house, rushed upstairs, and bursting unceremoniously into No. 10—which happened that moment to be in

SOME DINNER AND AN ALARM   47

gloom—" Lepidus ! " I said bitterly, " are you mad? A child would be ashamed to go on like this. Don't you see the men are laughing at you down below? They will think you are out of your mind. Why don't you dress and come down to dinner like a man in his senses ? "

" I am sorry," said a smooth, pleasant voice from the darkness, "but these lights of yours are so fascinating, and the bath too! I have been turning your taps on and off for the last twenty minutes, and am not half satisfied yet," and suiting the action to the word, he put on the electric lamps again.

As the light flashed up, and the radiance filled every corner of the room, I saw before me, not the dusty mummy I still somehow expected, but a stalwart fellow in modern evening dress, so like to me in the main, that I fairly staggered against the doorpost, and stood gazing at him in blank astonishment. Like, I have told you before, we were, but this was my reflection, my copy, the very mirage of myself —a little paler perhaps, a thought larger in frame, a trifle stiffer in bearing, with hair not cut like mine —and yet myself, my very, very self! He had bathed and washed and come forth rejuvenated— who could have dreamt there was such a healthy skin under that crust of centuries? He had got very correctly into a suit of my own evening black; the handkerchief that dangled from his pocket flaunted my initials, the socks showing above his patent shoes were twin with those I wore; he was the very copy of me, and I gazed at him, as well I might, with speechless amazement for a minute or two.

This, then, was the meaning of the strange familiarity of his face—dull and slow that I had been not to recognise it! I covered my eyes with my hand for a minute, and every incident of the last forty-eight hours rolled back before me—the mound under the fir-boughs, how I lay chest to chest with that dusty *thing* in the forgotten crypt, filling his shrunken frame with my breath, and his empty mind with thought and speech by the very ardour of my desire that he should live again. I remembered the dim, uncomfortable resemblance he bore, even then, to something I knew as well as I knew myself; I remembered the finding of the sepulchre, the very book I was reading just before—ay! and the very passage in that book wherein an old philosopher, rummaging the wastes of human thought for any scraps of truth the gods might have dropped there, wrote how one man lived many lives—was it possible I and this other were one, was it possible?—But my mind was too confused to reason, and, before I could think any more about it, the Roman's hand was on my shoulder, and speaking in that charming way he

SOME DINNER AND AN ALARM   49

could use when he chose, he was asking lightly what was amiss. "Been waiting too long for dinner, comrade? Jove! you look as though you had—just come and see yourself," and he led me over to a tall glass by the window until we stood there side by side, the duplicates surely of one common individuality, staring hard into that polished mirror.

Had I waited too long for dinner? was my liver out of order? As I stared it seemed to me that our two identities ran together on that surface, blended like drops of rain upon a window pane, and all the reflections of the common-place about us stranded out like mist, to rise again into the likeness of a Roman street, a street of porticoes and wide pavements, a deep blue sky overhead, and dirt in the marble gutters; yonder a peep of brown Tiber water through the olive trees, while nearer by, in the busy foreground, two-wheeled carts creaking down the open, and men and women, slaves and freemen, jostled each other—it was only a flash, a thought, a breath upon the glass, a glint of a sunny ancient street, bright and busy, yet though I had never been out of England in all my life, every detail of that place was familiar to me, every incident of the motley throng was of everyday knowledge!

"Well, come along," said my friend, "you will never cure an empty stomach by staring, and there are better remedies somewhere below, unless my nose deceives me," whereon he led me arm-in-arm into the corridor, and so downstairs to the hall where our guests were still waiting. Beautiful, if quaint, was the sweeping bow with which he saluted the company on the threshold of that great black oak ante-room. Such a bow had never before been seen in Caster Manor: it was all-embracing, at once gracious, yet dignified; it was the sort of salutation an emperor might have made on coming into the presence of a group of captive kings. It was outlandish undoubtedly, yet somehow you could not smile at it. The unfaltering ease of that stately bending conveyed the silent certainty of equality, the unhurried elegance of the recovery seemed like that of one who was certain beforehand that, be they who they might, he saluted no better man than he who came amongst us. My dear, simple-minded mother even attempted something like a reflex of that salutation, it was so fetching; while all the others bobbed and blinked in polite awkwardness, and then, when it was over, there was Marcus Lepidus standing in our ancestral hall eyeing the company with an air of the kindliest patronage.

Of course I took him round the circle, introducing him individually to those frigid elders, and in an amazingly short space of time he was at his ease—

SOME DINNER AND AN ALARM 51

long, in fact, before the others were—smiling his spacious smile, and answering the veiled wonder of their questions with a general success which made me marvel. At times he tripped, no doubt. Thus I overheard the Bishop's wife say—

"You came by the express, of course, Mr.—ah—Lepidus?"

"Oh yes," said the Centurion, and thinking of mounted military stages and that horse "express" he alone knew of, he went on cheerfully, "and a rough time we had of it, too! We got off into a bog twice——"

"Into a bog!" gasped the episcopal dame.

"Yes, and when we got out of that it was as black as our mother-wolf's mouth; we could not see where we were going, and plunged headlong into a river——"

"Good gracious me!" gasped my mother.

"And when we scrambled out of that, we got lost in the copses just outside the town, and went snorting and plunging about till we caught a sight of the station lights by the merest chance; in fact——"

"In fact, sir, the only wonder is there was not an accident," observed the Bishop's wife coldly. "Cecilia, dear"—this to my parent—"will you come and tell me about your Dorcas meeting last week? I hear it was very successful." Nothing daunted, my Roman bowed, and went on to the next group, and everywhere I saw the fascination of his presence light the eyes of his listeners, while rising wonder, amusement, and surprise flitted over their countenances.

All went reasonably well, until presently, far away in the corridors the gong sounded for dinner. You know that long, low muffled sound? It appeals both to the hollow interior of the expectant diner, if I may be forgiven for saying it, and to his mental imagination, should he possess any. It is a singularly lugubrious sound, and no people with the slightest sense of compatibility would ever let themselves be called to a cheerful festival by such a means; but there it is! That brassy rumour rolled sullenly up into the hall, coming, it might have been, from a mile away, so hollow it sounded; it gathered volume and strength, until the house seemed full of it, and as the first knell died away, and suppressed gladness shone upon the faces of our guests, my Centurion leapt to his feet: "Hullo!" he cried, excitedly turning to me, " did you hear that?—a British war-drum, as I live!"

"Nonsense, man!" I answered; "it is only——"

"Don't tell *me* what it is! Haven't I listened

SOME DINNER AND AN ALARM 53

to war-drums since I first scrambled down from my mother's knees?—to the ramparts, you laggard, to the ramparts, I say, or the barbarians will be on us before we can strike a blow!" and quick as thought, my plucky Roman leapt to a trophy of arms upon the nearest wall, tore down a broad-bladed German boar spear and rushed towards the curtained entry. Just as he approached it, our portly butler drew aside the arras to announce soup was on the table, and there he met the German steel! Blue, sharp, and a good eighteen inches long, it glistened for a second against the full rotundity of his white waistcoat, and with a yell of terror he leapt back, catching his foot in the curtain and falling heavily among the folds. Away went Lepidus along the corridor, and down came brass cornice pole and rings upon the bald scalp of the luckless servitor with a crash which set our teeth on edge, and gave him a worse two days' headache than my mother's most experimental port.

"Lepidus! Lepidus!" I cried, leaping over the wreck and rushing after the truant, "come back, you fool! Lepidus, you are mad—" and so on down the corridor, across the pantry, through the servants' yard, and out into the open starlight, where I fairly ran him down, panting and hot, his fine eyes dilated with martial eagerness, and his better ear bent groundwards to catch the tramp of those armed men who he thought were coming on us.

It was only with the greatest difficulty I got him back into the house, and made him look at the gong as it hung on its bamboo framework near the butler's room.

"So that is all it was," he said, indignantly staring at the little disc. "Well, if folk will have a battle-call sounded to tell them dinner is ready, sane men are bound to reach for their weapons. Here, you pink-legged slave, hang that up again," and tossing his boar spear—sharp end first—to a frightened footman who stood near, he thrust his arm through mine, and as we walked back towards the dining-room, asked in my ear—was it question, was it affirmation?—asked whether *I* had ever heard a British war-drum sound.

Had I? Yes!—at the touch of that strange hand on mine, and the whisper of that voice in my ear, it seemed as though the long forgotten leapt into remembrance; the tough walls of that old Manor house shredded out as fine as summer mist, and blew away from before my reeling brain! I was on the grassy rampart of a Roman camp; on the low hills opposite, the dawn was hanging like the lip of a ghostly sea. The near glens were purple in the shadows, and the willow bushes were shivering along the stream in the breath of the coming morning. And then I heard it—heard the dull wail of hatred and oppression go up from the trembling British drumheads, and mount and mount, till my inmost fibres seemed tremulous with the sound; then listened while it died away again, listened while the bitter and sullen tocsin rolled over the peat hags and faded away on the folds of the brooding shadows. Ay, and I saw them—saw the thin yellow flush over the eastern moorlands beaded with foemen, saw the glint on their brass, and the plated chariot-poles twinkling like streaks of fire, saw their helms gleam, and the fine small lightning from their spear-points lead down into the hollows! Behind me, the Roman camp started to life as I stared: I heard the phalanx wake with a single long-drawn sigh in the darkness; the clatter of steel on steel, as a sleepy fool stumbled over his armour; then the cry of a startled child, the bark of a dog, and the voice of a Tuscan sergeant cursing his men in a guttural whisper. I saw the foemen swing out right and left upon the heather, and the Roman eagles spread their gold wings overhead on the last of the black night-time. I heard my heart thumping—then the roar of the British onset —fifteen years of shame and bloodshed and terror expressed in the yell of a moment, and—drowning its echo—a wild derisive shout of defiance and welcome from the throats of the Romans behind me!

"My dear, will you please pass the celery salt?" said the mildly reproachful voice of my mother, and looking up from my reverie with a guilty start, I found I was seated at dinner at the head of our table, her ample ladyship of Pewchester on my right, a buxom matron on my left, my dear kind parent far away through the vistas of wax candles and fern, and Lepidus, that splendid waif from the past, near her, beamingly gracious and discoursing abundantly —good Heavens! what might he not be discoursing on?

CHAPTER V

THE CENTURION PLAYS CENTAUR

IT is usual to speak of early rising as a Spartan habit. Had you known my Roman you would have altered the geographical equivalent of the virtue! Marcus Lepidus could not sleep after cockcrow, and what is more, if the cocks were not punctual in the discharge of that duty he was quite capable of going down at the proper hour to inquire into the cause of their remissness.

The first morning after I had introduced him into the house (and a lovely autumn morning it was, by the way) the idea seized him to bathe in the lake before anybody else was astir. So he let himself out in the dewing on to the terrace walk in a pair of sleeping trousers and a blue velvet smoking coat I had lent, and with a bath towel over his arm, went down to the weed-grown pool. There, alone in the splendid sunshine, naked and not in the least ashamed, he frightened the moorhens from their earliest meal to his heart's content. Then he sauntered back over the lawns, glittering with a thousand dew-drops flashing gold and blue, the mavises on the green pine steeples flooding the moist coppices with the glamour of their songs as he passed, and hungry, as all healthy bathers should be, that follower of the imperial standards broke into our larder through the kitchen window, and set to work to refresh himself with common plebeian British bread and dripping.

Thus it came about that our stout old cook, who had been in the family thirty years, gave us notice, for when she came down from her room (sleepy, and perhaps a trifle irritable, as aged dames of her standing will be at such an hour), and opened the foresaid larder door, a semi-naked gentleman, insufficiently arrayed in flannel trousers, the foresaid jacket, his abundant black hair rolled up in a bath towel, and a large slice of bread and dripping in his hand, fell out upon her.

" This is what comes," she said, as she recovered consciousness twenty minutes afterwards on the horsehair sofa in the servants' hall, " this is what comes of master's bringing wild Indians into the house "—to that good lady, everybody who had not been born within the British seas was a " wild Indian "—" I, at my time of life to be knocked into the fender the fust thing in the morning, and scared out of my senses by a *gentleman* as ought to have been waiting upstairs in a Christian way for Mary

THE CENTURION PLAYS CENTAUR 59

to take him his morning tea, instead of prowling about my kitchen for bread and dripping." And so Lepidus, the nephew of the Emperor, cost us the services of our dear cockney dame before the sun was over the plum trees in the kitchen garden that morning.

But little the Centurion grieved when, strolling about the garden an hour later, I pointed out the result of his escapade.

"After all," he said jovially, "what is one slave more or less? Why, my uncle Marius fed his lampreys with his stupidest bondsmen; ay, and when his own supply ran short one day, he borrowed a favourite butler from a neighbour, and on that sullen fool asking for his domestic back, Marius sent him round a dish of those fat and dainty fishes!— a right down jolly fellow was my uncle, the best hand at a brew you ever saw, and hard to match for humour." And that light-hearted soldier, plucking my mother's best rose for his buttonhole from the verandah trellis, led me laughingly in to breakfast.

There he was, as graciously irresistible as I was supine and helpless. My star seemed to have set in the splendour of that southern sun that had ridden suddenly into our skies. Never in my life had I felt so worthless, so washed out, so mentally sapped and soulless, as I did at this time. As for the Roman, he grew fat on my leanness, he waxed magnificent by my eclipse, and the strangest thing was that I recognised there at the breakfast-table, as I had done before so often in his talk, my own figures of speech, and in his knowledge (often blunderingly drawn upon) my very own experiences. In fact, there could not be any doubt to me, as I stared and listened, that Lepidus was using my mental raiment as certainly as he was inhabiting my best tweed suit, and though of the two perhaps the homespun fitted him the best, yet, as I have said, he did marvellously well in both. So much I frankly perceived, while, for the rest, I could but sit and marvel to see the old knowledge, and the borrowed new, jostling each other with varying fortunes in his mind. Everything was strange to him. The damask tablecloth with a pattern that was light or dark, according as you viewed it up or down the table, was a more magic web than any Penelope ever wove. The silver cruet seemed a chemist's shop, which he turned admiringly upon his thumb without the slightest knowledge of the ingredients within. When they offered him a fricassee of duck he helped himself with his fingers, and the sausages on toast he declared were the most singular kind of fish that ever swam. Then again, when my mother asked him whether he would take tea or coffee, he paused upon those unfamiliar words, and said with studied graciousness, " A little of both." She gave him tea without the shadow of a smile, and sending the sugar to him, he courteous in everything, took half-a-dozen lumps upon his plate, sucking them one by one as occasion offered with the frankest simplicity.

And it was all done so charmingly, he was so obviously at his ease and happy, that no one laughed. His very blunders were endearing in the shine of his gracious presence. Yet Lepidus could bare his teeth at times for all his smoothness, and under that velvet manner, a word now and then would show that a touch of the old Imperial blood still tingled in his veins. We had nearly done breakfast when some chance allusion put us on the subject of game-fowl.

Thereon Lepidus, turning to my Lord Bishop of Pewchester, asked, " Are you fond of cock-fighting, sir? There are some fowl outside who I fancy would make a set for us if you liked the sport." But the Bishop's worst hour in the twenty-four was this one sacred to coffee-pots and buttered toast, so he answered severely that fighting of any kind for pleasure was low and debasing. At this the Roman haughtily answered—

" Ah, I had forgotten that slaves—and Christians

—only fought in the arena." Then turning to me: "Dear cousin Louis, would *your* stomach, too, turn at seeing a cock put to their proper use the weapons with which the gods have lavishly provided him?"

I tried to smooth the matter over, and jestingly said that our cocks had too many domestic differences on hand to care for artificial combats.

"And how interesting it is," observed the irrepressible Lepidus, addressing himself pointedly to the Bishop's wife, "that the sex which inspires us with courage and ambition before marriage should be our excuse for a white liver after it."

"The characterisation of white livers describes most men so seldom," put in the vivacious widow from across the table, "that it would be comforting to think even matrimony could confer it on them."

"Dear Mrs. Milward, you put the wrong complexion on my meaning," answered the Roman, helping himself to some more sardines with the bread knife. "I might jestingly observe that one may have a white heart and a black liver, or worse still, a black heart and a white liver, or none of either, or too much of both, but you know what I meant, and my respect for your digestion prevents me following a complex subject further. I yield myself into the hands of our sprightly cousin Louis, here, whose shining modesty has alone pre-

THE CENTURION PLAYS CENTAUR 63

vented him from speaking all breakfast time. Whatever he thinks will amuse you best this morning, will delight me above everything."

"What is it, mother," I said to the gentle matron at the other end of the table; "what are we to do to-day?"

"Well," answered that lady, "I will not venture to plan for you young men—we women folk have many things on hand. But before you go anywhere I want you to come and see the foal which came last night—Osborne says it already shows many good points." So to the stables we presently went, but Lepidus contrived even then to force another incident into the brief interval between breakfast table and manger.

We had sauntered out into the conservatory in ambiguous after-breakfast ease, and the Bishop, being a man of peace in practice as well as preaching, had tendered my Roman a very choice cigar by way of peace offering for the snub he had administered an hour before. Lepidus took the strange-looking article with grave courtesy, and having surreptitiously watched the others set theirs to their mouths and light up, turned aside to do likewise. Now I foresaw that, being absolutely unaccustomed to "the weed," this first experiment must make him suffer, and in the softness of my heart, not bearing to see him shamed, I took an opportunity of whispering hurriedly to him as we stood among the orchids, "Don't use it, old fellow, it will make you ill," and accompanied my warning with a meaning look.

The Roman started, and a fine Imperial flush of anger swept over his open countenance. "Make me ill?" he repeated in a whisper.

"Yes," I answered, "make you sick to death at the shortest notice——"

"Now by the splendour of my uncle's throne," scowled Lepidus, catching my arm with a grip that left five blue indents there for many an hour, "do you mean to say that round-stomached hypocrite, that gaitered villain in black yonder would try to poison me—me, just risen from a common table of friendship! Louis, he dies—dies before the world is five minutes older; give me down that brass squirt there, and I'll send him spinning into Hades!" whereat the angry Roman stretched his hand for the greenhouse syringe, the nearest weapon he could see.

"Hush, hush," I whispered, "I did not quite mean that. It is a sort of—well, a soother for the nerves, a kind of medicine only deadly when you are unaccustomed to it."

The Centurion frowned, and stared incredulously at me. "A medicine for sound men, and one which

THE CENTURION PLAYS CENTAUR 65

kills or nearly kills those to whom the physician prescribes it! Surely, Briton, this is complex?"

"Ay, and you will find," I laughed nervously thrusting my arm through his and dragging him out of harm's way; "you will find the older you grow the more complex truth becomes. That is right! chuck the cigar into the water-lily tank, and come along with me to the stables; I will be bound you know more about horses than tobacco."

To the stables we went accordingly. My dear mother joyed in horses, regarding them as others regard rare pieces of china, for she never rode now, though she had once been a fine horsewoman, and in her brougham cared little what beasts were matched against the pole. But she loved that display of glossy haunches which rewarded endless grooming with the shine of new-shelled chestnuts in October. She liked the neatly braided straw under those nervous hoofs, and the long array of gold-emblazoned names on blue labels above each manger. She relished the savour of corn bins as few women do, and could tell if there was a musty peck of oats in the store-room quicker than any miller ever born. As a result, the stable cat on the overturned bucket loved her too; the stable boys entertained for her a respect which they withheld from all the rest of her sex.

"Are they not beautiful beasts?" she said proudly, turning to the Roman as we strolled down the array of friendly quadrupeds.

"Beautiful, indeed," he answered; "but why do you keep them all ranked like this—tails outward, dear madam? Surely the beauty and intelligence of such noble pets shine at the other end—all these glossy buttocks are well enough, but in my uncle's stable we know our horses by their heads——"

"Have you ever been on a horse, Mr. Lepidus?" asked cousin Alice, in her sweetest tone.

The Centurion smiled, and mildly observed that he had mounted once or twice.

"Then," quoth his sweet tormentor, who for some reason had got the idea into her silly British head that no foreigner could ride, above all no Italian, "then do borrow something very quiet from dear Mrs. Allanby; the last Roman I saw on horseback made the fortunes of a dull day for us in Florence!" And Lepidus in reply, with modest humility, "doubted whether there was anything staid enough in the stable for him."

"So I might have guessed," said my cruel little cousin, firing a parting shaft; "it is as difficult for another person to get you foreign gentlemen on to a horse as it is for you to stay there once mounted!"

THE CENTURION PLAYS CENTAUR 67

and picking up her skirt between two dainty fingers, the little lady went forward with a toss of her head.

"I say, mother," I took occasion to whisper as we two stood back a minute; "I wish Alice was not quite so rude to Lepidus; it is most marked."

"Yes, I have marked it, and it makes me anxious."

"Oh, I don't see why it should make you *anxious*."

"But it does, and just because it means that she is very much struck by him, and is trying in that way to show herself she is not. My dear boy, I know more about girls than you do, and I always feel that when one is exceedingly rude to a young man without cause or reason, then it is time for her guardians to be careful."

"I had never thought of that, mother."

"Louis," said she, slipping her soft arm into mine, and speaking in the playful nursery way we had never outgrown, "there is so much you never thought of!" and she led me after our guests.

They meanwhile had gathered in a group at the further end of the stable, and were peeping and peering into a loose box, whose outlooking was hidden by a curtain, while exclamations of surprise and admiration rose amongst them.

"Oh, what a lovely beast!" "What a back,

what loins, what shoulders!" "Just look at his neck: it arches like a rainbow—" "His coat is like satin—see how the veins stand out through it." "And his lovely little ears; why, his whole expression goes from one extreme to the other as he pricks or tucks them back!"

It was, in fact, a famous stallion that our head man in a fit of reckless enthusiasm had persuaded my mother to take off the hands of a neighbouring lord, who joyed in seeing how much wickedness and "blood" he could breed into a single equine carcass. A magnificent fellow few could manage at stall, and none mount in the open; a glorious and useless brute, outside his limited sphere of action, that we had christened "Satan" in awful wonder—and after a month's possession would gladly have parted with for a third of his value. There he stood quivering with suppressed vitality at the back of his crib; rank with corn and want of exercise; eyeing the faces intruding on his privacy with wrathful wonder; his broad silky muzzle showing red nostrils as he sniffed at us; his fine silky skin drawn tightly over the strong muscles beneath, and his fretful fore hoof pawing the straw, while he shook his keen head in anxiety and displeasure—the embodiment of well-fed strength and unmastered pride.

"Oh, what a lovely beast!" cried Mistress Alice.

"Oh! I would lose my heart to any man who could mount and ride *him*," adding hastily, as she caught the reproving glances of the matrons, "but then, of course, there is no one who could do that."

Now Lepidus had been standing a little behind, eyeing the great horse silently. Whether he heard my cousin's remarks or not, I do not know, but he came to the front, and turning to my mother, said, "A nice animal, Mrs. Allanby, a little heavy, I think, in the shoulders, but then there is so much draught-horse blood in all your British stables. Do you ride him much?"

"He is never even saddled, Mr. Lepidus; no one dares to get upon him."

"Then I think, with your leave, I will give him a breath of fresh air myself"—and turning to where three grooms stood watching us at a respectful distance, he called in his fine imperious way, "Here, you slaves of the manger, saddle this beast and bring him outside."

"My dear Mr. Lepidus," expostulated my parent, "it is impossible——"

"It is not only possible, dear madam, but may perhaps be amusing too," and he gave a half glance to where my cousin stood balancing her emotions. Then he led the way outside as though the matter were settled beyond dispute, and while we waited anxiously, amused himself by rescuing flies with a straw from the open water-butt by the coach-house door.

Presently the great horse came. A stamping and a scuffling on the hard floor of the stables, then a struggle in the doorway, and out burst the black stallion with two struggling grooms hanging on desperately to his nose and headgear, while a third clung to the stirrup leather. He sprung out with a snort of joyous defiance, and was with the greatest difficulty brought to a standstill near us. But first, let me explain that the stable-yard was a roomy expanse a couple of hundred yards long by half as many wide, fenced in with tall walls, those opposite the buildings being under the shade of a row of lime trees. At the further end were chicken-houses and coops; at this, the double gateway opening on to the carriage drive. We had come through those gates by a side postern, the main portal being fully seven feet high, heavy, massive, barred with iron, and overtopping the walls on either side by a good twelve inches.

Well, the big horse was brought out, shaking his head in wrath at the unaccustomed trappings, and pawing the ground as he eyed our group suspiciously. Everybody again admired him—from a **respectful distance.**

"I really wish you would not try to mount, sir," said my kindly mother to the Roman; "no one has been on his back for weeks—it is really dangerous."

"Then surely, madam, it is high time someone got astride of him," laughed that descendant of Imperial Rome, and receiving a whip from one of the grooms, he strode forward, gathered the stallion's bridle-reins in his hand, taking up a knot of the sable mane as he did so, and having cast a swift glance round the limits of the yard, prepared to mount. But the big brute did not lend himself kindly to the idea. With a shiver of indignation and a toss of his tremendous head he swung away, hurling a groom head over heels across the cobble stones as he did so, being with difficulty brought to a stand again—fuming and defiant.

And on the cheeks of Marcus Lepidus the hot Tuscan blood burnt in two bright red spots. He followed up the horse, took the bridle and mane again, and laying a hand lightly on the saddle crupper as though meaning but to try the tightness of the girths, quicker than we could think flung himself sheer astride of the horse.

Thereat began a fight worth going many a mile to see! With a furious bound that sent the grooms flying like chaff on a threshing floor, and a quiver from head to tail, the big beast let his temper go.

Here and there he bounded as he worked himself into a fury, sending the gravel spinning, and the startled pigeons in a cloud from the stable roofs. We thought the rider must come off, and held our breath. The horse gathered himself together, then swung round as though he were suspended on a pivot. But little it mattered to the Roman, who went round with him as though horse and rider were one piece. Next "Satan" stood up straight in the air, a sight of wonder and dread, and pawed the linden trees, it seemed, our splendid guest watching his endeavours from between his ears with a contented smile. Up the other way, heels in air went that corn-eating devil till the rider lay flat back along his quivering haunches. Then "Satan" shook his mighty head till all its brass and leathern furniture rattled like a dice-box, pawing the ground and whinnying with shame and rage, but still nothing it mattered to Lepidus! At last the great horse bolted down the yard, scattering the fowls in mad panic from his thundering hoofs. At the stone wall he pulled up perforce, and then we saw the Roman suddenly take the initiative—swing that great black stallion round, wave his armed hand above him, and bring down the heavy riding crop with a thud across his flank that made one's own skin quiver.

Back like a black thunderbolt came the mighty beast, straight at the walls by the main gate; surely Lepidus would never try to jump them? Yes, he went by us across the yard like a whirlwind, hands down, chin up, and then, just as " Satan," feeling the master-hand upon him, shortened his stride for the dangerous effort, just as he was rising to the brick and mortar, that addle-brained cousin of mine, that fluffy-haired little jade must get in his way, and stand there right in the brute's path, courting death, irresolute which side to run, with her cowardly little hands outstretched and her eyes dilated with terror. It looked for a second as if nothing could save her, and then, almost before we had had time fully to realise the peril, the Centurion took the situation in at a glance, and without a moment's hesitation, without a change of countenance, swung the horse round, just as he rose on his haunches, straight at the higher seven-foot carriage gates! The stones rang under the steel shoes; we saw Lepidus bend like a green withy as the mighty body rose beneath him, the white splinters flew from the gate-top as the triumphant hoofs cut two grooves in it, and with an irrepressible yell of delight the stable boys behind us screamed " He is over! He is over!"

We poured helter skelter through the wicket— my dear mother, the Bishop, the grooms, myself—

with no regard to seniority or precedence, to pick up the Roman's dead body, and were just in time to see him thundering down the avenue, and disappear over the yew hedge into the lane beyond. Over stubble and plow he went like a black dot here and there between the distant trees. He galloped round behind the fir-covered mound, so full of memories, over the ridge and up the pastures, at the same break-neck speed, riding with glorious ease, and ended up by coming like a tornado through my mother's thickets of cherished rhododendrons, and jumping the moat and rose fence straight on to the tennis-lawn (Lepidus knew nothing of tennis!), where we stood in a breathless and admiring group.

I shall not readily forget the picture that noble Roman made as he reined his smoking stallion back upon its haunches—the great steed smothered in white foam, his veins pulsing in a moving network under his silken skin—and tossing back his own disordered curls, turned his flushed and handsome face upon us, laughing at his victory.

"An excellent horse, madam," said the Roman, dismounting, "with no faults except those of his training."

"And well matched," observed my parent graciously, "by his rider."

We watched the steed, now as humble as anyone

could wish, led away to the stables, and then turned, chatting towards the house. On the verandah steps I noticed Alice standing apart, and as the Centurion passed near her she held out a small white hand, while in the one glance she stole at him there was a something no man could misunderstand.

"Oh, Mr. Lepidus," she said gently, "I am so sorry!" But the nephew of the Emperor did not or would not see, and lightly chatting as he passed, left the lady there unrecognised, unforgiven.

CHAPTER VI

AN INTERRUPTED EXPLANATION

IT would need a busier pen than mine to follow the days minute by minute, to express the delightful sense of novelty the stranger brought into our hum-drum society; the vitality—my vitality—he radiated out; the infinitely quaint perversions of established fact he expressed, and the imperial grace by which he made us feel that his very blunders were more commendable than the strict proprieties of ordinary folk. He fascinated us, and the very fact of his sociability, the way he was ever present, all pervading, prevented much of those criticisms or cross-questionings which would have been so awkward for me to meet alone.

The good Bishop did indeed observe that morning, when Madeira and biscuits in the conservatory had softened his heart, and the Centurion was out of ear-shot: "A most singular and interesting man, this cousin of yours, Mr. Allanby. Obviously a scholar; strangely, I might say almost flippantly, familiar with some of the classic authors; so saturated with his studies that one would think at times he had actually *known* the bearers of the great names he uses so lightly! And yet with all this, with a personal knowledge of ancient usages, and ways of thought which startles even me, who—well, *ahem!* am sometimes considered to be of fair scholarship, with all this bent-shouldered learning, I say, he is a fine fellow, an athlete, a rough-rider of the first category, as we saw an hour ago—the very ideal of one of those bold Roman adventurers who made this country their own, and regarding whom history is as silent as our imaginations must always be active."

I bowed, for it seemed as though his Lordship were praising me personally. He helped himself to another half glass, and having carefully felt for the crispest biscuit in the silver dish at his elbow, added: "And so like you too! Anyone would know you were cousins, if they did not take you for brothers; his very speech is yours; his turns of expression; one could almost think he had borrowed part of your identity, was thinking with your brain, and living with your life!" whereat the worthy Churchman replaced his glass carefully on the tray, little guessing how near he came to the truth.

A few outside comments like this I had to stand. They were easily evaded. But you will guess how I longed to be alone with Lepidus; how I sighed to pump him: to get below the surface of his courtly ease, to hear what he thought of the present and the past—the splendid past that he alone could bring up glowing and palpitating to the eager vacancies of my mind. I grudged him to those pedants who after lunch cornered him and tried to get his opinion on the place of Michael Angelo in art, or St. Xavier in political theology—individuals it made them giddy to find he had never heard of. I was jealous of those laughing girls who stole the great Centurion from the wise men and essayed to teach him tennis or croquet—just fancy the nephew of an Imperial Cæsar at croquet! Late in the evening, when an after-dinner hush had settled on the company, I did indeed find myself alone with the Roman in the billiard-room, and determined to ask him some questions about himself, but the result was disappointing.

I was diffident about beginning, for one thing; it seemed such a big subject, and it is awkward commencing a conversation on eternity with a man whom you suspect of having just arrived thence. Lepidus I knew was a frank open-hearted fellow who would not hesitate to answer anything I might ask, but I felt a prig beside him, weighted with prejudice, and full of the scruples of my narrow rearing. So I lighted my cigar in silence, and we settled down to

AN INTERRUPTED EXPLANATION

a game of a hundred up, the Centurion handling the cue all the better for having played a game something like billiards in that long ago about which I itched to ask him. But our hearts were not in it, and soon we were both sleepy and bored.

"Let's sit down and have a talk," I said, taking another cigar from the box on the side table, while Lepidus took a pull at a deep silver tankard of ale, a drink he had recently discovered, and already venerated with an affection which respected neither time nor place.

"What shall we talk about?" he asked, throwing himself on the couch next me, and propping his handsome old-world head upon his hand.

What, indeed? I scarcely knew how to begin, and stared for a time at the opposite wall through my blue curling smoke.

"Lepidus," I said desperately, "tell me about yourself. Think how I burn to know something of what you know—speak to me, speak, I beg you."

He was silent a minute, then replied: "What shall I tell you, good comrade, to whom I already owe so much? Is it about old Rome you wish to know, or about these misty hills of yours—how we came and conquered, digging the fosse, staking the palisades, and kicked our heels on yonder green knoll, while we cursed your British climate and sighed for home? Why, man, it would take a dozen nights to tell but half of it."

I waved my hand impatiently. "All that I can fairly imagine for myself. It is not of the gold and glitter I want to hear, not of sunshine and blue skies. I can picture your red horse-hair plumes waving amongst the green fir branches. I can hear your laugh, you and your brass-bound comrades, as you splashed mud-stained chargers home through barbarian bogs after some bloody foray, the captive British girls hand-fast to your saddle-bows, and the burning villages crimson and black against the sky behind you. It is not about all that, Lepidus, not how you lived, and drank, and fought, but about the after, the crypt—surely, surely there must be something of all that long interval stored in your dusty mind—something left behind by all those long years of waiting; a single remembrance *then* were worth a library of ancient history, fascinating as even that would be from your lips. Come, surely you can remember at least something?"

"Remember!" said the Centurion. "By Hercules! I should think I did. All that grey sleep, as you once called it, is a tangle of remembrances, a web whereof the woof has gone amiss and the gaudy patterns dropped into disarray. Sometimes I think I could patch it out again; a bright dream of the

AN INTERRUPTED EXPLANATION 81

manifold nether worlds of death leaps up for a minute or two, and if I could speak while it lasts, and you could jot it down——"

"Lovely, lovely!" I cried in delight. "Lepidus, this will be worth the doing; lord! what a book we will write between us—you the one traveller returned, and I the scribe! Sit you there as tight as a rock while I run and get a note-book from the library; we will begin this very evening."

Away I went, eager, as you may guess, to set down that immortal narrative, possessed myself of a fountain pen, and then hurriedly searched the writing-table drawers for a blank note-book. The first one that came to hand was half full of old tailoring accounts, and one cannot well run a narrative of the outer world on to details of trouserings, or the price of under-vests. The second my mother had three-fourths filled with recipes for pickling walnuts and preserving rhubarb, while yet another was a washing account book—and I shut it up hastily, since for some reason my dear parent never permitted me to look at *that*. What a shame that the Roman's splendid narrative should grow cold upon his lips, while trivialities of this sort hindered me! Finally, after many precious minutes wasted in fruitless search, I snatched up a sheaf of note-paper, whereon was emblazoned in gold, besides our address, the best way of reaching us by train or telegraph, and with this bolted back, red-hot, to the billiard-room.

It was empty and deserted. There was still a wreath or two of cigar smoke under the lamps, and the score board pointed emblematically to the record of the unfinished game, but Lepidus had disappeared. Deeply chagrined I turned to the doorway, and there a footman met me, "Please, sir," said the man, "Mr. Lepidus has gone upstairs to play poker with the Bishop; the mistress sends her love, and would like you to join them at once."

A bitter, an irreverent expletive coupled with him of Pewchester rose to my lips—he a Churchman to rob the world like this of knowledge the Church has groped and probed at for unnumbered generations; it was shocking, but what could I do? With a groan at the malevolence of fate, I threw the paper down, straightened my white cravat instinctively in the mirror, and heavy hearted went upstairs.

They set me down to whist at a side table, and I suppose I was about as deplorable a partner as had ever revoked or trumped his partner's cards since the world began. As for the Centurion—that false repository of splendid secrets—he was in his element. He leant over to me and shouted for the loan of a handful of silver in the most shameless way;

AN INTERRUPTED EXPLANATION

he cut and shuffled, and—with pretty little Mrs. Milward behind his chair to prompt—played his picture cards with boyish pleasure. Was it possible, I thought to myself, as I dealt the odd card into my neighbour's lap, and nervously stirred my coffee with the scoring-pencil, that that broad-backed fellow scooping in the pool, and clamouring for his penny "points," knew more than all of us put together of the great knowledge; that he could, if he would, say that which should send a shudder of awe and wonder through the sentient world, toppling philosophies, shaking religions, and altering the very foundations of society—and would not! Never was a player so delighted as I, when my partner rose and said that as we were hopelessly beaten we had better cease play for the evening.

Later on there came tea, with stronger drinks behind for the men, and while we sat grouped round the fire, the talk turned somehow to town and country fashions in women's frocks, and the curious process of devolution by which rural linendrapers come to possess what Regent Street, or Picadilly, has done with two years back.

"Ay," observed my mother, presently, "but there is a girl coming here who will put all our country fashions to shame;" then turning to me with a quick, malicious little glance, "Louis," she added,

"I have a letter here from Miss Priscilla Smith, to say she will be with us on Thursday afternoon. She can give us only a short time as my invitation clashed with another already accepted, yet that is better than nothing, isn't it, Louis, dear?" and the kindly mother, after bending upon me grey eyes that stirred the secret of my soul, sent a private whisper round the circle.

"Better than nothing"—vexation and chagrin dropped from me like a mantle at the mention of that name; why, one day with Miss Smith was better than a year's enjoyment without her. The most beautiful girl you ever saw, at least to my mind; not one of those pink-and-white human dolls that are sometimes called beautiful by some unacquainted with beauty, but a girl with a face like a great book that you could go to again and again for tenderness or inspiration, and renewed assurance of the dignity of your kind. A face that you could go to merry and not be quenched; or downcast and find your sorrows less than you thought them; or bad to hate your badness; or good to feel yourself lifted with a glorious elation into her sweet comradeship. No, Pris (I cannot call her Miss Smith any more) was not, perhaps, beautiful at first sight; I doubt if even I, who am somewhat of a fool in general things, thought her so until that day, alone with her in the garden, when, stormy and discontented, I abused my kind and the world for five minutes, then, looking up for the first time, found her eyes fixed on me with a look of such splendid compassion, such tender understanding and better knowledge, that the spleen died away from my tongue, and I was shamed without a syllable of reproach. It suddenly flashed on me *then* that she was beautiful, and the belief went on increasing, until it became a deathless certainty that day a month ago, when in the same rose-walk she let the hand I had captured rest in mine, and, giving me a glance out of those speaking eyes, revolutionised the world for me, and (barring some fits of boredom I was subject to when she was absent) made me one of the happiest men alive. A tall, stately girl, with classic features, a gentle upbringing, everything perfect about her, except her name, and that, thank God, it was easy to change.

All this my mother's words conjured up while, oblivious of the amused eyes bent upon me, I sat, as Lepidus said afterwards, " like Narcissus absorbed in his own *reflections* "—not so bad a pun, considering the Roman's recent knowledge of our vernacular. I saw the good Bishop reflectively twiddle his thumbs, and heard him, with modest triumph, say to my mother, " My warm congratulations, dear Mrs. Allanby, and my wife's—a charming girl, I have no doubt; a support and a comfort, I trust, to you in the years to come, and a most faithful and, ahem!—improving helpmate to your excellent son here."

For the rest, I only know I returned a dozen friendly hand-grips at bed-time that night with enthusiasm, submitted to a good deal of patting on the back and gentle sarcasm, and went to my room happy and delighted with everything and everyone—even Lepidus.

CHAPTER VII

THE ROMAN REFLECTS

THERE will occur at times, episodes of dulness in the best regulated country houses. It may be the barometer, or the host; it may be an indiscretion of the cook over last night's dinner, or the approach of the day of departure; but the solid fact remains. Every now and then a fit of silence descends on the country house guests, an interlude of stagnation when flirtation becomes tedious, gossip no longer fascinates, and a gentle melancholy broods over minds and tongues that yesterday were the devoted slaves of flippancy or folly. It is a deplorable experience, since the modern host or hostess regards it as his or her sovereign duty to let no one think while under a friendly roof. They may laugh and frolic, make love, or play havoc with their digestions, but reflectiveness is as much an offence against countryside morality as shooting a fox, or coming down to dinner in a comfortable coat.

The day after the events narrated in a previous chapter, such an episode beset us in Caster Manor. In vain my mother led off the ladies in parties to her dairies, her larders or preserve manufactures; in vain she dangled before their eyes the newest parcels of crewels from Welsh warehouses, or strove to interest them in brand-new consignments of hymn books, gold-edged, limp-bound, wherewith one might be devotional with the utmost convenience and gentility. In vain I suggested walking, riding, shooting, cigars, billiards, battledore, petty larceny, arson, abduction—anything, everything (except sacrilege) to the good bishop and my other male guests; they, like my mother's, were civilly but hopelessly melancholy. There is no cure for such a state of things except that sovereign remedy Time—a remedy which the gods in their mercy have lent us to numb the remembrance of griefs, great or little, such as their potency could not prevent. Time, like one of those medicines our cousins over the sea are fond of inventing, will cure everything, from a chilblain to a broken heart; it cured our dulness in due course, and by lunch that day we were fairly cheerful again. A rebellion in the kitchen, promptly suppressed, afterwards opened the hearts of the womenkind in a glorious exuberance of sympathetic experiences; and two bottles of port in the smoking-room convinced my own comrades that life, after all, was still worth living.

Then arose the question what were we to do during the afternoon, and as we lounged idly by the windows, we fell to making suggestions. One was for ferreting the barns, another stood out for a cock-fight, until it was explained to him that we lacked the rough material, our poultry being bred with a view to the table and not the amphitheatre. Other ingenious suggestions were that we should kill one of my mother's pigs; act some play; go blackberrying; or dress us as minstrels and serenade the ladies in the drawing-room. There were objections to all these plans, but when the boy Binks, who had been fetching cigars, and overheard our conversation, volunteered the suggestion, on permission being given, that we might run the water off the lake, which was already very low, and see what fish there were in it, everyone's face brightened.

"Why, you chubby imp of wickedness," said the Centurion to the page, "this is a golden solution of our difficulty, and I for one am all for it. We will make you a graven image, Binks: the Page and the Pike with the black clouds of discontent rolling away behind. To the lake, comrades! I am as hungry for fish as an otter in a January thaw!"

So it was settled, for whatever pleased Lepidus, somehow seemed to please all of us; and a little later on we were taking our way across the lawn, armed with baskets and bags for the removal of such spoil as Providence might allot to us, and a marvellous assortment of articles for baling out the remains of our summer-spent pool. It was a foolish and boyish enterprise, and I fairly blushed for the exuberance of my Imperial Roman, who, with a tin dipper in one hand and a clothes-basket under the other arm, strode along in front of us gleefully telling the sculptor how he, when a little urchin, had once fished for prawns in the Tiber, and taken his best catch from the interior of a drowned dog, an episode that made his fame as a sportsman amongst his comrades, but diminished his fondness for prawns at dinner. But after all, to be happy one must be boyish. To manhood is given the consolation of effort, and the sober satisfaction of success, perhaps; but true, unhampered pleasure is the privilege of those alone who occupy the state of youth, or can revert to it, and Lepidus infused us all that afternoon with his juvenescence. At times it is true he would be serious for a moment or two in the midst of the wild sport which followed, and on one of these occasions, while we were fishing, I noticed him standing, as the falconers say, "at gaze"—looking this way, and that, up the stream, and then across from side to side where it narrowed at the end of our lakelet, until, presently, seeing me watching, he came over and, touching my elbow, said in that low, impressive voice he always had when he was interested—

"'Tis strange, cousin Louis, but hereabouts I should have said was the place where a fugitive maid very dear to me, and I and such of her slaves as were left, crossed the stream one night long ago when her father's home was burnt. There was then no villa where yours is; no sluice gates; no neatly margined lake. But down by yon sloping bank on the right we came, flying through the dark, tangled coppices in our haste, with naught to light us but the red glimmer through the trees behind. It was *here,* I would have sworn, we half dragged, half carried that tender lady through the winter flood, losing as we went a stupid, treasure-laden slave or two; and up yonder pine-covered knoll we toiled on our way to look for safety—surely, surely I am not mistaken!" And the Roman glanced about with a wistful eagerness in his expressive face, until after a time some incident of the sport claimed his attention again.

But, to return to the regular sequence of our narrative, down to the lake we went in procession with all that gear, and round by the margin where my mother's Alderneys were standing ankle-deep in the shallows, endeavouring to ward off the swarming midges; and so round to the lower end of the narrow sheet of water, where, indeed, nothing but a moss-grown hatchway under a foot-bridge separated it from the river proper. Here Binks, who was in his element, pointed out that by putting down an old net he had brought, and lifting the hatch, we could let off the water faster than the springs and mill-pool a mile above could fill the lake, and with the assistance, perhaps, of a little baling, all the luckless fish in the place would be ours. It was a base poaching project, but down we put the net across the face of the sluice, and opened the hatch, and with the awed delight of schoolboys bent on mischief, watched all that the summer had left of our lake go tumbling in a turgid flood into the stream beyond.

In twenty minutes the panic-stricken coots and moorhens were flying over the meadows to quieter places, while our tame ducks had gone off hurriedly to the farmyard to inform their friends the Dorkings that the end of the world had surely arrived, and from where we stood, almost back to the lawn, was nothing but a desolation of black ooze hemming in a melancholy succession of diminutive pools. Then began a wild scene of boyish riot, a horrible debauch of fun, and fish, and mud which I should have been ashamed to chronicle but for one little incident at the end which has saved it in my memory from utter shame.

The water as it came down, brought with it all the fish that had grown and battened under the lily leaves for generations, and these with the exception of a few which still plunged about in the upper pools, were now collected in the last of the series, an ankle-deep sheet about half an acre in extent just above the sluice gate. This was literally seething with them! Enormous pike rolled in the stream like logs of grey birch-wood, golden carp tumbled in yellow splendour in the sludge; speckled trout, such as none of us ever dreamed the lake contained, jumped indignantly from the plebian press; lazy tench strove to burrow into the soft bottom from which the struggles of their comrades in misfortune constantly disinterred them; keen perch, barred black and green, set their angry spines in defiance of all comers; lithe eels passed through the throng like gleams of light, and shoals of lesser fish, shivering in silvery brightness against the darker mass like aspen leaves in the breeze, flew here and there. What man, in whose veins the food-winning instincts of remote ancestors had ever tingled could see such a sight unmoved?

With a shout the Roman rushed into the water, and immediately sank nearly up to his knees in the soft black alluvium; we followed him in, as a matter of course, and once we had dimmed the immaculateness of the white tennis flannels in which, for some perverse reason, we had dressed ourselves, we became indifferent to all further consequences. We soon saw there was no opportunity for baling, as this, the last pool, was obviously shrinking of its own accord, and narrowing down to the channel which led to the floodgates, the fishes perforce following the falling water, and more and more congregating in the one spot still remaining to them. So we threw away tin pannikins and dippers, and went for the big chub and tench with a fine disregard of consequences.

It was a sight to see the Centurion plunging after a giant pike with joyous fervour, to watch him edge the fish into the shallows, and then rush upon him, only to receive perhaps a slap of the broad tail and a squirt of liquid mud, as the victim dodged back, between his legs, into comparatively deep water. Mullens, too, did heroic things, tossing the little fish out on to the bank, and having at least one encounter with a gigantic tench, which Lepidus said the gods themselves might have watched with interest from Olympus. Nor was I, or the men from Oxford, idle. And as we all floundered and staggered and reeled, growing every moment more unrecognisable through a mask of dirt, perspiration, and fish scales, the scene became wild beyond description. All that was left of the pool and its oozy bottom became churned by our feet into a perfect cauldron of muddy foam and reeking water, and in this horrible bath men and fish wallowed and fought under the quaintest circumstances. Never had the bottom of that placid lake been so disturbed before. Now one man would rise victorious from the foam clutching a struggling chub, perhaps, to his breast, and then another would slip and go down into the vortex amidst shouts of unsympathetic laughter, which were redoubled as he came up inky black from head to heel, dripping and bedraggled, but still undaunted!

Never had the bottom of that muddy ford been so diluted. We had been hard at work for nearly an hour; had filled three garden water-barrows with specimen fish to be returned to the lake when the wild frolic was over; and had thrown an incredible quantity of lesser fry over into the lower reaches of the river, when that incident happened which is my only excuse for putting all this upon paper.

I have said the water had drawn down until it was the stream which it had once been, rather than the lake which artificial needs had made of it. It was flowing again, in brief, as it had done long years ago, and our rough sport had taken place just where a natural constriction of the course had suggested the situation of the ancient ford and the modern sluice gate. We had scuffled and stirred the sediment of ages, while the water had carried the resulting fluid over the weir, until we had actually worked right down to the ancient gravel bottom itself. Lepidus was still joying in the mêlée close to me, wet to the skin, a fact which he heeded little, and scarcely recognisable for weed and mud, which he heeded less, when he struck his foot against an object imbedded in this shingle, and something about the feel of that unseen thing arrested his attention. He felt it again with his foot, and then put down an exploring hand into the still turgid water.

"It is not a stone," he said quietly to me, as I splashed over to his side, "and it does not feel like wood."

"Perhaps," I answered derisively, "it is some of the treasure those slaves of yours dropped that night you were speaking of!"

"You laugh, cousin Louis," said the Roman, "but stranger things have happened, and here it comes at all events to answer for itself." And the strong muscles tightened, the broad soldier back stooped to the effort, and the next minute, with a swirl and a splash, out of the gravelly depth he lifted into daylight—a box!

A leaden casket it was, about a foot square each way; old, dulled by long ages, dinted, covered with caddis worm and water slime, yet so perfect that the lettering on it, the scrolls, and doves, and pretty dancing cupids of the lid could easily be traced. We stared at it for a minute or two in blank surprise, and then the Centurion, turning those grave black eyes of his upon me, said:

"A right good guess of yours, comrade. It *is* some of the booty from the villa. I remember the casket well: remember the very rogue who had it on his head, and tripped, and fell here, that evening of many memories. Lend a hand, and we will see what is in it."

So I took one handle, he the other, and between us we dipped the ancient coffer once or twice in the stream, rubbing its venerable scrollery with our fingers, till it was all clean again, and then staggered to the bank with it. There, while the others left their fishing and crowded round us, we forced the lid and peered into the depth of that strange link with the long forgotten. It was full of money, nearly to the brim! Quaint, handsome old money, bearing the images and superscriptions of dead Cæsars: gold, silver, and brass, all lying side by side, though you could guess by the way the separate metals stood somewhat together, and by certain mouldering traces of ancient fabrics amongst them, that they had once been in bags that were snatched in haste from some strong hiding place and thrown in here in the panic of a midnight flight, just as we found them.

It was a wonderful sight, and the Roman laughed a little scornfully as he recalled, perhaps, the fierce labours those things had cost to win. Then—knowing nothing of manorial rights, or the legal niceties of treasure trove—he turned to the muddy, wondering men about him, and said gaily, " By the immortal Jove! our cousin Allanby here keeps the best fish in his pond till the last. Shall we share like good comrades, sirs? Well then, here's for you, Mr. Sculptor; and here for you, Sir Scholar, and you, and you, and enough still remaining in the bottom for you, Binks, to buy up all the sweetstuff on the village stall, and incapacitate yourself from further mischief for many a day," and suiting his actions to his words he plunged his hands into the casket again and again with lordly generosity, and poured the ancient coins so liberally into the palms of those about him, that when he turned to me there were none left.

" Now this is hard lines, good friend Allanby," said he, shaking the casket as he spoke, " that we should plunder your preserves and leave you nothing of the spoil; yet wait a minute—surely something rattled then?" and peering again into the now empty coffer, we saw within it a second lid, and lifting it cautiously—he and I, the twin inheritors of a strange past—there hidden in the false bottom was found a *golden wreath.*

Such a lovely wreath, made for a lovely woman's head! All of the purest, palest gold that no time or age could dim. Fabricated by some cunning pastmaster of his craft in the ages when men worked lovingly on such things as these—two dainty myrtle sprays in bud and blossom, knit at the lower end by a golden bond, and open at top, where the wearer's forehead would shine under the soft glimmer of those leaves and buds—an ornament of ten thousand that would grace even beauty's self, and I gazed at it with strange feelings rising within me, until the soldier lifted it and taking me aside, out of earshot of the rest, said—

"This for you, dear comrade, whom I already like so well. You are nearer, maybe, to a wife than I am, so take the chaplet and let it be my tribute to her, whosoever she be, and in part payment of all I owe you. 'Tis a pretty trinket, and no light gift for me at least to give, for the last time I saw it, it circled the brown head of that lost maid I told you of."

"Lepidus!" I exclaimed, "are you sure of that?"

"Quite, quite sure, Louis! It is, as I say, a gift from the head of my lost girl to your living one. Put it in her hair that day she is yours, and if the giver is not there to see it so worn—why, spill a drop or two in friendly libation to his spirit as the wedding cup passes from her lips to yours!"

And I took the chaplet, and all happened as he wished.

That night we had two or three people in from neighbouring houses to dinner, my whole attention being given to putting my shoulder to the conversational wheel, and helping it out of the ruts liable to beset it under such circumstances. The tendency of a gathering of this kind is always towards extreme provincialism. The inhabitants of ancient Hellas divided into diminutive nationalities by mountain barriers, were surprised to hear from their conquerors, that organised humanity existed beyond their parish boundaries, and in somewhat the same way your rural neighbour in England if you permit him, will talk of cabbage-bed and mothers' meetings, the latest highway tax or the inquisitiveness of the local church-warden's mother's aunt in a way that condemns your other friends to silence from soup to celery. By dint of dragging the good bishop in that evening neck and crop to our burning question of church government; by stirring up the secret wrath which I knew slumbered in the breast of the sculptor, Mullens, against the masonry decorations of our village school-house, and basely inviting Mrs. Milward to teach our Vicar's wife how to organise free kitchens, I blended the imperial and the parochial, the general and the particular, in our table talk and earned my mother's gratitude.

Of Lepidus I saw nothing till we met by chance alone in the billiard room about ten o'clock. They had been twitting me upstairs with regard to Priscilla, asking whether it was on her account I had sent for the village barber to cut my hair that morning?—and so on. The Roman, of course, had heard that banter, and laughed again at me in his friendly way, as he sat recumbent on a corner of the billiard table, questioning about the lady, her height, her colour; whether "Smith" was the patronymic of a powerful gens; and offering to wager me a hundred silver coins to nothing that he would convey her affection from me to himself within a week of her coming. It was only in play, but you know how tender lovers are on such scores. Besides, Lepidus was undeniably big and handsome; he had a most persuasive way with women; a keen eye for female comeliness; and his upbringing had, I feared, not been conducted on strictly Anglican principles; consequently my brow clouded over at his banter.

Seeing that, the Roman clapped me on the shoulder, saying it was but his fun, and "no men were worth much who were not fools in love." He himself could sympathise with me, for over and above some transient flames, some light friendships of march and camp, he had himself once dearly loved a girl, Prisca Quintilia he said she was called.

"Such a girl, Britisher," he exclaimed, warming with his subject and swept away on a sudden by the remembrance; "the daughter of one of our Roman Prefects here by a British mother; a southern fruit ripened under the northern skies. Gods!" he cried, jumping from his seat and pacing up and down the room, "such a girl—tall, fair, stately, her brown-red hair like a crown upon her head; the woman and the man twin in her spirit; her father's pride and her mother's gentleness shining in her face; a fury from hell when spears gleamed on the rampart; a touch of velvet on a wound when the day was done; a silken step, and a voice like summer streams where sick men lay about.

"And I loved her, loved her fiercely, Britisher, and had her troth here in your holly coppices!

It was for her I, a fameless soldier, painted my name in blood across these endless moss hags; it was for her I gutted every hut and village from Isurium to the western sea—pouring out golden British spoils before her—well content if a smile and a touch of those fingers repaid a month of danger and hardship. Do you remember," cried the Roman, forgetting time, and place, in the full flood of his waking recollection, " how the barbarians stormed her father's stronghold that night in December, and how I saw the glare from my hut on the next hill-side, and, half naked, sword in teeth, swam the ice-choked river to her rescue? Gods, what a fight we made of it! and when the place could be held no longer, our way back over the snow to the shelter of the forest was littered with black corpse of dead foeman, and puddled with blood, like the track of the wolves who drag their spoil away to caverns on the Apenines. I sometimes think," said the Roman, laughing low to himself, " that we of the Tiber shall never get the taint of that fierce foster-mother's milk of ours out of our blood," and he stalked to and fro through the tobacco smoke with changing passions on his face—the very embodiment in mufti of the emotions he spoke of.

To and fro he went for a time, while I, doing

the wisest thing, never said a word, for I feared even by moving to break the thread of the recollection he had chanced upon. To and fro he went, finely agitated, then coming and sitting down suddenly by me, stared into the opposite shadows.

"But she died," he ran on, gripping my wrist, and pulling me as it were towards the void he saw before him, "she died, and I died; and then—years after, a hundred years after—two hundred, I know not—as I lay in the crypt, her spirit came to me from the world of the living. It was a windy night and a wet one, and your knoll there was covered with pine and with spruce; and between the damp shadows, and over the dead leaves that scarcely lifted to the draught from her skirt hem, she came drifting through the tree-stems to me. And I knew she was coming, and smiled in my dust and loneliness.

"'What ho! sleeper within there!' she said, between the gusts of the storm, beating with clenched fist on the sod of the hill-top.

"And 'Enter' I answered, and down through the turf and the solid flag-stone she sank, till she rested, a violet cloud, on my bosom. It was pretty to feel the dove in her breast fluttering against mine, but I would not look—knowing it was easier for her so—until she had taken shape, and then I looked, and the crypt was full of splendid violet light, while at the bier-foot, dangling her dainty heels against the stone, and laughingly shaking the night mist from her braided hair, was Prisca Quintilia in the dress of a Saxon.

" ' Why, sweetheart,' I said, getting up on my elbow, ' 'tis a poor night to be out; art not afraid of the wind and the rain?'

" Whereat, laughing merrily, she shook her head for answer, and I knew I was a fool, for the silver drops she had gathered as she came, fell with that merry gesture in a shower through her gauzy substance and pattered on the floor of my chamber, where they vanished.

" Then we fell a-talking till the rain had stopped, the pine branches overhead began to scrape together in the breath of the morning, and the rustle of the night worms drawing home from above sounded soft on either hand. And she was as merry as a cricket on a hearth, that shadowy lady sitting dangling her feet on the stone the while she talked of her thanes, and thorpes, and burghers, drawing, as she chattered, a necklace of amber beads to and fro across her pearly teeth. Then all on a sudden she stopped and listened as it were—' They call me!'

she cried, and in a thought the lady had shrunk to a round of pallid light, and was but a bright spot upon the further wall; deeper and deeper she sank unto it, until you could see the joints of masonry rising through the shine; and then the gravels and pine roots stood out as she, making the solid earth transparent for a moment, passed beyond—then masonry, earth and fir tangles closed up, and she was gone.

"Again I slept a century or two, keeping little note of time, and dozing on the brink of oblivion. And many others that you know not of came and went across the dusty walls, some in friendship, some still frowning over old wounds—for friendships and wounds outlive empires—until presently my love came down again.

"This time she had dropt her green Saxon tunic, wearing instead a tight-fitting Norman gown of purple stuff, her shoes up-pointed, her sleeves puffed and slashed with white satin, and round her dainty middle a splendid cincture flashing with gems and silver—a lovely sight, and she was standing over me before I knew of it (so many hundred years were making my perceptions dim), tapping on my chest, and crying in my ear—

"'Up, sleepy one! By sweet St. Denny, you are

the only man in England who would doze like that when Margaret de Lisle stands unattended beside his couch '—and then, for though her voice was high and her eyes sparkled, her look was gentle, she stooped and kissed me. Those fair lips roused me at once. They smelt unconscionable of sack, while on the girl's cheeks the flush of new excitement was burning unmistakably.

"'Why, sweetheart,' I said, 'what is it now? It is but a span since you were here before. How do the gentle burghers? Is aught the matter with your friendly thanes?'

"'Phew! what do I know or care for thanes or burghers? I tell you, Sir Mole, I am Margaret de Lisle—Norman heiress of Stackley and Brabourne, and to-day Queen of Beauty at the great Tournament. See here?' and taking if off from where it hung in the crook of her elbow, she held up for me to note a lovely crown of myrtle and orange flower cunningly twisted with silver threads. 'There! how does it look? Young De Vipon, whose bloody gauntlets laid it a few hours since upon my forehead, said he had never seen myrtle so wellbecomed!' and the girl with swift woman fingers placed the crown amid her gleaming hair, and turned upon me a face that shone with happy excitement.

"'De Vipon, lady, would seem to be a capable judge, as well as a bold soldier.'

"'And you are not jealous of him? He loves my body up yonder.'

"'Let him have it, sweet lady. It no more concerns me than who owns the green kirtle you came here in last time. You smell of supper——'

"'And good reason. They have fêted, petted and pampered me since De Vipon gave the crown, till my head fairly spins. They put me 'tween him and the king himself, newly come from wars abroad, at the joy-feast, and what with lights, music, flattery, and sack, I was near distraught when my serving-women bore me off to bed an hour ago.'

"'It might well be so,' I said, and there the lady stood and talked, sometimes a mere violet shadow, as her restless body tossed, half awake, under silken counterpanes somewhere above, and sometimes, as it slept, clear and defined as that body itself."

Here Lepidus himself seemed dozing, and I half feared this strange confidence into which he had dropped, so unreal and yet so picturesque and vivid, was at an end. But I kept still, my hand on his, and everything was as quiet as could be, save the ticking of my watch, and the sound of an under-footman whistling as he cleaned the dinner glasses in his pantry across the yard—

> "For she was one of the early birds,
> And I was an early worm."

Then the Roman suddenly roused again, and went on:

"I slept and slept—every rustle of brown leaves overhead marking a passing winter, until presently across my sleep there fell the sound of someone sobbing. It was away back in the darkness, perhaps a mile back down the thicket path, but it roused me. Nearer it came, while I kept my eyes tight shut, till at last the light shone through my dusty lids, and the smothered sighs of a woman in grief were but a pace or two from my feet. Then I roused, and there again was she, whose soul, affiliated to mine, came to me thus, time after time, while her bodies tossed to and fro on the thing you call life. That night she was all in rags, her russet brown skirt frayed at the hem and full of burrs; her poor feet bare and muddy; her hair tangled and wind-blown; her face as white as the stars overhead; and her arms, as far as I could see them, scratched and bleeding. But in the clutch of those arms, shrouded by a faded red shawl twisted across her shoulders, was something bulky and valuable! She stood there, leaning against the grey stones for a time, rocking softly from one foot to the other, and cherishing that bundle, without noticing me, while her tears ran down the ragged shawl. Then suddenly she came across, as softly as the mist over wet meadow grass, and standing by my side, said without preface, 'They turned me out, Lepidus! I knew they would,' and the tears gushed out anew.

"'Who turned you out, sweetheart?'

"'My father, and brothers, and harsh Janet, my sister. They turned me out a week ago—me like that! And if it hadn't been for the food my mother hid next day in my path, I had starved outright by this.'

"'Why,' I said, 'this is a different tune to the one you piped last time; but things cannot surely be so bad. What have you in the bundle? More trophies, more gems and jewels?'

"'Gems,' cried the little lady indignantly flashing up behind her tears with fierce mother-pride. 'Infinitely better than *gems;*' and dropping her voice she whispered proudly, 'Look! isn't he lovely? Didst ever see such cheeks or such a rosebud mouth before?' and turning back the flap of her weather-stained shawl, she showed me a sleeping babe but a day or two old.

"I spoke her softly after that, but of De Vipon and the tournament she remembered nothing, shaking her head, and saying she was just plain Alice Selby, whose father was woodcutter in King Harry's forests here—'if I did not believe it, I might go and ask—everyone for miles round knew rough old John Selby, and his pretty daughter Alice,' and the poor girl blushed and sighed as she uttered her own name.

"Later on there came another puppet in the soul-show, a merry, brown-eyed merchant's wife, who talked of tallow and hides; and then another—only a spell or two ago, it seems—who hurried in, her hair piled high, and powdered white upon her head; her shoes steep-heeled and coral red. She swept in hastily and anxious-looking, her flowered silk skirt clutched in her jewelled hand, and touching me with an ivory fan—

"'Lepidus,' she said, 'dear Lepidus, they have kept you waiting here too long. But 'tis near over; to-morrow—or some soon to-morrow—the respite comes; I was sent to tell you—good-bye, good-bye' and in a thought she too was gone."

"Who came next?" I asked. But this time my Roman had stopped in earnest, and when presently he roused and shook himself together, it was but to declare he had never in his life felt so sleepy before; so seeing there was no more to be got from him that time, I led the way to bed, and tossed about all night haunted by the strangest fancies.

CHAPTER VIII

SHE COMES

WE went rat hunting next day. Lepidus was up before breakfast, and took a swim in the lake, much to the alarm of the Bishop's lady, who saw him drying himself far away amongst the fir trees—the Centurion was no more ashamed of his body than he was of his soul—and indignantly reported the circumstance to my mother. After breakfast, Mrs. Milward and my cousin carried the Roman off to our tennis-courts, where, though his play robbed the game of much science, it added immensely to its excitement. There was a splendid vigour in his rushes, such as would have carried dismay into the defenders of a fort threatened with escalade, while his "services," though not always exact, came from those sinewy arms with almost the swiftness of Jove's own thunder-bolts.

Then, as I said, when tennis was over, the ladies went off to read indifferent novels, or devise methods of spending their kinsmen's earnings, and Lepidus, prompted by that boy Binks, invited me to come and see one of my own corn-stacks thrashed.

"You must come," he said, beaming with the enthusiasm that marked everything he did. "We are going to take sticks, and all the terriers, and Binks says he will get us the biggest jar of ale in the cellar—the butler being asleep—though privately I believe Binks had drugged him with this very object. Mary too has promised to pass us out a basket of bread and cheese through the pantry window—so you must come."

"But my dear fellow, why this secrecy? Surely I have influence enough with Mary or the butler to get you lunch without such illicitness?"

"Ay, good friend Louis, but to Binks and me the food would lose half its savour if it were come by honestly; so on with your oldest jacket, and we will wait just five minutes for you by the stable gate."

Now I hate rats and love rat hunting. Theoretically I reverence life in every possible shape, not knowing where it came from or whither it goes, and can quite sympathise with those Eastern devotees, who refuse to sit down abruptly on the bare ground for fear they may thereby inconvenience a centipede or earwig. But you will find everyone's philosophy has a weak point, and that of mine in this connection is rats. Fierce and valorous I know they are; conceited over their young as any human mother, arrogantly holding, like her that the true pivot of the world is their own particular nursery; tender to the infirm of their own species until tenderness becomes weakness; bold in design, abundant in resource, resolute and skilful in execution; venturing their lives in fulfilment of that destiny to which, through no choice of their own, Nature has appointed them, and dying when the time comes with their backs to the wall—all this makes my dislike shabby without amending it.

So that morning I put on my oldest coat, took down a blackthorn kept for the special purpose from the rack, and set off to the meeting-place with the utmost cheerfulness.

And a jolly time we had of it. The stack-yard, like a giant's camp, with a new harvest's stacks in place of tents, was tremulous with the busy roar of thrashing machines when we arrived. To left was a broad pond, framed in by mighty oaks which had seen as many generations of harvesters come and go as we have seen harvests. To right was a fine old farmstead, a village in itself of dormer windows, steep roofs, mighty piles of chimneys and sunny walls whereon snap-dragon and wallflower flourished, as ruddy and bright-toned with time and weather as the ripest of those pleasant-scented pippins lying mellowing in its great apple lofts. On the pond ducks were swimming round the legs of horses leisurely taking their mid-day drink; on the lichened farm-house roof white fantails were slipping and sliding, while in the yard itself all was activity, dust, and noise as the heavy corn shocks tumbled in a steady stream down the hungry thrasher slopes, coming out at the other end a tumble of bent, earless straw by one exit, and a flow of clean round grain by another.

Binks was general in command. As the special stack being operated upon began to get low, he placed the representative of Imperial Rome at one corner, myself at another, and scrambled up on top himself. Our three terriers, their limbs fairly quaking with excitement, and deep sunk in the litter of spent straw lying round the stack, took places between us, and then we were ready. Whirr, whirr, whirr, went the big wheels of the machine, while a hundred flails within it, separating corn from husks, kept up a deafening roar. The three or four men feeding the shoot were invisible at times as they staggered about under their burdens of corn, but slowly they sank lower and lower, until the rats found their stronghold no longer tenable, and began to move. "Fritz" the terrier got the first one. It leapt out almost into his ready mouth: a snap and a shake of his head, and he had secured "first honours." Then another bolted towards the Centurion and was settled by a blow from the blackthorn which would have unloosened the soul from a bigger body than that of the poor "vermin." At the same instant Binks on top was hotly engaged; his rat, after dodging about the shocks for a time, came over the six-foot side with Binks in company right on top of the terriers, who, mad with excitement, were waiting eagerly below. While I was watching the extraordinary scramble that followed, a shout from the harvesters made me look round just in time to see a giant amongst rodents slip silently by me into the strong cover beyond. Then Binks, fighting on his knees like Witherington at Chevy Chase, was aiming blows at quarry on either side of him, while Lepidus, in company with the spare dogs, was wildly chasing something round the stack, I myself being engaged, it must have seemed to an onlooker, on some private thrashing operations on a particularly bulky heap of corn into which I could have sworn a rat went, though I neither saw him leave it, nor could find him in it, alive or dead, afterwards.

The lower the stack sank the more furious the fun became. I will not say the sport was greatly to the credit of our good bailiff, for on an ideal farm there are few rats, and in an ideal wheat stack there are none at all. But the harvest had been hurried, the corn was piled on a foundation of faggots instead of being, as it ought to have been, raised on those stone mushrooms every countryman knows so well—and we were not for the moment agricultural economists. When there was but a foot or two of straw the rats fairly streamed out, and not a moment's respite was allowed to dogs or men. The slaying-stir, as our picturesque-tongued northern ancestors called it, spread to the labourers, work was thrown aside, the ganger put away thoughts of evening's wage bills, the neglected thrasher thundered along on an empty stomach, the last few trusses were thrown aside, the faggot foundations torn up, and for a few minutes the ruins were a wild pandemonium, an inextricable medley of straw, men, dogs, rats, steel-pronged forks, and blackthorns; a confused babel of machinery, shouting, squeaking and barks! Then we rose from the dust and the riot, perspiring and dirty, and under the noses of the sniffing terriers, laid out in two lines three dozen "tails" as a result of the fight.

It was sanguinary, it was perhaps ignoble, but cruel it was not, for there was no room for wounding; the luckless little beasts died in the open and for each of them the game was not lost till it was over. What better terms does Providence ever give to the best of us?

SHE COMES

While they unthatched the next stack and worked it down we had our meal in the neighbouring barn. Binks had been as good as his word, or better, and had provided an ideal stack-yard lunch. We had the farmer and his foreman in, and it would have done your heart good to see how the nephew of the Emperor and they fell upon the beer and cheese, each seated upon an ample truss of hay, while they made the dusty drapery of cobwebs shake on the rafters overhead with their stories and laughter. For my part, I ate in silence and stared. Was it possible, I asked myself, that that jolly gaitered, rat-hunting country squire opposite, nursing the great stone ale jug on his knee, and shouting with laughter at the countryman's musty stories, was the man who last night had called up before me terrible and beautiful visions from the nether world, who for me, his newer self, had lifted for a moment the curtain we all long to lift, and had shown me, I dare not say the truth, but something that he at least took to be that thing?

Well! I was getting accustomed to surprises, and Lepidus at least seemed to have absolutely forgotten the talk of the night before. The lunch ended presently, whereupon we plunged into a new bout of slaughter.

All this time you may be sure I had not lost sight

of the fact that Priscilla—my Priscilla—was to come to us to-day. With the jealousy of a lover I had scrupulously refrained from mentioning the fact, but it was not forgotten, and after lunch, in the midst of rat hunting, when Lepidus had no thought but the sport he was pursuing with such boyish ardour, I took many a surreptitious look at my watch, calculating with secret joy and those tremulous misgivings peculiar to the lover's malady, the time when I should see my lady again.

My mother had elected to meet her at the station in the carriage, and my idea was to slip back to the house (leaving the Roman of course, to his unworthy sport)—have a comfortable wash and brush up, and thus, after getting into that new suit of clothes, as to the peculiar suitability of which to my person I do not mind confessing much recent thought had been given—thus washed and rehabilitated I should be able to receive *her* in our porch, as she ought to be received, with graceful dignity. I felt that would be giving myself a fair chance, and when Lepidus, of whom I already cherished a deep instinctive jealousy, arrived at tea time, dirty, dishevelled. and probably smelling of rats and farm-yards—why, I hoped, and thought, the comparison would not be all in his favour. So I kept an eye on my watch, and when there was just enough time left to carry out the little scheme comfortably, I went over to the Roman, telling him that the severe demands of duty called me home to receive my mother's guest; there was no reason whatever for him to cease his sport. "The sacred cause of agriculture absolutely demanded his presence at the ricks for the present," later on we would meet at home, but at the moment, much as I deplored it, I was bound to get back quickly.

The Roman laughed; perhaps I had rather overdone the apology and he saw through my simple artifice. Be that as it might, he contented himself with good-humouredly excusing me, sending his love to Miss Smith, and advising me to hurry, as he had heard the train whistling a little while before in the next valley.

Just as I was starting, Binks came up to ask if I would mind carrying up half-a-dozen rats for the ferrets at home, as no one was going that way for some time? The task was not a particularly welcome one, yet I was in such a profoundly dirty state already, and smelt so aggressively of vermin that a little more of either characteristic would not matter. The rats were consequently handed over, and I started off at my best pace for the Manor House, whose red chimney-stacks could be seen over the tree tops.

What Lepidus had said about the whistle in the next valley had been taken at the moment merely as a jest, but by the time I got into the lower part of our mile-long drive his suggestion made me uneasy. There *had* undoubtedly been something like a whistle down there—could I have made any mistake? The watch was pulled out again, consulted nervously, and—think of my horror—it had stopped! It pointed to exactly the same time as when I was still ratting in the yard half an hour ago. And at that very instant, still standing dumbfounded, I heard the sound of approaching wheels coming round the curve. There was no mistaking that sound, it was my mother's Victoria and highstepping chestnuts without a doubt; and with a groan of chagrin at being caught in such guise I hurriedly stuffed the wretched rats into my coat-pockets and glanced round for a hiding-place.

Just there the drive was bordered by a tall thorn hedge, beyond which was a spruce copse. If the latter could only be reached unseen the bath and clean suit might still come off. I ran down the drive like a poacher flying from six months' hard labour, and plunged desperately for something that looked like a gap on the right. But our hedger carpenter was a good man, and conscientious; a perfect barricade of thorns met me. Reeling back, scratched and foiled, I caught a sight between the trees of two ladies in the swiftly approaching carriage, and, what was worse, as I subsequently heard, they caught a sight of *me* behaving like a March hare out for a holiday! Ten yards higher up there was another gap. I leapt the muddy ditch and jammed myself head first into it. A swishy bramble snatched my cloth cap off and waved it derisively aloft, a hawthorn spike, a good two inches long, penetrated the tenderest part of my leg, while another bared my knee with a six-inch rent, and just as the friendly shelter beyond was almost gained the cruel bit of timber I was clutching gave way, and I rolled helplessly into the muddy bottom of the drain.

My mother has an absolute confidence in my sobriety. She often boasts to other mothers not so fortunately situated, that she has been able to trust me with the keys of the cellar since I was ten years old; but even *her* kindly face clouded over for a moment as the carriage drew up five yards away, and I crawled on hands and knees out of the docks and stinging-nettles.

" My dear Louis! " she exclaimed, "what *are* you doing? "

" Oh, it is just nothing, mother; I was only walking back from the farm, and—ah, slipped into the ditch as you came up. Miss Smith," I said, turning to the beautiful girl by her, in whose face surprised amusement was struggling with gravity, " you must forgive the guise in which I come before you—I was hurrying home to meet you."

" Thank you, Mr. Allanby; I am sure your haste was most eloquent of your good intentions," and she smilingly held out a hand to me.

" But what," quoth my parent, who embodies all the virtues except tact, " what have you been doing to make yourself so dirty—and what are those strings hanging out of your pockets ? "

Alas! in my haste I had forgotten to tuck away the tails of those odious little beasts we had been killing, and my mother ran on—" Good gracious me! they are rats' tails; oh, how horrible! They are not alive, are they ? "

" No, mother," I answered, humbly pulling out a couple of gory victims to reassure her, " we have been ratting down in the stack-yard, and I was taking these home to the ferrets."

" My *dear* boy!—but why carry them in your pockets like that, with your handkerchief and tobacco pouch? Well, never mind; I don't think we will offer you a lift in the carriage just at present "—this with a meaning sniff in my direction—" but come straight home like a good fellow," and then she called back as the carriage swept on up the drive—

"and for heaven's sake, dear Louis, have a wash before you come into the drawing-room to tea!"

Those ferrets of ours went supperless to bed that night.

Lepidus was late home. He had gone down in the twilight to see some cocks that were to fight a private main in the back parlour of the village inn next day, and came back just in time to dress for dinner. Then happened that which I record briefly and prosaically, but which was surely as strange an incident as ever came to be recorded in black and white. It altered the whole current of our lives for the time, and led directly to that tragic comedy, that strange and dreadful episode, every incident of which still tingles in my blood, casting a shadow of sweet and bitter remembrances over my waking hours, and filling my dreams with fancies splendid but sorrowful.

We had both put on the garb of social servitude, and met, clean collared, black coated, and ample in shirt fronts in the lobby on our way to join the other guests. My heart was softened towards the stranger within our gates, for Priscilla had been very gracious to me at tea-time. Was I not the successful lover, with that incomparable lady under my roof, while he, poor fellow, was separated from his mistress by who knew how many hundred years, or how many circles of immeasurable space? I was tender, I say, to the Roman, and linking my arm in his led him light-heartedly down the passage, chatting as we went. The arras hung across the doorway at the end, and lightly lifting it, there across the great black-oak hall was my dear girl standing by the fireplace, half turned towards us, and talking to the Bishop of Pewchester.

You could not have seen a prettier picture for twenty miles around. She, that tall, sweet lady, had put on a dress of shimmering white satin, that fell soft as milk and tender as moonlight from her graceful shoulders to her feet. Behind were the ebony shadows of the panelling, against which that fair lady stood out like a splendid star on the black forehead of the night. The distant lights twinkled through the banked palms and flowers, the pine-logs cracked and sparkled throwing a lovely changing glow over her white robed figure, the air was full of pleasant scents and harmony, and in an ecstasy of delight I touched the Roman on the arm.

"Look, look!" I whispered, "there she is. Surely, dear Lepidus, nothing new or old was ever better than this sweet, modern girl of mine?"

Then Lepidus looked—and as he looked again the red southern blood rushed to his forehead, and then fled back to his heart. Again the fierce red current swept round his brawny neck and filled the swelling veins of his temples, while his eyes flashed and his breath came quick and short.

"That *your* girl," he said in a minute, when the first gust of his surprise was over, "that *your* girl, your *modern* girl? Louis—you lie—that is *my* girl —Prisca Quintilia!"

For a minute we stood silently by the doorway. Knowing all I knew I durst not answer him; remembering all he had told me I durst not argue it; and then the Roman, recovering first, signed to me to go forward. Stunned and bewildered I obeyed mechanically. We went over to the fire, and there, again mechanically—scarcely knowing what I did, but prompted by a look, I approached the lady, and said—the very words sounding absurd and unreal in my ears:

"May I have the pleasure of introducing my friend, Mr. Marcus Lepidus?" after which, turning to the Incomprehensible One by my side, "Lepidus," I faltered, "let me introduce Miss Prisca Quintilia; no, no!—Miss Priscilla Smith, I should say."

And she smiled, and he smiled, and we all smiled and bowed!

CHAPTER IX

THE OLD LOVE AND THE NEW

A LITTLE time ago I might have taken Lepidus's exclamation with startled disdain. Priscilla his!—my Priscilla, who had grown up as it were under my mother's eye, the beloved of that Roman swaggerer I had brought in a thankless moment from the tomb! It would have been a manifest absurdity, looked at in its mildest light. But now everything was changed; a few hours had taught me the shallowness of my understanding. I was numbed by wonders, dazed by the self-assertion of that other one, and miserably weak with a strange weakness that was neither distinctly in my soul nor in my body, but pervaded me hour by hour with growing intensity.

Thus, when I had blundered through my introduction, and the Roman, looking abominably handsome, had turned the full splendour of his presence on Pris, I drew back, and inwardly consumed with jealousy, but doubtful how to act, took refuge behind the person and tongue of the perennially cheerful

Mrs. Milward. But over that comely widow's sleek and powdered shoulders you may guess how, ever and anon, I stared at the group standing by the fireplace. And as I stared, one grain of comfort came to me. There had not been, nor was there, a visible sign of recognition in Priscilla's face, and the Roman, open as he was with me, was apparently keeping from her, as he withheld from all others, the wonderful secret we two alone knew of. Had it been otherwise, had he spoken, had there been any remembrance of him from the long ago, she must have turned colour, or screamed, or opened her arms, as dead Abelard opened his when dead Heloise was lowered into his tomb. But not a flush went over that gentle face, not a sign of more than womanly approval of a tall, well-featured stranger came into those bright eyes, that looked so frankly into everyone's face. No, Pris at least knew nothing, and this was something gained; as for the Roman—I sometimes thought he did actually forget, either from policy or from some peculiarity of his condition, when with strangers all that he remembered with me, he was absolutely himself again as I looked: bold, bright, unembarrassed, just the sort of man to win his way straight into a female heart, but nothing about him in the least suggestive of what he was, or had been—and then the gong rang for dinner.

I trust I did my duty fairly at the meal, although I splashed more gravy about than usual, and answered most inconsequently when the Bishop's wife spoke to me. For they were so abominably handsome that pair! I tortured myself, and fanned my rising jealousy by bitterly saying to myself that at last my diamond had found a setting worthy of her; here at last was someone matched to her in everything, I said, savagely confiding my sorrows to the soup. Perhaps the same idea came to the rest of the table, for the conversation flagged at our end, and presently all eyes were turned to where those two sat, facing each other across the cloth, and engrossed in some blithe discussion; yes, they were undoubtedly a handsome pair, and as my betrothed bent forward under the shaded candle-light to listen to the Roman beyond the maidenhair and roses, I could see the colour come and go upon her cheek and her white bosom heave

—"With her laughter or her sighs,"

and I asked myself whether her eyes would have sparkled like that had *I* been talking to her, whether she would have followed my words with the rapt attention of a disciple sitting at the feet of a saint; and the answer to both questions was distinctly melancholy. I hated everyone for noticing them

THE OLD LOVE AND THE NEW

so pointedly, and leaving me in gloomy silence, and when Mrs. Milward who loved scandal, looked first at me, then at them, then back at me again, with an almost imperceptible lift of her eyebrows, I hated her. It was only a well-bred lift of a hair's-breadth, but for the moment I hated her for that hair's-breadth, as much as a man may hate a woman.

At the Manor we do not very strictly observe the separation of sexes after dinner. It is an old custom, but I do not know that there is much else to be said for it. In the most remote periods it was no doubt a matter of expediency, as the post-banquet hours were liable to brawls, in view of which a careful host naturally sent into inaccessible places his most easily damaged goods. In the time of our grandfathers, again, it was a matter of decency, as that interval was sacred to drunkenness and obscenity. But since at the Manor my mother foresaw neither of these contingencies as the finish to a satisfactory meal, the ladies remained with us, or rather, we rose simultaneously, distributing ourselves through the hall, billiard-room, conservatory, or drawing-room, as we fancied.

That evening I was button-holed by a worthy rector from a neighbouring village, who wanted me to use my influence to get the Bishop to do something or other for him, and it was nearly an hour before

I tore myself free. Then my first thought was of Pris. Where was she? Surely, on this, her first evening here, she ought to pay me a little more attention? But the lady was nowhere to be seen, and what made her absence worse was that the Centurion was missing too. They were not in the billiard-room, where a couple of men were playing amongst the wreathing tobacco smoke, and they were not in the hall. As I passed into the drawing-room, the grass-widow looked up from a group she was amusing with stories of Indian cantonments, and reading my face, said wickedly—

"They are in the conservatory, dear Mr. Allanby; do go and fetch them; they have been there *such* a long time."

So thither I went, across the soft Turkey carpets and between the archipelagoes of furniture wherewith the modern housewife dots her rooms, my mind divided between a schoolboy jealousy, and a curious wonder as to what the nephew of Vespasianus might be saying to the girl whose other self he had told me he had loved and wooed in Imperial Rome. Was he recalling to her, with a touch or a look, some desperate love scene by the distant Tiber? Was he bringing to her pliant mind, as his mesmeric presence had brought to mine, some vivid picture of the past? Then all of a sudden there impinged upon my inner sense *the unmistakable odour of roasted chestnuts!* The carpet under my feet turned into tesselated pavement, and in front rose upon my vision a red and white striped awning with under it a little brown-skinned urchin sitting roasting those nuts at just such a brazier as we see nowadays at the street corner, while a fellow in brass and scarlet, with his back turned to me, was sorting them on the hot iron with his square scabbard-tip before he purchased.

The vision, or whatever it was, went as swiftly as it came, but the odour of burning husks was still pungent in my nose as I peeped through the open doors of the conservatory. Yes, there they were in a dim nook amongst the camellias, and for a moment all the blood ran back cold to my heart, for the Roman was on one knee before the girl, and either holding her hand or giving her something! It was a pretty scene enough to a disinterested spectator, no doubt, but I did not take it so, and just as a rush of anger was coming back with the blood to my head, Priscilla laughed lightly, and said—

"There, let me pin it for you; those collar studs are always treacherous things, and how you men, who boast yourselves above all fashions, can consent to wear such uncomfortable neck-gear I cannot think.

"Down lower, please, Mr. Lepidus—lower still, and

give me the pin," and down went Imperial Rome upon one knee, while the girl bent over him, and for a minute her white fingers were busy about the back of his broad neck. Then they sat down again, and neither spoke. Priscilla, with true feminine coquetry, allowed that silence to last just long enough to be impressive, then broke through it with a smile.

"You were talking two or three minutes ago of chestnuts, and how to cook them, Mr. Lepidus," she said lightly, "and do you know, as you spoke I could see the scene you described as vividly as though I had been there myself: the little Roman boy under his awning, his fir-cone fuel by his side, his goatskin bag of chestnuts—you did say, by the way, he kept them in a goat-skin, did you not?"

"They were in such a skin, Miss Smith, but I did not mention it."

"I could actually smell the chestnuts as they roasted on the grid; the whole thing was as clear to me as though I had myself sent you across the Forum—the street, I mean—to buy me some! What a charming power of description you have. Do tell me some more about Rome; have you lived there long, and when did you leave the great city?"

"It was some time ago," answered the Centurion, calmly, "some considerable time ago." Then, adroitly changing the subject, he went on to speak of other things of present interest.

It was clear neither of them wanted *me,* I told myself gloomily, as I turned on my heels; let them enjoy themselves as they chose. If Priscilla preferred spending the evening with a stranger of unknown antecedents, *I* did not care, or at least, was not going to show it—and I went away to the hall, and sulked ostentatiously all the rest of the evening.

CHAPTER X

A CHAPTER OF ACCIDENTS

PERHAPS it was that fit of ill-temper which made me sleep late the next morning; be that as it may, the sun was abroad and strong on the windows before I woke, and there was that savour of breakfast in the air which will penetrate at such an hour to the upper regions of even the best regulated households. The man who looked after me had twice rattled the brass hot-water can in the basin before I could get my senses together, and then when he had arranged my things to his liking and left, my opening eyes fell on the clean white shirt he had placed on a chair by the window. It was vexatiously dazzling in the sunshine. Why did he put it just there, I said to myself peevishly? "These pampered domestics, drawing high wages for trivial services, are mostly nuisances," and I shut my eyes again, wondering as I did so, with the melancholy philosophy of the sleeper awakened, what it was that made me so irritable.

Then all of a sudden a thought of Lepidus and

last night flashed across me. Yes, that was the cause of my ill-ease, and cause enough in all conscience. In a moment I was sitting up in bed, my chin upon my knees, angrily staring at my reflection in the mirror opposite. "Yes, it was Lepidus who had upset me —how badly he had behaved! And Pris, too, a woman like her, versed in the regulations of society, ought not to have overlooked me on the first night of her coming. It was not civil to me as a host, let alone from the point of view of my other claims upon her. No doubt she had twice tried to draw me from my sulks later on in the evening, and had been twice repulsed for her pains; but did she think I was going lightly to forget her visit to the conservatory with Lepidus, her pampering and talking with him for heaven only knows how long—why need she talk to anyone but me? She never pinned down *my* collar; never found *my* conversation interesting enough to make her forget her sense of propriety and good behaviour," and I stared moodily at the angry, shock-haired fellow cuddling his knees in the looking-glass opposite.

Still debating these things in my mind and wondering whether my displeasure might be emphasised most to the individuals concerned by going breakfastless for a long lonely country walk, or by refusing to get up at all—for jealousy was making a perfect girl of me: while still thinking of these things, there came presently through the open window, along with the sunshine, and smell of late roses the sound of footsteps in the verandah below, followed by a pleasant woman laugh, and then a voice that was certainly the Roman's, saying—

"I am afraid I have tempted you to make your feet wet."

"Oh, no," replied the laugher, who was equally certainly Priscilla Smith, "I always wear thick shoes in the country, and besides—they say to be out in the morning dew is the best possible thing for the complexion."

"It would indeed be a sovereign specific, Miss Smith that was able to improve yours!" Then more pleasant laughter, and the speakers passed through the French casement into the house.

I got out of bed immediately, and going over to the window, leaned out, lightly clad as I was. There was nothing to be seen; but a very distinct odour of fried kidneys, and other good things, which at a happier time might have mollified me, was coming down the light morning breeze from the rearward of the Manor buildings. The morning itself was golden; the sunshine bringing up the still damp foliage in vivid contrasts over the shrubberies and distant hillsides; the stream course in the hollow marked by thin strands of opal mist that died away in prismatic attenuation as I looked; the cedars on the lawn heavy with moisture hanging in glittering beads upon every needle point; the lawn itself, silvery with dew —and across that tell-tale surface leading up to the verandah steps, a man and woman's footmarks!

Where had they been, and how long were they out? What a fool I was to lie between my frilled sheets while this swart adventurer made love to the girl that was all in all to me! I turned at once and hurriedly dressed, but never had my sleeve-links been so reluctant to do their duty, never had my razor seemed so bloodthirsty, or my collar so cruelly cantankerous as on that morning. However, I was ready at last, and going downstairs found them all busy at breakfast in the morning-room, Lepidus more than usual elated, and only Pris (who had found her way into the seat next mine) silent and thoughtful. In response to her distinctly gracious welcome I made a return which was barely polite, plunging into the interior mysteries of an egg and buttered toast, as though they were far more interesting than anything she on my left could say or do.

I let Lepidus babble on, and coldly satisfied my mother's distant inquiries as to the general state of my health, until after a time, under cover of an outburst of laughter at the other end of the table, that fair and false lady at my side, leaned over and said to me in her gentlest voice—

"I hope you slept well, Mr.——Louis?"

That last word she had in her maiden pride rarely used as yet to me; now, though it was spoken so low as to be scarcely audible, there was both apology and wistfulness in it. It went right down into my heart, for I loved her greatly, and looking up for the first time, I saw her kind great eyes bent on me with a strange look I had never seen in them before. She was certainly very fair, and her morning's exercise had brought a lovely colour into her cheeks; well might the Roman have doubted whether any dew that ever fell from heaven could have improved them. Her thick soft hair was piled up on her shapely head, and tied with a pale green ribbon, the colour of a beech leaf in April; her dove-brown dress was trimmed with the same hue, there was not an ornament about that winsome wife-to-be of mine save the fresh red rose at her throat—and that was *wet with dew!* The Roman had given it to her, for certain, and the sight chilled my admiration to the bone. I jerked my spoon angrily into my empty egg-shell and blurted out my answer:

"Thanks, Miss Smith, I slept well enough, but did not wake so early as you did, or to such pleasant appointments. I hope your feet are not wet after all?"

For a minute she looked at me in surprise and wonder, then, as the Centurion's before-breakfast remark came back to her mind, not knowing my bedroom window overhung the balcony, she jumped at the conclusion I had been eavesdropping somewhere. The friendliness disappeared from her face, and a flush came up instead.

"Yes," I went on, foolishly imagining I would win a wordy triumph of her, "a lovely morning for a solitary ramble with a friend; a trifle wet underfoot perhaps, but if dew is a disadvantage there it adds to the value of a gift-rose like that of yours."

"I *have* been out early this morning, Mr. Allanby," said the lady, looking me straight in the face, "and by chance I met your friend Marcus Lepidus. He *did* pick me this flower, and I took it, because the time has not yet come—it may never come—when I shall have given up my right to accept so simple a civility without applying for permission. I am glad to see your mother is getting up from the table; I think I will go with her."

And to the mother she went, chin in air, and heart, if I could but have known it, all in a woeful flutter. As for me, I watched her across the room with the firm conviction of a lover that the passing disagreement was the beginning of the end, and as I stood irresolute, eyes on floor, and cursing my boorishness, half impelled to go at once, and apologise, half urged by my pride to wait for her recantation, there came the fall of a broad hand on my shoulders, and a manly voice in my ear—

"Admiring your carpet pattern, eh, cousin Louis? A right good invention, this coloured web of yours under foot, warmer than tesselated pavements by a long way, even with our heating flues thrown in, but nevertheless, not good enough to keep one in such a lovely morning as this. Come, they are talking of game and hunting yonder by the window—will you take us out? I used to be rather a good shot with a cross-bow, and, if you can lend me one, should like to try my luck again."

"We don't use cross-bows now," I exclaimed, my sporting instinct rising superior to my spleen.

"What! slings then, like the Bœotians? Well, I have tried those too, and though I never killed anything with such a weapon, save on one occasion a slave who was sent to drive the game to us, yet I am not afraid to handle any man's weapons—lend me a sling, cousin, and show me how to use it," and thrusting his arm through mine, the Roman haled me off to the company yonder who were all agog to

A CHAPTER OF ACCIDENTS 143

get out and try our coverts for whatever they might contain.

Thus it came about that half an hour later the younger men of the party were busy donning gaiters, and filling cartridge pouches, while I had drawn Lepidus aside into the gun-room, and with a view to the safety of our life and limb, was giving him a hasty lecture on guns and ammunition. It was beautiful to see his grave surprise as I explained to him the properties of that deadly black dust—" seed of lightning " he called it at dinner that evening—which has revolutionised the world, and established for ever the sovereignty of man over beast. And his stoic pride would not allow him to show a tremor when I threw a spoonful of loose powder on the open fire, thereby filling the room for a moment with flames and smoke. I gave him an empty gun to handle, while I got down my own and then of course the Roman, as soon as my back was turned, must reach over for a full cartridge, load as I had shown him how to and pull the trigger! By the mercy of Providence the muzzle was pointed to the window, else had Caster Manor and all pertaining thereto passed " in tail male " to that distant swashbuckler cousin of mine who is cursing Providence and the laws of succession in a remote Californian township.

As it was, there followed a resounding report, a crash of glass, responsive female screams from various parts of the house, with a rush of feet in the passages, succeeded by an avalanche of anxious inquirers through the doorway—the only individual absolutely unmoved, and inclined to view the incident as a legitimate experiment in the property of explosives being the Centurion himself.

Well, I quieted their fears, disarmed the Roman, and hurried off to get into my shooting clothes. Now as it happened, my way led through the conservatory, and who should I find there but Pris herself, standing with her back to me, and that indefinable something about her whereby a woman indicates grief as expressively by her attitude as by her face. Indeed, there was the tag end of a cambric handkerchief peeping out from between the pretty fingers clasped over her eyes, while a succession of gentle throes shook her supple form from head to heel. Pris—and crying! what lover would not have been moved and astonished. I advanced cautiously to her, forgetting everything in the emotion of the moment, and, half surprised at my own boldness, slipped an arm round that inviting waist. The lady was not startled, as I had supposed she would be, she did not even raise her eyes from the depth of her handkerchief, but an audible sob or two rose thence, and slowly her pleasant scented head came over to my shoulder, nestling there while I gently took down the white wrists and supplied such comfort as my position warranted.

"And to what," I asked presently, "to what, may I ask, are these tears due?"

"Oh, I was so much frightened—desperately frightened," whimpered Priscilla, after a minute or two's work with her handkerchief.

"Frightened," I answered, staring round for a possible cause of alarm, but seeing none. "What at?—a mouse, a beetle—something trivial no doubt, for big things do not scare you women."

"Oh, it was trivial enough," exclaimed the lady, with another indignant sob, at the same time straightening herself up, and brushing the pretty hair back from her forehead. "I knew you two were together, and remembering how horribly jealous you were at breakfast just now, thought that perhaps you had quarrelled, and—"

"Had a duel with breech-loaders over the gun-room table?" I suggested, and my charming friend gave an affirmative sob as the touching picture rose before her, while her handkerchief went once again to her eyes. "Pris!" I exclaimed, catching her hand with a thrill of delight at the idea those tears were for *me,* and essaying that most dangerous manœuvre, the pressing of an advantage on a woman in retreat, "you thought *I* had been hurt? Pris, dearest, my beloved, it was me you were crying for, wasn't it? Put your head down again and whisper it, so——"

Whereon the charming enemy turned on my advances: "You!" she cried, taking her hand away, and drawing herself up. "Oh, how dense you are! Of course it was for the other one, Mr. Lepidus," and wriggling from my clasp, she walked away to the inner door, leaving me aghast and speechless at her cynicism. And at the door she turned—saw my horror-stricken face—and bursting into the prettiest little laugh imaginable, threw me a kiss, and disappeared.

So it was for *me* after all she was grieving. What a fool I had been not to guess it, or to let her escape so lightly! "Pris!" I cried, hurrying after her, "Miss Smith—stay a minute, I have something to say to you," and I rushed eagerly on her footsteps into the drawing-room, but only to find she was not there. Into the side boudoir I charged, to discover it equally empty, then into the corridor leading through a by-way to the hall, where a glimmer of a white dress showed for a second before it disappeared down the staircase lobby. After that

A CHAPTER OF ACCIDENTS 147

retreating skirt I went full tilt; it twinkled for a moment, at the top of the stairs where the open oak gallery runs across from wing to wing, and with my blood now roused I went up three steps at a time. It was not to be seen in the corridor, but it could not be far off, and was it likely I was going to give up the hunt with such a quarry afoot in front?

Thinking that I had never seen Pris so sportive before, and with the remembrance of that last bewitching smile dancing before me, I rushed to the opposite end of the gallery, glancing down a possible but empty passage or two, and then, deciding she had gone down a short flight of stairs ahead, bounded quickly down them.

There was a turn at the bottom, and across it one of those portière curtains my mother loves hanging from the ceiling to within eight inches of the ground. The two halves were drawn together so that I could see nothing beyond, but just underneath, close against the curtain, there was a bit of woman's skirting, and a pair of dainty shoes with silver buckles—Pris! for certain, in hiding and going to give me a surprise!—Gads! we would see who would be most surprised, and without a moment for thought I uttered an Indian war whoop and leaping forward, adroitly wrapped the curtain round the fair figure beyond it, pulling her to me, and between the folds in spite of a stifled scream or two, kissed the half-seen face again and again with boyish exuberance.

Then, and then only, was the fair captive allowed to escape, and judge of my horror, my consternation, when from the curtain struggled out in red-hot shame and confusion, not Priscilla Smith, but that winsome lady, Mrs. Milward herself! Worse still, as she swung the drapery aside, she disclosed a yard or two away a group of people she had been talking to when I made my onset, the excellent Bishop and his straight-laced spouse, my cousin Alice, and my mother, all in attitudes of the most picturesque alarm and amazement. We stood there, glaring speechlessly at one another for a minute or two, and then the good Bishop said—

"Ahem!"

It was a slight observation, but it let loose everyone's tongue.

"You horrible, abominable, wicked, *odious* boy!" gasped the pretty widow (though her eyes were not half so angry as her tongue); "you have hurt my wrist *horribly,* and half pulled down my hair——"

"My *dear* Louis," cried my parent at the same moment, "are you out of your mind this morning? If you are going to let off guns and play at brigands like this all over the house, I shall really have to——"

I think she was going to say " send you to school again."

As for the Bishop's wife, she let off a little overdue scream which had apparently been delayed by the stress of her emotions, and subsided into a convenient chair.

" Mother," I said, advancing into the room, " I am dreadfully sorry. I thought it was—well, I saw a foot under that d——, that hanging curtain of yours, I mean, and thought it was—well, Miss Smith's."

At this the great lady of Pewchester looked inexpressibly shocked, and the fair widow visibly pouted. Turning to her, I blundered wildly on: " I owe you very many apologies indeed, dear Mrs. Milward. Indeed, it was an utter accident: I had no idea it was you—I would never have done it, believe me, if I had."

" Oh! thanks," said the little lady sarcastically, " and since you are so very, very sorry, you had better go down on your knees—both, please—and tie my shoe-string which has come undone in the struggle—I shall, of course, fully report your playfulness to Miss Smith; I am sure she will be gratified."

And humbly I had to tie the lady's shoe-strings, under the mild laughter of her friends, and then, crest-fallen enough, as you may imagine, to go in search of my shooting things, and the Roman.

CHAPTER XI

A STRANGE DISCOVERY

WERE this a diary of human sport I should joy in describing what we did that morning, for I have in an extreme degree that common power of shutting my eyes to the suffering of lower things when such suffering ministers to my own pleasure, being at once the most compassionate and bloodthirsty of individuals. But, alas! it is my duty to write here as the hunted, not the hunter; as the helpless quarry of the gods, the plaything of their moods, the sport of a strange chance; so I must pass lightly over my own humble pleasures that the chronicle of their superior sport may not be kept waiting.

We shot the rhododendron coverts first, finding a fair sprinkling of pheasants there, with more rabbits than should have been so near my mother's cherished flowers. For the first shot or two Lepidus had been a terror to me. A gun, of course, he would have, and equally, of course, I kept close at his elbow, on the watch to protect the safety of my guests and my own humble life, but, as a matter of fact, the anxiety was needless. With that quick comprehension which he sometimes seemed to draw from my understanding, rather than from his own, the Centurion learnt how to manage his weapon, as he learnt everything else, in a marvellously short space of time.

"What!" he said, as the first rabbit dashed out into the path in front of us and sped away with its little white tail twinkling between the dead grass stems, "what, shoot him while he runs; no, not if I know it; that would be a shocking waste of your bolts, my good cousin. Let us wait patiently, and we will find him in the nets you have no doubt spread lower down, and there we will shoot him with twice the certainty."

With a shameful glance round, to make sure no one had heard this scandalous proposition, I pointed out its error, and after a good deal of persuasion, got the Roman to try a moving shot. Twice he fired far behind, as was only natural, but the third time he made a brilliant hit. It was a cock pheasant, and I saw Imperial Rome's face light with pleasure as he bent over it. "Jove!" he said, "you must be a rich man to shoot such birds as these. Why, when I was last down in Gaul there were not more than a couple of dozen in the country, every one of them valued at a freeman's ransom."

"Then," I exclaimed, "if there were so few as that, you probably know how the first came over—it is a problem that has stretched the imagination of a hundred sporting writers."

"Everyone knows that."

"No, but everyone who handles a gun would be glad to."

Whereon the Roman, plucking the pheasant's tail feathers out, to the horror of the keeper behind us, said, as he arranged them artistically in his hatband, "It was all that insatiable glutton Marius—you knew him, perhaps?"

"No!"

"Well, never mind. He had the smallest heart for fighting they said, and the biggest stomach for quaint provender of any man we ever brought over. He had a fancy one day to give a feast to the local barbarians, and of course, some of these birds had to figure at it. A dozen were sent alive in a crate all the way up through Gaul, and though eleven of them died on the road, and were far gone towards our common distintegration when they arrived, Marius ate them—he would have eaten a satyr chop itself had it been fashionable or costly enough.

"And the twelfth one?"

"Ah! she, poor beast, had turned prolific on the journey, and when the crate came to hand was sitting, with the deathless instinct of her sex, on some few eggs in one corner of it. Marius ate her too, of course, but the eggs his steward put under a common fowl, and three or four hatched out in time. They bred, and, as I say, had multiplied to a score or more when I was sent up here."

So that was how it happened, I thought to myself as I dropped two more cartridges into my gun, and listened to the solution at first hand of a riddle that no one but Lepidus could have answered. How strange that the appetite of one vainglorious glutton should have given joy to a hundred generations of sportsmen, and an income to every English shire from Thames to Tweed! Poor hen, great-grandmother of all pheasants since, and to be! And all that afternoon I religiously abstained from hurting any of the sex, in reverence of her memory.

Well, we shot through the coverts round the garden, then over a furzy ridge to the right, and afterwards towards the ridgy lands along the river hollow about a mile from home. The Centurion, as soon as he learnt the art of aiming well ahead, and not dwelling on the shot, had distinguished himself greatly, his victims adding materially to the bag. For the most part he seemed altogether absorbed in the sport, and deeply engrossed in the working of the dogs—my pet spaniels—whom he had commenced by calling weakly, velvet-coated curs, having heaven knows what ancient breed of shaggy boar-hounds in his mind's eye. For the most part he seemed absorbed in these things, but now and then, as we rounded a corner or crossed some bluff, he would stop to stare uneasily about him, while enjoyment gave way to perplexity in his expressive face, and his eyes roamed from hill to hill, or up and down the glen, like one who strives to recognise some dimly remembered locality and but half succeeds.

He looked here and there wistfully for a time, until we came round a shoulder of the low hills, and saw right before us a grassy spur jutting out into the river flats. It was dead level on top, with brambly thickets rising above it where it started at right-angles from the mainland ridge, while its two sides were grassy, and dropped down by easy slopes towards the stream, which here took a sharp bend and thus nearly encompassed it. Down the glen you could see right away into the dim mountain borderland in the west, while in the opposite direction the view went back to the wooded knolls surrounding the Manor House, and the trail of the great main road over which for unnumbered generations the traffic of many shires had passed to and fro. I often thought what a fine place it would be for a house, and time and again had taken a book out to sit for hours under the honeysuckle tangles of the hill above, delighting my eye with the scenery, and submitting happily, through long summer afternoons, to the influence which, like the soft crooning of a mother in the ear of a sleeping babe, filled me with unexplained contentment. You may depend on it we are more closely connected with the good mother Earth than we know of, and I for my part feel her pulses in my veins now and then with strange distinctness. There are places I can never go to without sadness, though nothing unhappy associates with them, and they are often enticing in every other respect; there are others where there is elation in the very soil, and pride and inspiration in the air that no surroundings explain. There are still others, and this grassy peninsula was one of them, that whisper wordless stories in my ear, strong and real, though they are reducible to no shape or speech.*

We came out presently on the hill behind that bluff, its smooth grassy top below us of four or

* Omar Khayyám seems to have experienced something of the same feelings:

"I sometimes think that never blows so red
The Rose as where some buried Cæsar bled;
That every Hyacinth the Garden wears
Dropt in its lap from some once lovely Head."

five acres seared, as pastures will be in autumn, by much sunshine, and at once the Roman walking by my side stopped as though rooted to the ground, while his eyes stared fixedly at the meadow in front.

"The place," he said excitedly, in a minute, "the very place! I knew it was; and the house, the very house—surely you see it, or is it only in my mind?"

"What house? I see none."

"Not see it," cried the Roman, pointing his hand eagerly towards the knoll. "Why, the villa, the Prefect's house. Jove! it fashions on my remembrance until I know not whether I see it in substance or no. Look at the long white sweep of hall and colonnade against the dark of the woods beyond the pillared verandah; the steep, red tiles above; the peep of wide inner courtyard through the portico; the blue doves on the roof; the mangy boar-hound yawning on the terrace steps—surely you see it?"

"There is nothing there, Lepidus."

"Nothing! how strange! No cluster of reed-thatched slave huts nestling in the coppice beyond? No trim garden between the villa and the slope? No war-stakes half hid in roses all along the brow, and zigzag terraced paths—good for defence or loitering on a summer evening?" And the strong Roman in his agitation gripped my arm, and stared in front of him as though indeed he saw that thing he spoke of.

Then he stared up and down the valley again for some minutes, eagerly drinking in the remembered scenery, until, when his eyes came back to the grassy promontory once more, apparently the vision had gone.

"Perhaps you are right, after all!" he said, in a quieter tone; "nevertheless the hard ground does not lie, if my mind does. Come, and I will show you."

Fortunately the other shooters had gone far ahead, so sending our gun-bearer, a dull unobservant fellow, after them, with word that they were not to wait, for we would catch them up later on, the Roman and I walked towards the plateau. About fifty yards from it, where the miniature table-land, dotted with golden-flowered rag-wort spread out beneath us, and the path dipped down through the overhanging bank, he stopped again and pointing to the level acres, scorched as I have said, by summer suns, cried out: "I was right! Look, see how the foundations show, look at the lines and patches lying like a map on the meadow—I was right!" and then for the first time I saw with vague wonder that it was as he said. The summer had been hot and dry, the short vegetation indicated, as it always does under such circumstances, by its varying tint the depth of the soil lying on broken wall-tops and pavements below, and there to my astonished eyes was the complete plan of a great house laid out in browns and greens under our eyes. "Come on!" cried the Centurion, flinging my forty-guinea breech-loader into a ditch, "come on, Britisher," and seizing hold of me by the wrist, he raced me down the slope. The great roan cattle lying in the hawthorn shade glared at us as we broke into their seclusion, then floundered hurriedly to their knees and feet, staying for one parting look of amazement before they broke in panic down the hillside. But Marcus Lepidus had eyes for nothing save the chequered field before him. As eager as a sleuth-hound on the trail, he dragged me round the grassy plateau, tracing each line or patch where the sun-burnt grass indicated foundations lying just below.

"Here was the porch!" he exclaimed, striding up a tiny southward slope, "and here the peristylium—see the great square on its further boundary, marked by yonder line of parchment grass; and that green, swampy patch, with the damp grass and sedge, lies where the foundation was. And here beyond we had our store and sleeping-rooms. Here was the tepidarium, and next it the cold-water

A STRANGE DISCOVERY

bath—often and often my teeth have chattered on this spot as the slaves dowsed me at dawn in your accursed March weather. Here was the further court, the great cryptoporticus around it, the stump of a marble column under every grassy hummock there all along the edge."

Going for a minute to the green brink of the escarpment, he looked eagerly up and down the valley, then turned back to the villa and wrung his hands, more moved perhaps than I had seen him yet. "All gone!" he cried; "gone the red-boled fir-woods on the hillside, and the white-stoned meadow path to the water-holes! Gone the villa, and the colonnades and the people! Where are they, comrade?—where are the brass-clad legionaries; and the naked British children; and the tall dogs quarrelling over yesterday's refuse; and the white oxen munching their hay by the stone-wheeled carts in the courtyard; and the hucksters in their sheds bartering Gaulish stuffs for new-plucked boar fangs, or wolf skins?"

"Who knows?" I answered, trying gently to soothe him in his moment of grief; "but we at least are here, and that is something."

"But where are *they*," cried the Roman, stamping his foot on the hollow turf, "where are those brown-skinned villains I led in many a blood raid, where are my jolly comrades of the XXth Legion, the drunken Marius, and Postumus, whose spirit not even a northern winter could kill? Where is old Carinus, where that sweet lady Otacilia, his wife, who squeezed the British of tribute from here to Solway? And where is Prisca Quintilia, light of foot and dimpled with laughter? Jove!" he exclaimed, quite carried away by the inspiration of the place, " I remember that last evening when the barbarians burnt the villa, as if it were yesterday. We had no thought of them when the sun went down, and when it got up we were ourselves on the way to be forgotten! Red it went down in the west, and as the fiery stain climbed up the marble pillars and made the tiles blaze for a time, all the far hillside, there across the stream, was smitten with copper. And the cattle coming home to stall were monstrous golden beasts before they dipped into the valley shadows; and the shepherd on the bare grass ridge towered gigantic over a golden Jason flock. Near at hand the clustering pigeons' wings were dipped in blood—good omen of the coming fury—the very fountain in the open inner court where the fading daylight came to it through the porticoes spurted blood eaves high. It was such an evening as one remembers sometimes; and I had come home from the hunting, and crossing the trim-kept garden flat, there was the maid herself, subdued by the evening quiet, standing like a statue done in ruddy metal against the white alabaster lintels. And I went to her; and she was kinder and sadder than her custom; and whereas before she had kept me at arm's length, now she came to my strength, nestling like a bird to me, so that my heart swelled over her.

By all the gods she was nearly mine that night! I led her back into the shadows, where a stone Cupid on a marble block gave us shelter, and there I had her in my arms, while the gold fire turned to purple dusk above—wooing her to my hungering wishes all I knew—had her head upon my shoulder, felt her bosom beating through my hunting tunic, and the fluttering of her white fingers in my prison hand. Were we not the only two of our kind in all these marches; near in quality; alike in age? She came to me as the river comes to the sea, devious and coy perhaps, and maiden slow when the inevitable loomed big ahead, but just as certainly. And that night she was all but mine; I knew it by the red stain the sunset had left upon her cheeks, and her trembling.

"And then, as I waited in the dead hush of the evening for her answer, her fingers lifted to my lips, my head bent to catch her assenting whisper, there came a kern upon a ragged pony, flying down the near hillside. He burst through our palisades, and, smothered with mud and foam, gasping with haste and news, galloped to the very portico and screamed out—'The dogs are on us! The Britons up; and all the moorland roads crowded with foemen!'

"You know the rest," he said, after a minute, "how they came and surged here round the palisades, trampling the flower thickets into bloody mud, like a pack of hungry wolves; how we cut our way out by the light of those burning roofs, that made another crimson sunset on the hillsides; how the slaves screamed on the British spear-heads; and burning flesh smoked in the cool courtyards where an hour before that girl was hand-in-hand with me—" and the Roman bent his head and, from old habit, made as though he would hide his face in his toga.

I spoke to him as best I could, though for a fact the things he described touched my perception to the quick with a sharp instinctive appreciation of their truth. How could I doubt that his ancient home was here under-foot, and yet how wonderful it was that he should be by me, he who knew that immensely ancient Britain, and whose tantalising, disjointed scraps of memory were like illuminated pages torn from some great story book wherein you could see the same scheme, though the sequence was all astray. There, as I looked, along the level sward were the long lines of the courtyards and walls slightly ridged and marked by dried-up grasses. On the steep river-ward slope faint indications of the terrace showed even now amongst bracken and bramble, and even the path to the watering spot he had spoken of could be followed here and there where an ancient flagstone lay bare and broken in the soft green meadow sward. "I believe!" I said, "it is as you say, Lepidus, for certain." And then, not daring to give the emotion in me play, I turned after a minute to the practical: "It is as you say, for certain, and to-morrow we will dig it all up to make certain doubly sure—shall we, Lepidus?"

"Oh, dig by all means," he answered, coldly; and then, as I saw he was still brooding deeply over the thing he had chanced upon, and as the afternoon was getting late, I led him gently away, joining the other shooters later on, and eventually getting home without further incident.

That same evening I sent for our bailiff, a most devoted man, who would have exhumed his own grandmother had I expressed a wish to inspect her bones, and to him I briefly explained the nature of our find, with my wish that ten men should set to work to uncover it the first thing in the morning. When the story was done he appeared buried in thought. "What is it, Andrews?" I asked. "Are you surprised at a Roman house being there?"

"No, sir, it's not that," answered the man, reflectively turning his hat in his hand. "I was thinking what we'd do with the red heifers if we dug up all that pasture; it's as sweet a bite as any in the country. You see, sir, there's as many sheep on the twenty-acre croft as it will carry; the high lees haven't sprouted yet, for what rain we have had has run off them like water off tiles, and the low meads I was saving till keep got scarcer. There's Farmer Morgan's ten-acre pasture by the mill pool—he would rent that——"

"Good," I replied, marvelling how different the same subject can look to diverse minds, "let the red cows go to the mill pool, and, Andrews, mind you, tell the men to dig tenderly to-morrow, and to save anything they light upon, though it is but the paring of a Roman toe-nail."

CHAPTER XII

WE PICNIC WITH OUR ANCESTORS

THE following morning happened to be wet, and curiously enough, though I was all agog with interest about our find of yesterday, my Centurion was comparatively indifferent. That he had forgotten it was unlikely; there was indeed, a substratum of seriousness in his lightest remark, which seemed to show he still brooded over it. But he was not openly interested, and though I stole a visit to the excavations in my heavy mackintoshes, he preferred to stay and card wool all day with my enamoured but insipid cousin Alice. The others followed their inclinations according to the established usage of a country house in wet weather, and thus I was left to myself.

Smoking and idling about the Manor that afternoon, eagerly watching a patch or two of blue in the western sky blossom through the rain clouds, I presently found myself ruminating over some glazed cases of antiquities we had in our hall. I loved those things. They were to others dusty curiosities, in value according to the pence a dealer would give for them, at best mildly interesting to vapid minds, and at worst cumberers of space, ugly and pointless. But to me they were magic. The gloss and sheen came back to that colourless rag labelled "From a Tomb," as I looked. I could see the very face, and the interest in the face, of her who once appraised it on the mercer's bench; I could see her draw it through her fingers while yet it was brand-new from the looms, glancing as she did so at the huckster's eyes to read whether she was going to get it at her price or his. And that little cracked phial for tears; there was nothing in it now; it was a jest to many, but to me its iridescent surface spoke instantly of the parti-coloured life of her who owned it so long ago, the life which was certainly so much like that of any girl here about us; a little universe of time in itself between two great hushes; and as I touched the little phial tenderly for the sake of her who once filled it with the elixir of sorrows, my own eyes smarted in compassion for those long dead griefs!

And the dead finger crept back into that ring that had been found with the tear-bottle, a strong finger that had done its measure of work and play, had gone home and taken its wages endless ages ago. There was a space in it where a gem had once been. To my mother and the others I found that hollow was bare, but to me it was red, always red with the shine of the ruby that had once filled it. Where was that stone now? Such things live for ever; on whose finger was it, and what of its history between those wide sundered hands?

Then that bronze buckler again, with the neat velvet backing of our museum case showing through the ragged hole near the centre, and the green hue of ages almost hiding the twining letters upon it, like moss on a village tombstone? One who dealt in such things, a gentleman from Birmingham, once told me that that stab hole took at least eighteen pence off the value of the article—but he was mistaken! I did not tell him so: I merely said I was content. He knew nothing of the strong soul that had flitted out like a bat from that hole on the day it was made. To him the shield was but a lot on an auctioneer's catalogue, only worse or better than any others as it approached the full round perfection of a new tin pot, and there was an end of it. So it was with all the other things in those modest cases of ours. To others they might be trivial in value, meaningless in purpose, but to me they were very pages of the past, and as I pondered over the fragments, the inspirations which arose from them were like the fumes which made yesterday, to-day, and to-morrow all one to the Delphic priestess.

Thus trifling, I spent a wet afternoon, and on the following morning we were to go in a body to see what progress had been made with the practical work of excavation.

I had intended that the investigation of the Roman villa, if a public function, should at least be a grave and dignified one. The visitors were to approach with chastened minds the vestiges of a magnificent past, and I hoped that its sobering influence might act on even the most frivolous of them. But there are certain people to whom ruins always suggest ham sandwiches, and the silence properly dwelling about the sacred places of the remote an incentive to buffoonery. Mrs. Milward unhappily belonged to the first class, and Smythers of Balliol, one of our Oxford students, to the second.

"Ruins!" cried the little widow excitedly, as we talked the matter over at the tea-table. "Oh, how jolly! and the weather is clearing up just at the right time. Dear Mrs. Allanby, do let us make a picnic of it; we can have out the drag; Miss Smith and I will pack a perfectly delightful hamper to-night. Three cold chickens," she exclaimed, rapturously turning her eyes up to the ceiling, and enumerating on her round fingertips the things to be taken; "a ham, all the rest of that huge Melton Mowbray pie—I know there is plenty left, because I came down in my dressing-gown after you had all gone to bed last night, and got cook to give me another slice—a cherry tart, and pastry; bread and cheese, and lots of drink for these thirsty men—oh! we *will* have fun, dear Mrs. Allanby; please let me help to get everything ready!"

"And cigars to smoke, and cushions to go to sleep upon while Louis gives us one of his interesting lectures on antiquity," quoth Mullens, the sculptor, from the other end of the room.

"And we won't go home till morning," sang the ribald Smythers. "I will bring my accordion, and we will make a regular jolly Easter Monday, Bank Holiday excursion of it."

It is unnecessary to say this was not what I had intended. But nothing could now be done. The find had been announced, these dear barbarians had rashly been invited to inspect the dust of their ancestors, and there was no putting them off. So I groaned in spirit while submitting with as much grace as might be, and the next day, shortly after noon, we started.

Our party pretty well filled the drag, and there was a nice little quarrel for places during which I observed with grim cynicism that Smythers had not only brought his musical instrument, but had donned for the occasion the rôle of funny man, in that guise doing his utmost to deprive our "bean-feast," as he called it, of the last semblance of dignity. One would have thought also that the party were going for a month's excursion by the amount of wraps, small luggage, umbrellas, fishing-rods, sketching materials, and so on brought with them, but that is an habitual peculiarity of your picnicker. Eventually the miniature riot smoothed down, everybody being seated save the Bishop, for whom a place had been reserved close by the sculptor, and as he approached, the accordion-man struck up "Tommy, make room for your Uncle," to which classic strains we started.

What, I thought to myself as I helped my cousin into her dust cloak, and rescued Mrs. Milward's glove, which my mother's terrier was worrying in the thicket of legs and skirts under the seat—what would the brass-clad Prætorians, and the black-browed matrons, whose ancient dwelling-place we were going to see, have thought of us? What would they think could they see us now? Would they be proud of their descendants mentally, morally, or physically? It was a doubtful question. And what was *Lepidus* thinking? I had not noticed him all the day. Nervously tucking the carriage rug under me as these fancies passed across my mind I pulled it off the Bishop's legs, and had to apologise and straighten it again, before glancing up at the Centurion. I need not have troubled. The Roman was seated on the luncheon hamper by the coachman —Smythers being on the other side of him—beaming with fun and good humour. It was only in solitude, or with me alone, that the past came upon him; in the full shine of day, amongst men and women, he was one of them, aggressively happy in his borrowed vitality. At the moment, he had a cigar stuck in the corner of his mouth, his hat a little tipped to one side, and the accordion in his hands, wherefrom, under his companion's guidance, he was eliciting doleful music that made even the horses fidgety.

Leaning over to Priscilla I said, with a suggestion of contempt in my tone, "He seems happy, doesn't he?"

"Yes," she answered, without looking towards the Roman, and to my satisfaction I thought there was an expression of the same thought in her face. Thus encouraged—for there had been an uneasy fancy in my mind that the day was to be my rival's wholly, I pressed my advantage, and when presently some of us dismounted to ease the horses up a stiff bit of hill I made an opportunity of asking Miss Smith to take a short cut across the fields with me.

It was a lover's privilege readily gained when my mother backed me; the accordion-man struck up "Pretty Polly Perkins," as the coach went out of our sight—and I was alone with Pris on the well-screened hedge path.

How good the clover flowers smelt after yesterday's rain, how splendidly the lark sang somewhere under the silver canopy of the great clouds drifting away into the west! There was an indefinite tenderness I had never noticed in the summer air drifting over the thyme and parsley beds, and linking her and me in faintly eddying bonds; encouragement in the low musical babble of the stream coming up from the neighbouring hollow; and I was gently, diffidently happy. We sat down on a log under a hazel, and I had her ungloved hand in mine. A strand or two of her hair I remember, gleaming like red gold as the sunlight ran down it, blew across my face, and I lifted that hand and reverently kissed its finger-tips.

"You do love me, Pris," I asked presently, "you really do—better than anyone else?"

"Yes," she said, keeping her face turned away—yes, and yes again, under her breath, until it almost seemed that she was insisting on the fact to her own sweet mind rather than speaking to me.

It was enough: I was not critical, and lapsed into

happy silence by her side. Yet it was impossible for me not to feel that there was something between us; sweet she was, gentle, and yielding, yet the brave, truthful face was not altogether at rest as I should have liked it to be, and once when I looked up suddenly there were prospective tears glistening under her lashes. It was she that spoke next.

"Louis," she began with an obvious effort, "I want to say something to you, but *cannot*."

"Out with it Pris. What can there be you cannot say to *me?*"

"No, no, no!" answered my companion, struggling with her woman's emotions, "nothing in the world can make me say it; you would think me horrible, unmaidenly—and yet—oh! if it were said, and done with, that would give confidence and strengthen me——"

"Tell me, dearest," I pleaded, slipping an arm round her waist, "tell me—nowhere in the world could you have a more tender listener."

But she only shook her head violently, and now it was "No, no, no!" followed by a show of tears, and an almost fierce cry that she was "sorry she had ever come to Caster; she would go away the very next day"—and so on.

What man would possibly make anything of this? I could but comfort her in my rough way, until presently she eyed me through the corner of her half-dried lids and, seeing I was stupid still, made believe to change the subject—though in fact she did not—and after a pause, said casually, "The summer is going very fast."

"Yes," was my answer—glad to be on tangible ground again.

"And after the summer will come autumn. English autumns are very short."

"Why, Pris, 'tis a way autumns have—to follow close behind the summer."

"And then winter," said the lady, dropping her voice, and flushing curiously as she pushed a little grasshopper from her knee—"the winter, *when no one travels!*"

How it was I know not, but something in her voice and the mention of travel (I had promised her a lengthy honeymoon abroad) showed her meaning to my sluggish mind. "Good heavens, Pris!" I cried, leaping to my feet and blurting out my discovery with manly brutality, "you mean when will I—when are we to get married? Forgive me, dearest, but I have been so happy in the present, that I have never ventured even to think of *that;* but since you wish it——" Instead of resenting my bluntness, Pris merely replied with sweet gravity that "it was advisable." So I slipped my arm in hers, for she had risen now, and found myself, as we sauntered slowly towards the picnic place settling dates, places, and all the details of that episode with amazing calmness.

Only long afterwards did I know from her own self what had urged her thus to bring me to the point; only then did I find out that, like the brave girl she was, she had recognised with terror deep down in her soul the germ of a new love beginning; had felt without understanding the deadly fascination of that other man's ancient claim upon her, and had gone the straightest way she knew of to put herself beyond the possibility of doubt, and to settle the matter out of hand.

Down at the Villa we found things in full swing. The diggers had worked for two days in the light soil like ants, and the whole ground-plan of the ancient mansion was laid bare. Lepidus has described it for me, so I will say no more than that all he had told of was verified; every court and chamber in the palace was as he had said, though, of course, somewhat shorn of its splendour. The whole place was a wondrous labyrinth of crumbling walls and pavements, broken marble steps and fallen pillars. The main courtyard they had cleared, all except a small mound crowned by a hawthorn near the centre. Round that half-removed hummock spades and broom had laid bare a fine sweep of tesselated pavement, not quite perfect, for tree-roots had forced it up or subsidences cracked it, but still wonderful enough in its green and white scrollery, its vines and doves, and complex pattern centring towards that mid-spot under the hawthorn where, I guessed at once, the Cupid had stood by which my Roman had made love to Priscilla I scarcely dared think how many years ago. And there was that sprig of ancient royalty, as we came upon the scene, joyously indifferent to the things that had moved him so much a few hours before, helping to lay a modern tablecloth upon a classic spot, and shouting for the corkscrew or bread platter as he spread the meal, as though he had no other thoughts in the world.

"Come on, cousin Louis!" he shouted across the courtyard. "Every man here has got to earn his provender—to you falls the hearth-place. Sticks, man, and faggots! lots of them, please; plunder your ancestral hedges and the turf heaps. You will find the kettle in the verandah, and Smythers has matches."

So I set to work at that great recreation which makes happy children of the oldest of us, and, tossing my coat into a corner, was soon "wrestling with my ancestral hedges."

CHAPTER XIII

LOVE, THE IMMORTAL

FROM an outside point of view it was as good a picnic as one could wish. The kettle boiled without upsetting: the corkscrew had not been forgotten, and it was not powdered sugar this time in the salt-cellar or *vice versâ*. Also my mother had sent away the servants, so that we lunched in peace and enjoyed the trivial discomforts which it is their duty to minister to. Lepidus was presiding at the game pie, magnificent and radiantly happy. The sculptor spent the greater part of the meal in mixing a gigantic salad, which he then proceeded to eat. Mrs. Milward accumulated all the pleasantest things in her neighbourhood with unblushing assiduousness; Smythers played what he called appropriate music while the plates were being changed; and his own precentor would scarcely have recognised the good Bishop in his new character of general handy-man and useful "super."

That pillar of the Church had, towards the end of the meal, been sent off to the hampers to bring up a big cherry tart, of which my mother was justly proud, and approaching us with it screened under a napkin, much as John the Baptist's head was brought in to Herod, met with a slight mishap. We were all at the moment watching Mullens's struggles with a refractory claret cork, each of us giving him advice at once—advice we were secretly very glad we had not personally to put into practice—when a plaintive wail went up from the direction of what we called the larder, and there, as we hastily turned, before our eyes was his portly lordship, with the cherry tart still borne bravely at arms' length, slowly sinking into the solid earth. What had happened, what could be happening to him? It was so grotesque, so singular to see him shortening inch by inch, while he clutched the pastry, shouting for help the while, that I doubted my own senses: a terrible idea came upon me that for once I had done wrong to drink all that bottled beer and claret-cup, and was beginning to see a little crooked. Indeed, the same fancy must in some form or other have occurred to everyone, for none moved while the great Churchman " set " solemnly into the solid earth like a disappearing sun, gaiter-deep, knee-deep, thigh-deep; and only when he was up to his waist, and apparently still going steadily towards the lower regions, did the horror of the situation dawn on us, and, Lepidus leading of course, we sprang to the rescue.

"Oh! please, please, save the pastry," cried Mrs. Milward, wringing her jewelled fingers, while the Roman gave a yell that would have carried consternation into a British camp, and led us across the tesselated pavement. When we got to the Bishop, we found him belt-deep in a hole of his own making, and naturally somewhat agitated. It was only after we had laid hands on him from all sides, and dragged him forth with scant ceremony, that we found the explanation of the mishap. His lordship had walked, without knowing it, across one of those ancient hot-air chambers the Romans made beneath their dwellings, and the floor, rotten with time, had failed under-foot, letting him slowly down through the crumbling tiles into the space below.

"Why, sir," said Lepidus cheerfully, when at last we had him out and were dusting him over, "'tis said that we at Rome once had a gap in the Forum which might be filled by nothing less than a soldier in all his armour, but surely this is the first time in history that a yawning fissure was ever stopped by a saint and a cherry-tart!"

"He looked like a black demon in a pantomime," observed Smythers, who was devoid of reverence, and owed the Churchman a grudge for many well-deserved rebukes—"going down to Hades with something he had stolen."

"And, oh! to have had a photograph of him when he was half-sunk," quoth another, "with that dramatic agony on his face, and the pie-dish borne heroically aloft! All Pewchester would have gone mad over it. We would have had it in every shop-window round the Cathedral close, and built him a new portico out of the profits of the sale."

With incidents like this we "beguiled the way," until by the time the meal was over the hamper was very empty, and our men, if the truth must be told, very merry indeed. After we had cleared up with scrupulous neatness, for I cannot bear a litter or fragments left in a beautiful place, the Centurion drew me aside.

"Friend Louis," he said, "do you remember I told you how we had a Cupid on a column in the mid-court of this place, hard by the fountain basin in which your priest of Pewchester now washes up the spoons? Well, that Cupid stood just where they have left the bush upon the hummock, and I have a great liking to see if he is there still—'twas that Cupid, you remember, in the shadow of whose bow I wooed Prisca the night the barbarians rushed us; and who knows," he added smilingly, "but that the little beggar may still have another shaft in his quiver to spend on us!"

It was a very feasible idea; I myself wanted to

LOVE, THE IMMORTAL

see that stony little god that was so real to my mind's eye, and the workmen had left half a dozen spades in a far corner under a tarpaulin, so in a minute or two I collected the company, and after a brief lecture on Roman architecture, adroitly suggested that that interesting people were in the habit of adorning the inner court of their great houses with fountains and basins, such as we already saw before us, while in very many instances a statue of "the tiny lord of love" occupied that central position. "My friend Lepidus here had suggested such might be the fact in the present case, and as the workmen had left the very spot untouched under yonder hawthorn which would represent the site of the possible Cupid, he called for spades and volunteers."

Smythers said my lecture was the most moving thing he had ever heard, while my mother observed that she had no idea I remembered so much of my school learning.

In brief, we got to work on the mound—half a dozen of us—with the energy inspired by lunch, and it was a beautiful sight to see these unaccustomed navvies shovelling the light soil with might and main, while the Bishop and I wheeled the stuff in two barrows over to the escarpment. When we had been at work about a quarter of an hour, one shouted out he had found something, and all hurrying round to his side, there to our delight—I will not say surprise, for I at least was certain the find would be made—was the base of a small fluted column projecting from the soil! We had it out—it was only about three feet long—in a couple of minutes, and under direction of Mullens in his professional capacity set it up firmly on end under the hawthorn boughs in the very socket it used to occupy in those days so immensely long ago. That fired our enthusiasm, of course, and the diggers, crowding to the place where the column had been found, set to work with redoubled zeal to unearth " the little beggar with the bow and arrow," as perspiring Smythers said. I, not to hamper my guests, withdrew to one side and shovelled away reflectively, Pris near by, working at the mound with a fern-gathering trowel and a curiously eager expression of face.

Scooping the friable soil, mostly vegetable mould or fine silt washed from the adjoining hillside, away from the surface of the tessellated floor, and bringing it down by the spadeful from above, I presently struck upon something harder than the adjoining earth, and going upon one knee, uncovered *a baby fist!* It was the prettiest little fist imaginable of white marble, tight clenched upon what I saw at once was the centrepiece of a small bow, and, foolish as it was, a paternal thrill of interest in the buried urchin, who for certain owned those clenched fingers, passed through me. As for Pris, she saw me stop work, sailed to my side, and instantly seeing the prize, with a suppressed cry of feminine pleasure, went down on both knees and kissed that chubby fist again and again.

"Quick!" she said, with her fair cheeks aglow, "dig—get it out; oh, the pity that the little love has lain in the dark so long!"

Between the spade and fern trowel we quickly bared the mischief-maker, and just as the others discovered the object of our frantic labour he rolled out of his darksome cradle into Priscilla's arms. She was so delighted she could scarcely even show him to the guests. Whether it was all maternal instinct, or some reminiscence of the old passion of which he had been witness I know not, but there is the fact: she held that stony babe, with the akimbo arms and dimpled cheeks, to her bosom—most dangerous place!—as though he were her own offspring.

Then when the wonder subsided we took the infant to the grassy basin hard by, and Pris washed him clean; removed the dirt of centuries from his crevices with a pickle-fork, and anointed him with tenderness and smiles. She dried him on two table-napkins, and there he was as complete and dimpled a little god as one could wish for. It is true a toe had gone, his wings were missing, and there was no bow in those strong small hands, but their attitude implied it to all beholders, and we, hoisting him to his ancient pedestal where he was soon triumphantly poised against the shadow of the hawthorn bush, stood round adoring in diverse fashions.

Everyone is in love, or has been, or hopes to be. I think the force of that great truth was borne in upon us as we stood there, actually silent for a moment, round the shrine of the strangely recovered god, and felt his mesmeric influence stir within us those pulses at once so sweet and so vague.

Miss Smith—charming priestess for such a shrine—protected the Lord of Love, not allowing Smythers to outrage him with his wit, and when we had adored enough we broke up into small groups and separated, each to our several enjoyments.

Some went to sketch upon the sunny hillside; some to fish down by the brook where the trout were scattered, but of fair size, in the holes under the alders; some to flirt; and the Bishop, with his lady and my parent, went off to visit a neighbouring moor-man's wife. At tea-time we all met again to boil kettles and brew tea, and so the pleasant day wore to an end. Just as the sun was getting low, and rabbits were cautiously beginning to appear from their burrows in the hedge banks, while that fine scent which comes with the evening was rising from the coppices, the carriage was announced to be in the roadway beyond the brow, and my mother, having taken an impromptu roll-call, found we were all present save Lepidus and Miss Smith. The fact of their absence had not impressed itself on me before; I had been so busy playing host and discussing knotty points of Roman architecture with the Bishop, who entertained some opinions on the subject I could not and would not assent to. The knowledge that they were not amongst us had presented itself in a vague way to my eyes, but I presumed the two were close by somewhere amongst the ruins, or picking blackberries just over the slope, and it was impossible for me to play nursemaid to them all day. Now the fact was not to be blinked, and an awkward silence fell upon the waiting group. Mullens had seen them higher up the river an hour ago deep in conversation, and Mrs. Milward had watched them as they sat on a moss-covered boulder, "looking, oh, so happy!" as she said with pretty malice, and these items of information having been elicited, silence again came upon us who stood waiting to go home. Finally my mother, turning to me with vexation in her kindly face, said:

"Louis, go and find these truants and tell them—or tell Miss Smith, at least—she must come at once;

we are waiting. We will go to the carriage and stay there till you return."

There was something in my parent's tone not to be gainsaid, so while she led off her party up the grassy slope to where the moorland road lay just out of sight beyond, I turned my back upon the now deserted villa, its little picnic fires still sending up spirals of thin smoke into the quiet evening air, its strange yet familiar surroundings, and went down to the stream, meaning to follow it up until I came sooner or later upon those two wanderers. Before I had gone half a mile up the bubbling course Lepidus and Pris appeared on the moorland slope high above me, going back most leisurely towards the picnic place by a hillside path. So up I went, expecting to overtake them before they joined the others, but an impassible bit of boggy ground across my way put me off the direct line, and by the time their track was reached the truants were out of sight.

What a lovely evening it was! As I stopped after the climb to take breath and glance round, the sun was just going down behind the heather which burnt in his setting as though it were on fire. All away between that glow and me the pennons of the cotton grass on every hummock ridge shook in the light breeze like angry flags, and the steel-white bents wavered and flashed in the twilight till you could almost think that they were the glittering spears of a great army pouring through those fen-ways. And over them the fiery sky flushed and every cloud in the west gleamed as though it floated over an open furnace door. It was exactly such an evening as the Roman had described to me as that one on which the villa was burnt, and with the remembrance of his words in my mind I turned to the opposite side of the valley.

All that fair slope was lit up again, just as he had said; the copper glow was climbing amongst the tree-stems and plating with gold the upland leas there lying molten under a sky of deep untroubled blue, spotless and serene. The very shepherd, such as Lepidus had told me of, was coming, huge-seeming of stature, over the brow, "driving a golden Jason flock" before him by twenty grassy bye-ways into the valley, as he had done a thousand years ago! The river was saying the very same things; the very silence was the same as that I had felt when he told me how, on that evening long ago, he had wooed the girl he and I both loved; and that likeness, that ghostly repetition of time frightened me; it was as though I had been swept sheer out of my being into the void of unknown centuries, and, like a dog who hears in the darkness the soft feet of the dead passing to and fro, I turned from the splendid brightness of that haunted valley and slunk away.

A few hundred yards along the track led me into the thicket above the villa, while another hundred paces along the winding mossy path, already moist with dew, brought me to the very threshold of that forgotten mansion. Passing round where the granaries had been, and between rows of broken pillars still red in the western glow, I came suddenly upon the courtyard in the centre with its shadowy hawthorns, its broken fountain basin, and that laughing, leer-eyed boy we had set up on its pedestal again after endless years of darkness!

And by that Cupid, in the hush of the twilight and shadows, with the ruddy gleams dying out about them as they stood, were the Roman and the girl he had wooed exactly as they had been once before! I was rooted to the ground, and could but watch in silent horror what followed. Speaking eagerly into her ear at first, he soon pressed nearer and nearer until his arm was about her waist, and her hands in his. Even from where I stood I could see the heave of her bosom, and the colour that came and went in swift transitions over her face. It seemed to me she was in the throes of a struggle such as one may feel but seldom in a lifetime, and while half her nature was struggling for freedom, the other half was sinking under some strange, irresistible compulsion of fate. Closer and closer he pressed, whispering what I could not hear, but could guess too well by his impassioned face, while she struggled helplessly, tearless and silent, now one mood getting the better, then the other, and all the time the Roman drew her in to him remorselessly, just as he had told me he had drawn her more than a thousand years ago, speaking to her in fiery earnestness; twice her head was half upon his shoulder, twice her hands half-way to his lips. A third time she tried to resist, a fierce desperate struggle for herself, and then it was as if her strength broke all on a sudden: the sweet brown head went down in helpless surrender upon the Roman shoulder, the soft hands submitted resistless to a rain of hot kisses, and when I heard him whisper to her, in tones of which no distance could deaden the triumph, she buried her face in his broad chest and, helpless as a babe, burst into a flood of tears.

For my part I was absolutely and completely nerveless without volition or being, for those few moments, and now that I come to look upon it, I can but explain that astounding negation by the supposition that the Centurion in that moment of keen excitement was drawing so largely on the fund of life I truly believe we shared in common, that he was actually using my supply as well as his own, and leaving me for the time void and helpless. Be this as it may, there I stood dazed, my eyes fixed on the ground, and when I looked up with sudden furious energy it was too late, the two had gone on silently up the path, and had already been met by one of the people from the carriage.

So I followed them in a very medley of strange sensations, half doubting whether what I had seen was real, and so numbed, when presently the rest of the party were rejoined, by the laughter and prosaicness of those about me, that I could not bring myself to say a word.

Nothing occurred during the drive home; indeed, my mind is a blank upon the subject—and that evening we were all pinned down to separate tables for cards. When the cards were done, my mother took me into her boudoir to talk over some matters of the estate and accounts, into which I plunged with feverish eagerness—for in truth my head was in a whirl, my heart full of bitterness. So long we stopped over those knotty questions, ranging from high disputes with neighbouring lords of manors to discussions as to whether the second stable-boy was entitled to charge us for two dozen new spotted cravats per month, and, if he was, whether he could possibly wear them out in the time, that the guests, tired with the day's fresh air, sent in a deputy to say they were on their way to bed—and their deputy was Priscilla!

She came in like a soft cloud of whiteness, bringing the faintest, finest odour of her favourite scent with her, and the whole room seemed to light up with her gracious presence. She went over to my mother, and, delivering her message, put a soft arm about her neck, and in the prettiest way stroked the grey hair from her forehead, while with the familiarity of a daughter she gently upbraided her for working so late. Then over to me, flushed and miserable, nursing my anger with the horrible remembrance of what I had seen back at the villa, she came and lightly setting her beautiful hand upon my shoulder, stood so by me for a minute. That touch thrilled me through and through; it was like a blessed opiate to my high-strung nerves; it was mesmeric in its sweet sedate confidence; I felt its strong virtue in my innermost fibre; it was like the touch of the white-robed vestal giving life and honour back to the wretch on his way to torture, and with a gasp of contending emotions I looked up at her. Never, I think, in her life, had she appeared so sweet, so immaculate, so absolutely certain of her unruffled womanhood; and yet, and yet, I had not been dreaming away there by the picnic place! This same girl, who had that very morning chosen the day when she should be my wife, was the same who a few hours later stood in the dusk locked in the arms of a stranger, crying her eyes out, and suffering him unresistingly to kiss again and again that very hand she was now giving to *me*. Was it possible, after all, I had imagined the whole thing—but no! I *knew* I had not imagined it. Was it possible *she* had completely forgotten it? was it possible she remembered, and was a wanton, cruel, heartless, and unblushing?

I hated myself for the mere supposition; she was the mirror of goodness there as she stood before me; the epitome of sweet and tender womanhood; something was amiss, but it was not she, and my love came back with a rush upon me as she bade me goodnight, and allowed me to lift her fingers reverently to my lips.

Then we settled down to accounts again, and my parent, who was admirably frugal even in matters of detail, asked me seriously whether I thought it was worth while growing potatoes for the household ourselves when they could be bought anywhere for three-halfpence a pound wholesale? She pointed out the amount of ground they took up in the kitchen garden, their cost in labour and manure, and asked whether it was justified. I abandoned the potatoes without a murmur, and my mother at once wrote out a ukase for the head gardener expressing our decision. The mention of that excellent person reminded her that he wanted a hundred yards of piping laid down from the well in the back-yard to the melon-house. "Didn't I think a new water barrow would serve just as well, and be much cheaper?" I was of course strongly in favour of the water barrow.

"Besides," said the dear old lady, "if we had the pipes laid, that young man Andrews would always be in the yard pumping, and the girls would be out helping, or staring at him when they ought to be in the laundry." I agreed, with a sweet figure in white still in my eyes, that financially, socially and morally it was essential to suppress the insidious pipe scheme; and so my mother went on for another hour or more.

It was quite late when we had done at last; the house had been shut up, and all others long retired to rest. My mother, with a sigh of relief, set to work putting out the lights, and as she had a fancy for keeping some of her more important account-books in a strong box in her own room, asked if I would carry the goodly pile up there. So, candle in one hand and books in the other, I led the way a little in advance, sleepy, but happy in a renewed confidence in Pris. Her bedroom, No. 16 it was, lay on the way to my mother's, and I should pass that magic portal. I knew the number beyond all mistake—had I not passed it once or twice since she came to stay with us, and once even seen that sweet, tall lady on the threshold, speaking to an attendant housemaid while from within, over her shoulder, as I passed came a glimmer of mystic bed-hangings, flower-decked toilet-table, and all those dainty trappings of the female room that are so awesome to the bachelor? No. 16! there was no forgetting that ambient number, and there it was, half-way down the dim corridor.

No. 13 I passed, where blithe Mrs. Milward lay, doubtless dreaming of some one toiling on dusty Indian plains for her; 14, the Bishop's lady's tiring room; 15, sacred to my cousin Alice—and may heaven forgive me for the presumption, but I could almost see my dainty little kinswoman within, curled up in her snowy nest, as surely as I could see her shoes put out for cleaning on the mat; 16—here it was, the room of rooms, the innermost sanctity of them all to me—why! what was this? I staggered back against the wall, nearly letting the candle drop in sheer amazement, for there upon the mat before that doorway were two pairs of boots, a man's heavy foot-gear, soiled with a day's tramping, and a woman's!

I stared and stared again: was I mad or dreaming?

What extraordinary mistake was I making? There was no mistake; it was No. 16 as plain as black and white porcelain could show, and the boots were real, —grimly, unblushingly real in their naked simplicity. I glared at them, while a score of strained excuses rushed upon my mind. Perhaps the boot-cleaners had made a mistake, but no—the boot-cleaners had not yet been round; perhaps some man had put his there in sleepy error; but then no male guest slept in this corridor; perhaps, perhaps——. My mind fairly tottered with amazement, while over it there swept for an instant all the doubt and mingling of the villa, the soldier's burning words, my doubt, and confidence again. What did it mean?—and then as I groaned, unable to move a pace from the spot, there came my mother's step behind me.

"What is it?" she asked in a low voice so as not to disturb the sleepers within. But I could not answer or look up, I was too ashamed, only could I keep my eyes on those boots. And after a minute my mother perceived the direction of my gaze. I saw that gentle old lady start, staring at me in turn, and then to her comely old cheeks, to which mine in babyhood had been so often pressed, there rose a blush, a real blush, and—oh, a thousand shames on me for bringing it there! With her quick wit she had guessed my thoughts, and, coming close so that our shadows joined grotesque and gigantic on the ceiling, she said without anger in my ear:

"Louis, for shame! You are a boy, a very foolish and jealous one, not yet worthy of the love of a sweet woman, I fear. Yes, that is, or rather was, Miss Smith's room. But she came to me after the picnic to-day, and asked—though why I know not—to change it for another next to mine, that one with the door opening between us. And this room, No. 16, I gave instead to Mr. and Mrs. Mullens, who also wished to change. There! are you satisfied now? Give me those books and go to your room at once, Louis—think what *she* would say, my dear boy, if she ever heard a whisper of this."

For a minute those kindly lips were pressed in gentle reproach to my forehead, and then I did as I was bid—ashamed of myself, but secretly joying for the moment in a new gratitude and trust in Priscilla.

CHAPTER XIV

THE HERO TURNS CYNIC

THERE were two or three rainy days after that, and the dampness entered into my soul, as it will into everyone's at times. I sulked in my private smoking-room, knowing little of what the others did, or hung about the retired corners of the library, taking down only those volumes of which the repute indicated that they were likely to agree with my misanthropical state of mind. A book which is unsympathetic when your mood is pronounced is no good. There are some who believe that you can go to literature to be morally chastised, as a naughty little boy goes to his mother for the physical equivalent of that process. But in pain or pleasure give me the book that is like a gentle friend and will meet the waywardness of the moment half way, holding out, as it were, the arms of an understanding compassion, weeping with my tears and laughing with my laughter—that is the true friend, whether in broad-cloth or gilded leather, whether on two legs or between two covers; and amongst those old shelves, so near to the top of the house that the noises of the frivolous world were deadened under foot, and only the contented chatter of young starlings beneath the red tiles above broke the stillness, I had tier on tier of consolers. There I would muse how strange it was that the fountains of human sympathy should be sealed to most of us by a hundred adverse circumstances: that the friends who still were flesh, and talked with living tongues, should so often be worthless by reason of conventionality or passing moods, of distance or misunderstandings, while these dead ones, disembodied, purged of chance emotions, loosened from the petty considerations of life, should be always at hand, always equable, always as bountifully ready to give of their nature, good or bad, as wind and rain, or the blessed sunshine itself. Perhaps the human dead are like them, and the troubled soul in another sphere may wander through the great libraries of the spirit world, getting from a thousand great essences that which it asks for instantly, and bettering or hampering itself by their consolation just as the living human mind does from its books according to the advisers whose aid it asks?

Personally I made a poor use of this philosophy, and spent those wet afternoons in the ungodly company of all the dusty old tomes who harmonised most with my ill humour, more especially with those who

THE HERO TURNS CYNIC 199

laid themselves out in denunciations of that sex to whom, since the world began, has been given the dual powers at once to hurt and comfort mankind the most. And alone with them in the retired alcoves, I, the latest of angry lovers, fed my fires with the cold ashes of their long dead disappointments. I read and read until the loveliness that is in woman became in my mind the very livery of sin itself, and the gentleness that behoves them but the touch of the creeping serpent; and, as I joyed with those old fellows in their spleen, the scales fell from my eyes and I saw deep at last into the horrible wickedness of the sex; feeling a new strength arise thereby within me! No more would I be toyed with, it was beneath my manhood to fetch and carry, to hang on a breath of these tinselled dolls, these after-thoughts of creative invention, inferior and incomplete.

Never again, I swore on the third of those wet afternoons as I sat recluse in my library corner, never more would I be a slave, never again let my heart beat slow or fast to the measure any mincing jade should set it. I was free, the scales had fallen from my eyes, and rejoicing in my strength, like a young knight in his untried armour, I shut the covers of my favourite ancient cynic and, sliding him to the floor, fell into a reverie.

Then it happened that, while brooding over the

frailty of all women and the falsehood of those in particular with whom I had to associate, there came a gentle touch upon my shoulder, and starting up, there against my bench was the high culprit herself, the quaint essence of feminine frowardness, tall and graceful, and bending on me eyes of shameless interest.

"Mr. Allanby," she began, "I have come from your mother: she thinks you are reading too long, and stay too much indoors of late. She asked me to tell you the rain has stopped, and she wants you, if you will, to take me for a ride."

"I am sorry, but I don't care about going out to-day."

"So I guessed," answered the lady, ignoring my rudeness, "and it was just for that reason I came up—alone—to persuade you. Please do come, your mother really wishes it, and I shall not go without you; it will give me real pleasure if you will come."

"And you think, I suppose, that that is conclusive?"

"It would have had weight with you once, Louis," answered the girl gently, and looking up I saw the beginning of a tear in those eyes that I used to think so kind. What was I to do? She was as beautiful as a flower, standing there against the dim backing of the dusty shelves, and all my resolution ran to waste as I looked upon her. What an infernal shame that so much wickedness could look so lovely—could be armed at every point for the subjection of resistance? Fair hair, a little loose, and touched by a streak of sunshine; soft cheeks upon which the treacherous colour came and went; sweet mouth backed by speaking limpid eyes that illuminated every utterance of her mind with tender radiance—now was the time for that crabbed fellow on the floor to stand by me, in the hour of trial; but, coward like, he made no sign, lying flat upon his face and looking—oh, so ragged and tawdry beside her loveliness.

Thus it came about that, deserted by my allies, I had to let Pris sit down on the bench beside me, and take my hand in friendly fashion, and absent-mindedly mistaking my philosopher for a footstool put her foot upon him, and woo me back to slavery. I felt the chains closing, and had no heart to shirk them; I felt my fair captor rivet the links with her dulcet voice, and I submitted. All my philosophy went at the touch of that sweet Circe. She was so eager to win me again, that by accident or art her very reserve was forgotten for the moment. Nearer and nearer she came; we were all alone, even the starlings' chatter was hushed—nearer and nearer, till her piled hair at my shoulder shone in the rays like golden wire, and her pleasant breath was upon me; nearer and nearer, wooing me with those velvet touches of her fingers, speaking to me with a voice like the wind in the meadow grass, so near came that sweet aggressor, inviting capture, that the glamour of her presence thrilled me to my sluggish core. Three times I shook my head, and put her back, three times looked for counsel and encouragement to those glum cynics on the shelves, and then, forgetting everything but the fascination of the moment, threw my arms about the sweet deceiver, and drawing her struggling into my breast, gave her the kiss of fealty—not one, alas! but many, and so went back to slavery.

"Well, dear," said my mother's voice, as we came down the winding library stairs, "have you brought him?"

"Yes, Mrs. Allanby, he is here behind me," answered Miss Smith, with modesty becoming a worthy conqueror, and forthwith I was "produced," as lawyers say, the guests about my parent staring at me, who had been so long in hiding, as though I were a piece of treasure trove, or a small boy caught in trying to make a burglarious entry through an upper window. "I have told him we are going out riding, and he has very kindly offered to join us" (this, by the way, was the first intimation that Miss Smith and I were not going alone), and turning to me before I could express my surprise, she went on: " The horses will be ready in five minutes, Mr. Allanby, and your dear mother, who loves horses only less than children, cannot bear to see them wait—will five minutes be enough for you to get ready in? "

I bowed: having so newly surrendered at discretion it did not beseem me to question a first command, and I went off to my room for a warmer riding coat, trying to comfort myself with the reflection that if company had been foisted on us, at least Pris had shown a proper spirit in making me one of the party. Probably the other riders were one of our Oxford undergraduates, who rode a horse like a sailor ashore, and Miss Alice, who was very nervous in the saddle, or pretended to be when there was an eligible gentleman at hand. Why! it would be actually promoting my mother's matrimonial schemes towards those two empty-headed triflers if I could manage to separate the party—an absolute act of virtue to " get lost " and come home in detachments; how we would laugh over it to-morrow morning at breakfast, I thought, as I buckled on my spurs, and fastened my cravat down securely at the back. And we did have that laugh the next morning at breakfast, but not quite as I had arranged.

These thoughts put me into a cheerful frame of mind. Judge then of my chagrin when, coming up to the group in the hall porch, a glance served to show that besides Miss Smith, the only other person dressed for the ride was Lepidus the Roman himself. I was so taken aback that for a moment I hesitated; surprise, anger, and a half inclination in my mind to throw my whip into the fireplace even then, and return forthwith to my sulks. "You fool!" I said to myself bitterly, "after stuffing yourself with all that philosophy upstairs, and swaggering your new-got caution, to swallow the first bait a woman dangles over you, climbing down from your pedestal at a touch of her finger to be a laughing-stock to everyone. You a man of discretion, you an improvement on your sex—why no schoolboy enamoured of the mature damsel behind his sweet-stuff counter could be a more silly calf! There, go! they have done laughing at you for the moment; go and stuff yourself with more philosophy till you are wanted again." Though I told myself I deserved all that, yet I could scarcely turn back having gone so far; that would be too peevish, too like the foresaid schoolboy, and while I weighed the matter Pris espied me. "Oh, there you are," she cried, coming through the crowd, "and ready—how good of you!

THE HERO TURNS CYNIC

Here is Mr. Lepidus ready too, so we can start at once—I told you he was coming, did I not?"

"I think you overlooked the fact," this in my gloomiest tone.

"Oh, how stupid of me!" exclaimed Miss Smith, dropping a beautiful hand for a moment on my arm, and giving a look of bewitching plausibility; "but you know he wanted to take me out, and I would not hear of it, unless you came too. And there is another surprise for you—your friend is going to ride 'Satan.'"

"I am glad," I blurted out, the unholy thought springing to my mind that perhaps "Satan" would break the Roman neck. Whether Miss Smith understood, or not, is impossible to say. She led me out into the porch, where I and Lepidus nodded briefly to one another, and there, sure enough, was the big black horse for whom the Centurion had taken a great fancy and had ridden once or twice of late, champing his bit and pawing the gravel in the exuberance of his spirits. For Pris they had saddled a strong Irish mare, a handsome beast of good points and vast endurance, but uncertain temper, while my saddle was on an ordinary hunter, an amiable steed, good enough as a second mount in an easy country, but of no character.

Well, Miss Smith was hoisted up by a groom (for she would not show any partiality to either of us in this matter), the Roman, scorning stirrups, swung himself straight on to "Satan's" back, amid the undivided admiration of the spectators, and when I had clambered to my hack (clumsily dropping my whip in the process) we waved adieu, and trotted off down the drive and towards the open country.

It appeared that it was Miss Smith's intention to go for a ride on the moorland, though the weather suggested one by preference nearer home, where shelter was to be obtained at need. But neither I nor the equinoxes were consulted in the matter, and to the heather we took our way, emerging after a time from the park on to the black uplands, flecked as far as the eye could see with the pools left by yesterday's rain, and a dull sky overhead that seemed to be already repenting of the sunshine of an hour ago, and quickly closing up its watery gleams with banks of leaden clouds that curdled as they met and twined in serpentine wreaths about the low vault of the heavens, like smoke from giant furnaces.

As soon as she felt the springing turf under foot, Miss Smith made an end of the desultory conversation we had been maintaining, by giving her reins a shake and starting the mare off on one of those long wolf-like gallops at which your Irish horse is hard to beat.

I confess there was an extraordinary exhilaration in the wild free air of those uncovenanted pastures that stretched away from our snug valley, ridge beyond ridge to the very sea itself. It fired our horses' blood like our own, and we went pounding away mile after mile over the springy ground, little noting how dark the sky was growing overhead. The shaggy red cattle gathering in knots behind the grey stone escarpments stared at us in wonder; the curlews rose from the steely pools, and circled overhead, uttering plaintive cries full of the loneliness of untenanted spaces—but never a human being did we see in all those miles. At last we had gone so far that even Pris pulled up, with a splendid colour in her face, and after a moment to recover breath, asked with a glance around what we thought of the weather, and how far we were from home? As it chanced, we had come into a part of the fen country that was not very familiar to me, so I could only reply that we were probably ten or twenty miles from shelter; and as for the sky, it was black enough to make a water rat turn home for his mackintosh.

Nothing, however, would do but Miss Smith must go back by a new road. "A short cut, kind Mr. Allanby," quoth the beautiful girl, checking her fretting steed, and brushing back with the other hand those rebellious strands of hair the wind was blowing about her face; " you know one, I am sure, across the stream; and if we get a sprinkling of rain on the way home, it is not I that will mind."

If she did not shrink from a wet jacket, how could we? So I answered that there *was* a possible ford a little higher up the swollen river on our left, and to it at her eager request I proceeded to lead them.

This mountain torrent was a continuation of the one which ran through our valley, but between that distant spot and here it had received on its way to the sea numberless additions, and with them had become an angry stream, tossing its dishevelled locks as it ran over a stony bed under the black canopy of the sky in an extremely formidable way. We turned down its course for the ford I knew of, while the thunder rumbled overhead, and the wail of the curlews sweeping away down the wind sounded like the voices of disembodied spirits; and as we went, I told my companions a curious story of the lonely spot we were coming to.

It was a darksome place amongst scattered grey rocks, hoary with lichens and ancient fir trees, and marked even to this day by the vestiges of a dwelling

THE HERO TURNS CYNIC 209

place, half hollow mound, half stone-built cell, and there long ago a very holy man had dwelt. He had consecrated to Heaven the affections which some wayward damsel had rejected, and though he was civil enough to benighted travellers of his own sex, or wandering shepherds searching for lost lambs, the mere supposition of a female presence put him in an ungodly temper. Now one wild afternoon just like this, with the sky inky overhead, the pine branches tossing together in the gathering gloom of the wood, and the yellow flood at the hermit's door, lamenting in a hundred melancholy strains as it hurried away into the mist-shrouded hollows of the hills, temptation in the form of a charming little lady came to that good man. He was cooking his evening meal in the shelter of the mossy stone outside his doorway; the water was just boiling, the humble pottage ready for the saint's wooden basin, when the gusty wind blew the smoke into his face. He coughed and sneezed, as even hermits must under such circumstances, rubbed his eyes, and when he looked up again, there before him was that dainty lady—oh, such a woeful figure, all in a ragged green kirtle, muddy and travel stained, her poor feet bare and bruised with hard walking, her fair hands torn by brambles and sharp rocks, the strands of her pretty hair blowing about her tired face, and such a look of pathos and entreaty about those wild blue eyes, and that tender baby-mouth!

If the saint had been wise he would have left his supper to take care of itself, and fled to the shelter of his cell before the charmer could say a word. But he was not wise, he listened, and was lost! It was only a little thing that hunted lady wanted— only to be carried across the ford before the night came down, and the hermit knew every foot of the way, he was a strong, big man, and she the lightest, slimmest little shape that had ever worn a woman's form. Far be it from me to say what arguments she used, what deadly persuasion sapped the saintly resolution, but the fact remains, the hermit consented at last to break his rule, and taking the damsel in those arms, where never damsel had been before, essayed to carry her to the further bank. And black as midnight grew the heavens as they went down to the flood, and strange unearthly voices howled amongst the tossing branches overhead! Like hungry serpents the angry waves presently curled round the hermit's knees, and that fairy form that had been so light before, seemed to turn to lead as he advanced. To thigh and waist and shoulder the torrent mounted, and then, alas! for faltering saintship, white as a dead man's grew the fairy's face—for it was a wicked water sprite, of course, and not a mortal woman after all—her yellow hair blew away like the dun spume from the ridges of the foam-laced flood; those dimpled arms about his neck turned to grisly bone, the rose-bud fingers closed like iron fangs upon the shrieking hermit's throat, and down she bore him, gasping and crying, into the black tide, down into that icy, eddying torrent, down for ever into the horrible black oblivion of the hurrying water —and then the night drew its curtains about the bed that wicked lady had made for herself and the hermit!

Lepidus, who was in a cheerful mood, laughed at my story, and said in substance that nothing in the hermit's life became him like the leaving of it, but Miss Smith, with all a true woman's unconquerable belief in the supernatural, took it seriously, and when we presently came to the gloomy hollow in question, where the shepherds said the anchoretic spirit still waited in stormy weather to show the ford to tired travellers, she was obviously more interested in the remains of what had once been his, than in our passage home. The Roman and I went down to the stream to seek for a turf bridge, which a farmer had built the previous summer, the rain beating in our faces, and the thunder growling overhead, while Pris rode on a hundred yards to look at the ruined cell. Now I do not know why it was, but our horses were extraordinarily nervous. It may have been but the coming storm, or it may have been because animals know more of those who dwell in haunted spots than we, but there was the fact; all three whinnied with displeasure as we went into the dip, the Irish mare shook her fiddle-shaped head and glanced anxiously from side to side, my palfrey trembled with well-bred reserve, like the decorous park hack he was, while the Centurion's black charger tossed his mane in fear and pawed the ground angrily as we came to the river edge.

Lepidus was just saying to me, as he eyed the torrent, " Mighty little can I see of your bridge here to-night, cousin, and if it were not for the lady, one place would serve as well to swim as any other," and I was answering that " it *was* for the lady, and the ford must be found by hook or crook," when we heard Miss Smith scream, and turning our eyes we saw the Irish horse a short distance off, rearing up on its hind legs in front of the hermit's ruined doorway, terror in its very outline. The next instant, sheer overhead came a keen blue flash of lightning and directly after a peal of thunder that seemed to rend the sky itself. Down went the sorrel mare at that sound, she spun right round in a way that must have unhorsed any rider less ready than the one upon her, and in a thought had taken the bit into her teeth, and was bolting headlong from us towards the open ground and hills beyond. What she had seen in the hollow of the ruined cell we never knew, but her rider told us long afterwards that *something* there certainly was inside, something grey and shadowy —a sheltering hill sheep, perhaps—but whatever it was it had scared the horse horribly.

Then began a chase never to be forgotten. I had slightly the vantage in position over the Roman, and with a shout started off in pursuit of the fugitive. But the scion of an illustrious race was only a few yards behind, and infinitely better mounted. When he saw what had happened, like the hero of Macaulay's ballad—

> "—Never a word he spake.
> He clapt his hands on Auster's mane,
> He gave the reins a shake,
> Away, away went Auster,
> Like an arrow from the bow;
> Black Auster was the fleetest steed
> From Aufidus to Po!"

Up the slope I led, my steed rending the tangles of moisture-laden sedge at every stride, and on the top we viewed her—saw her whom we both valued above all things, on fifty pounds' worth of accursed horseflesh, flying headlong into the grey mist of the next " bottom,"—saw the black arms of the storm taking her in, and clapped our spurs into our horses' sides. And all down the next moorland slope, dotted with grey rock and heather clumps, we raced madly; we burst girth-deep through a brook at the hollow, and with a shout set our horses to the following rise. It was there that " Satan " came thundering by on my right hand, his hoofs spurting the bog-water to right and left, mane flying, and eyes as eager on the chase, I thought, as those of him who rode him—brave rider on brave steed. In vain I pressed the poor panting beast beneath me and inwardly cursed my luck; it was like chasing one of the storm clouds overhead struggling after those two, and Lepidus laughed as he saw my futile efforts. " Stir him up, cousin! put your heels into him; clear is the course, and fair is the prize. What! done, is he? Well, good-bye, then, and trust me, but I will take good care of the lady till we come again;" and stooping low, he slapped a hand anew upon Satan's great neck, and shot away as though I were no better than rooted to the ground.

All up the next rise I flogged my wretched hack, jealousy and anger raging in my heart. I gained the top just in time to see Pris, half a mile ahead, wave her gloved hand, half in entreaty, half in encouragement, as the brute she rode swept her into the heavy mists of the further valley, saw those shadows swallow her as if she had ridden though the portals of another world, heard the Centurion's answering shout of courage as he gained on her at every stride, saw those shadows engulf him in turn, and then the heaving thing I bestrode caught a front leg in a rabbit burrow and rolled heavily, stupidly over with me!

When I rose, dazed, to my feet and assured myself no bones were broken, a glance showed that save the disabled horse and myself there was not another living thing in sight. Miss Smith and the Roman had disappeared into the mists, and all around was a melancholy waste of moorland stretching for miles on every hand only relieved here and there by lagoons of mist in the hollows or occasional hillocks of rising ground crowned by rocks or dreary tangles of heather or bog myrtle. One of these, about a quarter of a mile away I recognised directly by the castle-like shape of its crags as a knoll called the Goblin's Den, and it settled my first instinctive inquiry, " Where was I? " with the chilling informaton that home lay a long twenty miles away over the darkening wastes, and the nearest village of any kind, five miles in another direction.

But it did not say where the truants were, and very bitterly I stared into the shadows, listening and watching in vain for a sign of their returning. Then, in a pause of the wild rain, I lifted my voice and cried out—

"Hullo there!" and to my surprise there came almost instantly the answer, "Hullo there!" Why, then, after all, they must be near, and greatly cheered I shouted again: "Hullo!" and again that voice answered "Hullo!" "Lepidus," I cried, "where are you?" and over the wet rush flats and sighing ling there came the slow, melancholy response, "Lepidus, where are you?" Then I knew that it was but an echo that took up my cries—the goblin was mocking me out of his rocky castle, and half in vexation, and half in anger, I laughed aloud, and instantly the goblin laughed with a hollow, joyless sound strangely weird in the gathering dusk of the twilight.

It was no use standing fooling with that shadow, so, very cold and wet, I essayed to follow the trail of my companions, and I did follow it for a mile or so, until it eventually was utterly lost in the long heather of a dreary tract that led up into the heart of a pine forest on the hills beyond.

What was I to do? The heroic course of conduct, that which fire-side philosophers would certainly expect of me, would be to scour the hillsides with unflagging energy until success at last crowned

THE HERO TURNS CYNIC

my efforts. But then these moralists never take such details as waning light and a crippled steed into account. If I stayed out here and beat the mosses to and fro like an owl looking for mice, I should certainly be benighted and almost as certainly fail in my object. If they did not hear my shouting, and my throat was already like a nutmeg grater, there was not one chance in a thousand of lighting upon them in the mist and rain. They might, indeed, have already passed me on the way home, and then what an egregious fool I should be to go howling about these wildernesses half the night searching for a couple of runaways who were already putting on dry clothes by the cheerful fires at home. To stay here shouting myself hoarse was heroic folly, to slink away to shelter, while my promised lady was perhaps braving out the storm alone with a stranger was plain cowardice. Long I thought of it, wandering to and fro, and crying on them until the very sound of my own voice bored me in those unsympathetic solitudes, and then I decided to take the ignoble course, and get to shelter.

So off I set westward, over the quaking grass and sludgy sheep tracks, dragging my limping horse behind, and shivering as every drop of cold water ran from my hat-brim down my neck. For guidance to the distant cluster of cottages, I had a familiar knoll far ahead, and at my watch chain a little compass—a gift of the gods to vagrant humanity, without which no man or woman should ever go out of sight of their cabbage-beds—and for comfort my own thoughts. What a fool I had been, I soliloquised, as the water soaked through first one thin riding boot and then the other, and my clothes began to cling damp and clammy about me—what a fool to come down from the retreat of my snug library, and wise old friends at the beck of that dear betrayer, whom in my heart I loved so greatly—what a fool to let her show me as her humble slave before her friends, to be taken a-riding, and then turned loose, to be presently made, no doubt, a laughing-stock to high and low! I cursed my folly, cursed Lepidus, cursed my floundering steed, cursed the weather, and the sodden bog that squeaked and bubbled under foot as I plodded miserable and shamefaced through the gathering evening.

It was a long five-mile walk, and at times seemed as though it would never end; but slowly the fir-crowned hillock grew tall and dim over the moorland track; like a well-known headland to a wave-tossed mariner it marked the way, and at last was rounded, and there below was harbourage.

To say I was glad to see the village, inadequately expressed my feelings. It was a grey and watery hamlet as I approached it in the last of the daylight, a poor row of humble cottages threaded on a very sodden bit of mountain road, but here was shelter at any rate, supper and a dry coat, which are cheering things even to your despondent lover. Further, there was a tiny telegraph office I remembered with delight, where they varied the sale of bulls-eyes and bootlaces by the supervision of such of his Majesty's mails as came into that region, and thence it would of course be possible for me to communicate with home, and discover if the truants had returned.

On to the village I went, and up the one street splashed my way, envying the truly happy ducks who were in glorious enjoyment of the gutters, and noting the curious faces of the weather-bound folk who stared at me from their diamond-latticed windows, as the good people in the ark must have stared at the amphibious monsters who swam into their neighbourhood during those dull months of theirs. At the inn, of course, they knew me, and were aghast with amazement to see the young squire standing there in the middle of the sawdusted bar, dripping like a newly landed walrus, steaming like a geyser. The stout host nearly choked himself with surprise and the beer he was drinking at the moment of my entry, his housewife all but dropped the babe she had in one hand into the cauldron of hot soup she was stirring with the other; the half dozen rough shepherds drinking the trestles stared with openmouthed wonder, the dogs set off a barking under the bench, and the cocks began crowing on the further rafters; the maid peeling potatoes, out of sight in the kitchen, cut herself and screamed, and never was heard such a pandemonium.

But the moment their senses came back, their rough but kindly welcome was overwhelming. Those good, bronzed fellows from the hills, who still wore undressed sheepskins over their shoulders, as their ancestors had done for unnumbered generations, led my poor horse to the stables; the host roared the yapping dogs to silence, and yelled quaint, peaty, north-country oaths at his noisy poultry; the injured damsel from behind, when the truth dawned upon her, rushed to kindle a fire in the little parlour beyond the homely bar; the mother scolded her indignant offspring into peacefulness, and seizing on me, took my wringing jacket from me as though it were the Cadmian shirt, and then, in the shelter of the parlour offed my sodden boots and socks. They lit me a fire in the one little guest-room looking out upon the street, they found me a mighty flannel shirt, designed for some giant shepherd boy, and a green coat, long tailed and brass buttoned, with a pair of the host's own trousers, short in the leg and monstrous in the waist. Thus equipped, my feet in carpet slippers so large I had to shuffle to keep them on, a hot glass of punch still tingling in my throat, and that æsthetic feeling which comes to the newly dried and warmed pervading my being, I presently found myself downstairs again confronting the landlord.

That worthy's manners withstood even the shock of my appearance thus clad, and forthwith I put to him the question in my mind. Firstly, had any two such riders as I described passed through the glen since dusk, and secondly, was there to be had for love or money in all the place, any beast on four legs that would get me home that night? Both questions were answered in the negative. Not one of all those keen hill-men who had come in from the moors an hour or two ago had seen a horse, man or woman ridden. It was not a sight to be seen every day in this wilderness, and they swore strange oaths that they would not be likely to have forgotten had such a thing chanced upon them. And to the second question the answer was equally certain; the only horse in all the village was the landlord's market pony, and he had done his twenty miles that day already—there was not another three miles' trot in him before the morning, though half the kingdom depended upon it. Thus there remained only one thing to be done. The village postoffice was still open; at least I could ascertain if the truants had got home; so on a fly-marked form which my host found for me between the leaves of some neglected blotting-pad I hastily scribbled out a message to my mother.

"All well, but have lost my companions. Have they returned? Answer paid."

It was brief and not romantic, yet how much it might mean! I sent the dispatch off to the little office down the street by a shepherd, and then fell a-ruminating while the landlord went back to his tap, and the wife came in to spread a frugal supper for me.

All through that meal I wondered and speculated. Was I a coward to sit here in a comparative comfort, eating and drinking, while the girl who was in truth so dear to me, whom it was the one ambition of my barren life to have for wife, and later on, if it should please the gods, for the honoured mother of my children, was braving the storm outside, alone with the man who loved her, as well perhaps as I, and whose very approach to her I had learnt these last few days to dread? Was she hurt? Had that cursed beast they had put her on broken her sweet neck and my heart at one and the same time? And if unhurt what had become of her?

While I still shuffled up and down the little room in my uncouth garments, listening to the wild rain outside, the answer came to my telegram. The yellow cover was tear-stained with the storm, and I tore it open with feverish haste. It was from my mother, and ran as follows:—

"Nothing heard or seen of your companions. Please change your socks if they are damp."

"There is no answer," I said briefly to the waiting messenger, and then as the door closed, dropped into a chair. No! there was no answer to that fatal little missive to-night—but there would be some answer to-morrow! What would it be?—good or bad? I could not tell, but as the anxiety and shame welled again into my heart I crumpled the message up in my hands and stared into the fire.

They were out for certain, out miles from home without a chance of rescue. What would they do? What should I do in the circumstances?

A thousand possibilities raced through my heated brain. At last, determined to think no more, I got up and stalked to and fro, until my nerves were somewhat quieted, and near on midnight I was able to take my candle and get to bed.

CHAPTER XV

LEPIDUS PHILOSOPHISES

DREAMING uncomfortable dreams, and starting up to imagine that the voice of the wind in the chimney stacks was full of horrible meanings, I spent a hectic night, and then, as so often happens, fell into a sleep of prosaic depth with the first streak of daylight.

Happily, for my reputation, orders had been given overnight for an early breakfast—early even as these moor-folk fix that ceremony—and for the village pony to be ready saddled immediately afterwards, and thus it happened I was called with the sunlight.

That summons interrupted me in the midst of a dream in which Priscilla, Lepidus, a funny old hermit, and myself were trying to cook oatmeal porridge in an iron pot. The pot was in a shepherd's hut, and the hermit fed the fire with tomes from my library at home. Lepidus, in trousers and vest, kept jumping hither and thither, and calling out that the cauldron would boil all right when the thunder stopped; while Pris bent, spoon in hand, so eagerly over our meal, that presently her long loose hair fell into the liquid, and went twining round and round in ever winding circles, till the pot spread out into a black river pool, in my disordered imagination, and hair and water swelled and foamed into a snaky all-embracing flood; the shrieking hermit on the bank wrung his hands and cried " Another, another traitress has come!" and Pris in my arms (for I had plunged in to rescue her) weighed heavy as lead, as with straining eyes and trembling limbs I struggled towards the shore that went back, and ever back, as we neared it. Lepidus on that bank was just in the act of wringing the anchorite's neck for calling Miss Smith a traitress, and I " at sea " was in the throes of drowning, when there came a respite in the shape of that knock at my door, and starting up with the suddenness of the sleeper awakened, I shook my wandering faculties together.

A lovely morning after the rain confronted me. It is the happy privilege of nature to emerge from her stormy outbursts not red-eyed and sore-headed, like we poor mortals, but refreshed and invigorated beyond recognition. Never had the moorland looked so fair as it did that daylight from my lattice, ten thousand acres of undulating heather and bog, with the rain-pools glittering in every hollow, and framed by the soft purple of the distant hills, while overhead the clouds were floating idly down a sapphire sky as clear as though it had not been ruffled since the world began. When the great mother thus smiles we, her children, must laugh. I breakfasted and mounted the waiting pony afterwards with a certain amount of confidence in the outcome of the day. For one thing, I had got my own clothes again, and that was much, since no man can be at peace with Providence in another man's trousers. Then again I had rested, and still again, my pony's head was turned homeward, where news and the opportunity of action awaited me—both god-sent things in time of difficulty.

So we jogged along pretty pleasantly, I the truant lover whistling at times to persuade myself that I believed all was well with Priscilla, until presently we mounted the last ridge and saw the dear, ever welcome roof amongst the trees below. I stripped my steed of saddle and bridle and turned him loose in the paddock by the park entrance to graze. Then, a few minutes after, with my hand on the shrubbery gate, stopped to collect my thoughts. What sort of welcome should I get—tragic or ludicrous? What news awaited me—good heavens! what a wide gamut of possibilities there was between the light banter I might meet with, and the horrible silence of the other possibility! The doubt was intolerable, and pushing through the wicket I strode eagerly over the lawns, sprang up the grassy terrace, and—I confess it—with my heart audibly beating, burst into the hall. No! there was no air of dramatic horror there, no funeral silence, no whispering groups! Instead there was a distinct aroma of breakfast, and a cheerful-looking tray of used plates and empty eggshells, resting for a moment on its way to the kitchen, caught my eye by the morning-room door. And through that portal came the sound of laughter that dissolved my last fears like summer mist.

"Poor wretch!" I heard Smythers say, "it is a shabby trick you two played, and I pay him the tribute to think he is fool enough to have spent the whole of a miserable night looking for you both on the heather."

Then a voice, easily recognisable as the widow's, remarked, "No, Mr. Smythers; I think, in spite of appearances, Mr. Allanby can be quite sagacious at times. He is not so stupid as you think, and when he found, his—well, I will say his *guest,* Miss Smith, had gone for an evening ride with a friend he probably decided to leave them to their fate, and went in search of shelter."

"I cannot agree with you, Mrs. Milward," said the

sculptor, from across the table, somewhat warmly; "a man's chivalry and sense of honour acknowledge no personal considerations whatever. Urged by either, he does the bare duty that lies before him, in this case to search for lost friends, with an absolute disregard of adverse critics or personal consequences."

"A beautiful rule," said the Bishop's mellow voice, "and befitting one who is accustomed to perceive the ideal ever rising triumphant through all the stress and labour of the moment."

"I do not know," I said, pushing open the door and stepping in amongst them without waiting to hear more, "whether my opinions on these matters are of any interest, but at least I may say I am very glad to see Miss Smith has taken no harm from her ride, whatever my part in it."

There, indeed, was that lady in white muslin, seated contentedly at the breakfast table, a little pale perhaps, but looking as splendid as only a lady can in her simplicity. And near her was Lepidus, spreading jam on buttered toast with irritating cheerfulness. It was he that hailed me first as I entered.

"Now, by all the Seven Hills, we are glad to see you! Where have you been, cousin Louis? When we parted, if I remember rightly, you were standing on your head in a peat hole, with that valiant steed of yours sitting on its haunches, and all the crows in the neighbourhood waiting to sup on your bodies."

Then the women got at me with pretty shrieks of sympathy, and I was stifled with questions, until my kindly mother came to the rescue, and after assuring herself that my clothes were dry, and none of my bones broken, said that all was well that ended well, telling me with sweet instinctive shrewdness, what I longed to hear above all else, that nothing untoward had happened, that Miss Smith and the Centurion had found their way back, wet and hungry, but safe, when it was far too late to send me word, and that I, who had been devouring my heart out with dreadful fancies, had alone been the object of their anxieties.

Thus ended outwardly a foolish incident, and it was not till long afterwards that I heard from the hesitating lips of the dear runaway herself how near comedy had been to sorrow. It was she who told me, when there were no longer any secrets between us, how the Roman had followed her into the wilderness of the hills, had ridden her down, and when they had got breath, there, amongst the dark pines and rocks, had made her dismount. She told me how in that lonely place, away from all help, save her own womanhood, he had proffered his love again, had asked her to ride on with him, pressed her to mount and ride with him " out of the little world behind them, out through the gleaming gateway which the lightning was making, into that new world his love would find for her," conjuring such wonders from the to-come, that the black night was prismatic with his fancies, and to her senses, trembling under the spell of his power, the twining mist opened, it seemed, on a fairy realm of delight; and the arcades of the forest, decked in the violet drapery of the storm, invited them to where the passing gleams filled unknown worlds with wonder. He pleaded for her love with all the vantage which the past had given him; wooing her body through her subject spirit, like another Jove come down to woo a hapless shepherdess; now filling her mind with such splendid imagery of passion that the world became unreal beneath her, and then, " turning mortal for her love," pleading submissively again, like a man pressing his suit on a woman who wavers.

Here in the story, she who told it me in the long after paused, and sighed as though for a moment the ghosts of the lost splendours came again to mind, then laid her hand on my arm, and whispered with averted face:

LEPIDUS PHILOSOPHISES 231

"He failed. I returned; I am yours."

It was not necessary, nor did I even ask her more; it was enough that she had escaped, and had made, it seemed, some compact for mutual forgetfulness of that wild half-hour which enabled them to meet again with smiling faces. But all this, you will bear in mind, only came to my knowledge long after.

That day of my return was peaceful enough. We men went down to the village inn to see a bull-terrier pup, which Mullens was thinking of buying for a cousin in Scotland, have its tail cut off; and the ladies walked across the meadows to see a new mangle at work, which my mother had set up, and held to be incapable of removing the frailest button that ever tempted Providence or soapsuds. We played croquet through the afternoon, and flirted platonically, and thus in divers ways we won our way to dinner-time, and the happy ease of the smoking-room afterwards.

All day long I had been philosophising on the follies of the day before, and—believing at the time that all had gone prosaically between Priscilla and the Centurion—marvelling at my anxieties and false presentiments. Thus I was in the mood for speculations when, we found ourselves in the snug after-dinner retreat, and I listened willingly when coming back from fetching a box of a favourite brand of my own cigars, I found Lepidus in talkative mood. Curiously enough he was saying, as I entered, that most of our mental pains were unnecessary, and much even of physical suffering avoidable. Both these things had their origin in the mind, declared the Roman, going off into that state of speculation in which I could never quite decide whether he was uttering his own convictions or but intellectually dreaming while half unconscious of what he said.

"It is quite possible," quoth Lepidus, "to bring one's mind under absolute control. In that state all circumstances of joy or pain are adventitious; they become the servants, not the masters, the playthings, not the whips of the controlled mind. And in a slightly less perfect degree the body also may be subjected. You hear of men on emergency performing great feats of endurance, of weaklings doing tasks of giants, and all the sensations of the material submitting to an imperative demand of the intellectual. It is curious you should not perceive that if you practised to rule your mind rigidly, and taught your body in turn to obey that intermediary, the miracles which startle you in a crisis might become the commonplace things of your every day. All bodily pain in this way could be reduced to discomfort, while you would not necessarily take the keenness off your pleasures, for the rush of the liberated hound is none the less glorious because he was flogged for riot yesterday."

Those other good fellows our guests never quite knew what to make of Lepidus, they were never quite sure he was not laughing at them; thus they sat in silence, and it was I that carried on the conversation. It wandered that evening, I remember, over an infinitude of subjects, human and superhuman, and some of the things Lepidus said were shocking, and some were strangely interesting to me especially, who knew from what strange source had come his inspirations. He lectured us lightly on living and dying, on birth and marriage, he passed lightly from Mrs. Grundy to the great primæval laws which lie at the back of time; and all the while there was that strange sense on me which they must have felt who out of the hollow mouth of the material Sphinx heard an unrecognisable voice addressing them.

At one time he spoke of marriage, and I was glad, on the whole, the Bishop had a cold in the head which kept him to his room that evening. Happy marriages, said the Roman, in substance, were those between associated spiritual essences, while unfortunate marriages were between hostile ones.

"I may take it," said Lepidus, "that you will

allow without argument and by the force of your natural instincts that it is desirable mutual souls should be associated here as elsewhere. And since these souls are anxious and ready to meet, like friends parted in a throng, any means by which they could be brought together would add immensely to the sum of human happiness. Hence arises the seriousness of the mistake you commit in making marriage so inviolable—oh, all right! do not wince, I will be discreet! What I mean is this. Your man and woman ill-wed is an abomination alike to society here and to the systems of the universe. The mistake such ill-assorted couples have made must be of inevitable frequency, but your blunder is in making the way out so difficult. I can imagine," said the Roman, leaning back and blowing a blue cloud of tobacco smoke up to the ceiling, " a state of society which has passed beyond all those conceptions of virtue based on the jealousies of remote ancestors, and which could give to this question the supernatural importance it deserves. I can imagine such a society allowing to the friend-seeker in the soul-throng an immense indulgence, and treating with wise indifference the mistakes he or she might make in the search. There might even be such a thing as a College of Love, where postulates could retire for mutual trial."

"My dear Lepidus," I cried, "think what Mrs. Grundy would say!"

"I know what you mean," he replied; "but, my gentle cousin, the systems of life and the universe were not constructed with a view to the susceptibilities of that worthy lady. There is your mistake; you are still so near to your ancestors, your ideas of virtue are so childish and trivial, that you cannot see life, its errors, and its objects in due proportion. There was evolved in the remote a code of rules, desirable and excellent in their way, but allowing nothing for that growth of understanding, that broadening perception, which comes as human life itself gets nearer to the great final understanding; and of this code you have made fetish. But I fear I bore you, and am not very lucid at that. How do you like my reasonings?"

And I answered, shaking my head, that I understood them little, and liked them less.

"Of course you do not understand them, my dear Louis; were it otherwise they would not be my speculations, but your accepted facts. You are a good-tempered prig, fully characteristic of your age; and who am I that I should jostle you into a riper state of wisdom against all your inclination and readiness?"

Then a little later on, when we had discussed

some other matters of kindred nature, he got upon the subject of souls, their whence and whither, and I was more than ever glad my lord Bishop's cold had sent him to bed.

"The soul develops, it seems to me," said the Centurion presently, "no less than the intellect and body—the realms of the invisible are peopled from the realms of the material. In that far-away time when man rose from the ignoble, that which he now prides himself on as his soul arose too. And in the rudimentary body of the babe, growing as it grows, is the nucleus of a soul ready to be affected by the circumstances of its surroundings during life, but as essentially the result of previous soul-growths as the body which clothes it is the result of previous generations."

"But," I said, mentally limping after him, "how then can one soul be continuous in many bodies if within each body there grows with it a fresh essence?"

The Roman hesitated as though he found the question difficult to answer rather from my deficiencies than from his ignorance. Then he replied, "The only answer I can give you lays me open to criticism on many points; I can but say, that though in general a new soul rises with each birth, and afterwards passes out to people worlds you do not yet even guess at, yet sometimes, for some special purpose—to finish some errand, to await some friend, to fulfil some compact—a soul will re-inhabit for as many generations as need be a succession of bodies, or, unlodged in that way, will hang about some familiar corner of this cabbage-plot of a world of yours—to your probable fright and its own inconvenience—awaiting fulfilment."

"Then you really mean to say there is more than one kind of soul amongst us here?"

"Yes, I suppose that is how you would put it. To you it may be startling to think of some souls that are quite new, as new as their bodies, making a virgin start; while others, their comrades and companions, are old stagers as it were, come back to keep an appointment, or for something they had forgotten. But even you yourself have an inkling of this. I heard you speak at lunch to-day of someone as having a great soul in a little body, while of others you talked as having lifelong 'antipathies' and obvious 'missions.' They *had* missions, friend Louis, if I recognised them aright in your chatter, they *had* antipathies; and great souls making shift for a time with poor bodies! They were the bronzed travellers of life, returned and mixing lightly in the throng of your green, country-bumpkin souls who have never been over their spiritual parish boundaries."

"And beyond that," I asked in a minute or two, "beyond the beyond—what comes then? You have spoken of the here, and the passing out, and the returning perhaps; but how about those souls who acknowledge contentment, who have no detaining causes, who do *not* come back. Tell me," I said eagerly, "what of them, where do they go?"

But the Roman shook his head. "There you ask me something which is as much beyond my grasp as to-morrow. Yet," he said, with a sudden softening of his tone, for he saw I was disappointed, "to-morrow will certainly come and bring its explanations with it. And more than that, when it comes you will certainly be there to find it as you have fashioned it to-day. If well, then well; if ill, then open to betterment. Why should you be frightened at the prospect of many spiritual to-morrows not unlike the yesterdays you have known of? Is it worthy of your manhood to sigh for one long eternal day of sleek enjoyment? Has this little span of life down here exhausted all your capacities of self-fashioning? For my part," said that splendid pagan, stretching himself in his pride and the luxury of his self-sufficient strength, "I could find it in me to pray to the gods for long ages of effort piled mountain high; and, knowing that pleasure dies when pain ends, would ask nothing better of them than to take my heaven and hell alternately as I went along."

Then the candles came, and, shaking the ashes from our pipes, we said good-night, and went to bed.

CHAPTER XVI

SOME REPROACHES AND A PROPOSAL

I SUPPOSE that strange guest of mine had to heart the axiom that all is fair in love and war, else I should be at a loss to know how he could have reconciled the terms of apparent good fellowship on which we existed with the implacable rivalry in love existing between us. Sometimes it had seemed to me that the Roman was unconsciously living a double existence, and therein lay the explanation of the anomaly. To love and win, fair or foul, the lady who was mine was by the strange irony of chance a matter of instinct with him, the deathless bequest of all those ages of waiting that had gone before. When occasion offered it became an imperious necessity in which he forgot all else. When the incentive was not present, he was but the bold, bright soldier of fortune, without fear and without animosity, the repository in his spiritual aspect of a quaint medley of heathen fancies, softened by the knowledge I had lent him along with more than half my vital force, and coloured by those strange inspirations which had come to him when he lay asleep many ages in the porch of death. Even now I cannot quite disentangle his philosophy, far less can I be responsible for it. To hear him talk in the evening was to inhale the mystic fumes which fired the Delphic priestess; to ponder on what he had said in the morning was like waking on a tantalising dream that excited speculation without satisfying it. I can but recall his strange heresies, though they lose in my telling all the magic force his personality lent, and leave them uncriticised as incidents of the narrative.

As for our personal relations, they were like those of two actors who are rivals before the curtain, and the best of friends behind; yet there again must I hesitate, and half disown my own explanations even as I make them, for our rivalry was as continuous as our friendship. Keenly as I foresaw the danger of his presence and knew the great stake we both played for, I never could quite rid my mind of the idea that it was some game we played at, some huge pretence which I was compelled by unseen influences to go on with in fear and trembling, though the terrors were imaginary and the forfeits lay in stronger hands than mine.

Yet it was all uncommonly realistic if Fate, after all, was only laughing at us, and the Roman, while still nominally my friend, laid himself out to win my lady from me in a way that, had the circumstances been less quaint, must have abruptly put an end to friendship and hospitality both.

I did not know, you will remember, at the time how he had pressed his suit upon Priscilla when he had her alone in the hills; perhaps even now I do not know the whole truth. But Priscilla had told my mother, who was more than a mother to her, of that episode; and my parent, with the anger of a hen in defence of her brood, had gone straight to the culprit, and put the matter to him in a way which, gentle as is that lady generally, was, I have reason to believe, a striking exception to the rule.

I was not present, but heard something about it afterwards—heard how that kindly dame faced the disturber of our domestic peace, and held his conduct up in a variety of most unfavourable aspects for him to select the worst from. Like all self-restrained people she had a very biting tongue when it was given liberty; and I could well imagine how she began paternally, lighting her angry fires as she went along, and treating the offender to a steadily rising stream of reproach, bitter enough to move the remorseful sentiments of most of the young men she knew, but strangely, quaintly unsuited to the drama whereof only the superficial aspects came within her ken. And I could fill up what I heard afterwards by well imagining the mild wonder with which the dark Roman eyes opened as the object of the interview was explained—the faint tinge of colour that dawned under a skin browned by suns that shone almost before history began, when my mother cast at him reproaches not one of which he would have stood unmoved from living man. I can imagine how his interest quickened as it always quickened where hearts beat high in pleasure or anger, and how he heard her to the end when, spent and not far from crying, she sat down at last. I can imagine how, one hand on thigh where his sword had used to be, the other extended open as he was wont to stand, he had set out to answer her.

That answer was not satisfactory. It was not entirely on the lines of unconditional apology for the errors of headlong youth, or humble decision to profit by her counsel, she had looked for. My cousin Alice, who by chance saw her leave her boudoir on the occasion in question, says she came out like an Inquisitor who had been put on the rack by some unabashed heretic, and was too dazed by the enormity of the incident to remember exactly what had happened.

It appears Lepidus had got up to make some half bantering answer, holding, as he said, the matchless attractions of the lady in question to excuse all his errors, and pointing out, perhaps, that by the laws of venery while game was still on foot it was any man's to shoot at. I could imagine how lightly he would begin; but, then warming with the subject, it seemed he somehow stirred his ancient other self, which always lay under his genial conventionality, as the hot lava lies under the pleasant olive gardens of his own Italian plains, and in a minute the courteous modern gentleman, mildly in love, disappeared in the fiery Imperial soldier, holding life, and even honour itself, as nothing compared to the furtherance of his passion.

My poor mother! How she must have gasped as the hot Tuscan blood got uppermost, and the descendant of a score of emperors poured out before her the full measure of his strength and love—called a whole hierarchy of pagan gods to witness that never mortal had loved and longed and waited as he had done; and was he now to stand tamely by and see another carry off the prize, the sweet-eyed Pretorian's daughter, for whom he had derided his royal uncle's anger, and taken a poor captain's place amongst the legions, that he might follow her into exile? For whom he had discarded all the glitter and luxury of the Mother City, and fought and worked with the meanest of the brass-bound rogues he led;

had walked through wild weeks of winter weather by her litter side, cheering the snow-bound Gaulish tracks with laughter and stories, happy only if he could lighten the tedium of her travel. Was he to give her tamely up for whom he had courted every danger of the northern seas and lain out at night on the British hillsides, watching over her safety in forgetfulness of all else? Was he to stand with head down-bent like a third-rate captive in a victor's show, while another went by in triumph with the prize, a knock-kneed, white-livered boy brought up on pap and psalters? He who had been first into Calleva, and hand to hand between watching hosts, had borne down Ambia and fired the palisades of Luguvallium, and had wrung honours and riches from the accursed British barbarians, all for the love of the white maid whom fate dangled forever before his eyes, and would never suffer him to touch? No! By the Black Tablet under the Forum stones; by every temple porch that catches the dazzle of Father Tiber when the sun goes down over the seaward marshes! by the honour of Vesta, and the belt of bloody Mars himself, he would wrap these hills in fire again, and paint every doorpost red from here to the salt waves of Deva sooner than be thus stultified!

Happily the torrent of his invective fell on my

mother's mind merely with a numbing effect. It completely quenched her own indignation as a larger conflagration swallows up a lesser, and while she gathered scarcely a word of his meaning, and missed, Heaven bless her! all his classical allusions, the general effect was to convince her that she was in the presence of a dangerous lunatic.

Nor were her views modified when Lepidus, after a few angry turns up and down the room, suddenly confronted her, and, changing his fierce exclamations to a tone of eager persuasiveness, asked whether, after all, the matter could not be settled in some friendly way, say by a gladiatorial combat between us two, each to choose his own weapons, and I, in view of those physical shortcomings to which he alluded with clearness but delicacy, to have any reasonable advantage that might be agreed upon. He reminded my parent, who had not opened the covers of an ancient history for forty years, that this was a favourite mode of settling little difficulties of the kind amongst the Bœotians, and he pointed out that life was apt to run too much in grooves at Caster Manor, and a gladiatorial display on the lawn—with nets and tridents, for instance—to which the gentry and villagers might be admitted at so much a head, would certainly be interesting. The body of the defeated would, of course, be at

SOME REPROACHES AND A PROPOSAL

the disposal of the victor according to ancient custom, and Miss Smith would hold her nuptial feast that evening in the lists.

Or, he ran on, without giving my mother a chance of getting to the door she was nervously eyeing all the time, if she feared to have her geraniums trampled on, or doubted whether his good cousin Louis's legs would uphold him through the onslaught, were there here no go-betweens to be had, no skilful experts in straightening these questions out, such as they had in Rome, who for a consideration would go into the matter and arrange it amicably? If it was dower the lady stuck at, he had friends at home who, between love and fear of him, would lend enough to buy up twenty British princelings. If it was position, why, his uncle the Emperor, though there had been asperities between them, had enough of royal discretion to accept a thing already accomplished; and once again in the imperial favour, there was not a viceroy or satrap, there was not a consul or prætor from here to Ind who would not welcome him as an ally and comrade. By all the splendours of the Seven Hills, Priscilla wedded to him, the merry tinkle of her silver harness bells should sound all down the Long White Street on gala days; black were the slaves she should have; and red and ankle deep the roses at her feet at dance and banquet. Libya should send her silks, and Neros gold, and Egypt sweet scents and tinctures—never lady should have shone so before; her beauty and fame should spread to every Court from Tiber to Euphrates, and none should share it with her. No! No other damsel that he might have taken before, or should take afterwards to soften his hours of soldier solitude, should ever come between him and this peerless light he sought!

Here my dear mother broke the spell and fairly fled. Happily for her peace of mind, she grasped little or nothing of the Roman's meaning. Not for her was his allusion to a sovereign kinsman or the dead city whose splendours still had life and being in his mind; not for her were his reminiscences of travel in dim ages, when no travellers went abroad except by sword point, or recollections of those liberal nuptial arrangements whereby the ancient masters of the world made the marriage yoke so light to bear. She heard nothing but the confused tumult of his eloquence, saw nothing but his passion, and only grasped the one plain fact that, against all established propriety, he was enamoured of a bespoken damsel—enamoured and unrepentant.

It was for that reason she fled as cousin Alice had seen her, and took me solemnly to task that evening on the indiscretion of cultivating chance acquaintances in general, and the desirability in particular that I should take an early opportunity of hinting to Lepidus that perhaps we were keeping him at the Manor from other friends who would be glad to see him in turn.

Other friends! Oh, who were those other friends; those shadows; those dim remembrances of valour and beauty; those dead human leaves swept out upon the void beaches of time, that he could go to? I heard her silently, and bowed my head to my dear parent's gentle logic, while I groaned in spirit.

CHAPTER XVII

SO AS BY FIRE

MEANWHILE we had a spell of ripening autumn weather, that climatic episode of the year which seems to be reflected in many who are not agricultural by a desire to garner the outlying fruits of the twelve months' industry, whatever it may have been, just as spring tempts the same people instinctively to sow the seeds of a future harvest. And possibly the gods, who have hidden knowledge everywhere for us to win by our own effort, have hidden the true reflection of life in the sequence of the seasons—the recurring ambitions of spring, the efforts of the prime midseason, the realisation of harvest, and the pause of winter, so that we may learn the truth from these great taskmasters as the luckless urchin comprehends at last the wisdom of those proverbs which his dear, dirty fingers trace in laborious repetition down the pages of his copy-book.

Lepidus, it seemed to me, was restless those days while the pears ripened slowly on the red brick wall behind the orchard. He was as restless as a migratory falcon who has lost the best quills in his wings just when the flight is on, and chafes to see how slowly the new ones come. He gave me the idea of being full of a strange disquiet, as though something in him that was not of the ordinary everyday world were preparing for a change. I cannot set down the impression his manner aroused exactly in words, but I felt it keenly nevertheless, and with duller comprehension than his waited for what should happen.

It was a spell of warm, still weather, such as that wherewith the autumn will sometimes close up its accounts with the vegetable world. The big yellow wasps dug juicy hollows into those pears on the wall quicker than my mother could pick and store them; the ripe red apples fell with audible thuds on the dry orchard turf in the still afternoons, the lowermost leaves of the elms turned yellow and began to fall for want of moisture, and the meadow gates shrank back a thought from their posts and shut quite differently to their wont in moister weather. Even the beasts in the field were not so hungry as they used to be; the swallows, in lines on the roof ridge, talked quietly, but all day long, of the coming exodus; the big ants swarmed from the path edges; and the thatch, the sparrows had loosened when making their nests in the springtime, slid in little glittering yellow avalanches from its place on the cowsheds, it was so dry.

As for us, we were rather bored by the sequence of those bright days. We developed an extraordinary interest in cooling drinks—even the good Bishop listened with obvious interest while we talked of such ungodly things as gin-slings and corpse-revivers; and when we were not drinking or making drinks we shook our heads in silent conclave over the prospects of the turnip crop, or wondered whether the grass on the croquet lawn would ever come to its natural hue again. We got quite angry over trivial things, and hated the man who invented linen collars.

One evening, after we had endured another day of refulgent brilliancy, when the grateful night came we spent it pleasantly enough in the verandah, watching the moon slowly climb out of the black undulations of the firs on what I had made up my mind to call in future " Mount Lepidus." The ladies went to bed at last, and as it was too hot for billiards we men still sat in the darkness talking slowly of casual matters, and finding I do believe, more pleasure in the companionship of each other's low-pitched voices than in any point of the desultory conversation. I think we had been discussing the right and wrong way of curing moleskins before making them up into waistcoats, and the Bishop had observed that he was certain there was a *wrong* way, because he once had a pew-opener whose moleskin vest crackled so loudly when he sang a hymn that no one else could keep their places in the service.

On this a voice, which I think was Smythers of Balliol, asked from the shadows what were the wages of a pew-opener, and whether there were many vacancies for ambitious young men in the profession. Someone else from another chair volunteered the information that he had once had a cousin who opened pews, and later on in life built himself a nice house down in Wales, but whether as the result of that calling or not he could not venture to say. This led us away from moleskins to a retrospective and historical inquiry into the antiquity of pew opening, which in turn merged insensibly into an examination of ancient Church history, and some speculations on the results of the interference of the Byzantian Emperors with what might be termed the native and indigenous government of the early Church considered as a concrete whole, and not as a fundamental part of the social establishment of the age. By the time the conversation had got as far as this everyone but his reverence of Pewchester, who felt the subject congenial, was half asleep.

For one, I was in a happy state of indifference—that happy state of contented drowsiness which comes over the voyager whose canoe glides with swift, sleepy smoothness towards the brink of the unseen falls ahead. I was watching the broad orb of the full moon perched delicately on the topmost twigs of the fir trees, and listening to the cry of the coots disturbed by a water-rat amongst the rushes in the lake, when presently a pause fell upon the talk of the company.

Then Smythers asked:

" I say, Allanby, are they burning rubbish somewhere in your garden at this hour of the night, or has Mullens lit one of those cigars he bought in the village yesterday? " Beyond question, as he spoke we were all aware of a faint pungent odour drifting over our nostrils on the light night air, an aroma not altogether unpleasant at first, coming as it did mixed with the scent of heliotrope and cooled by evening dew, yet somehow very striking and thought holding.

" It can't be Mullens' cigar," quoth the undergraduate, " it is not half so nasty."

" And it has much more body in it. This is good

strong rubbish anyhow, while Mullens' cheroots are neither." So we lapsed into silence again for a minute or two, until the sculptor, who was sitting with his face to the rearward portion of the house, started up.

"Hullo!" he cried, jumping to his feet, and pointing excitedly towards where the servants' quarters stood, "what is that yellow shine on the under sides of the walnut leaves?"

We all looked round, of course, and there to our horror was a sight not easily to be forgotten. Over that part of the rearward buildings, as I think I remember to have said before, there were some tall trees of the kind Mullens had mentioned; they actually overhung the courtyard and adjacent windows of the wing joining the stables to the main house in the complicated geography of our dear old Manor; and now, as we looked, an extraordinary thing was taking place. All the leaves of these trees, that had been a sombre cloud a few minutes before, backed by the blackness of the night only one shade darker than themselves, were now flushing on their under surfaces with a strange hectic tinge! They were becoming defined, turning each frond and leaflet to burnished rosy red even while we watched. Never did any vegetable in Aladdin's gardens look so weirdly magnificent as those trees of ours, and even as we gazed they came out refulgent and tremulous up to their topmost twigs. All down the servants' roof ridge, just visible from the lawn to which we had rushed, a dozen grey spirals a yard or two apart rose twining delicately into the night air, taking rosy hues on their upmost points, as though Aladdin's garden were being increased by the growth of some wondrous strain of magic creepers, more prolific than anything human gardeners ever heard of! We stared and stared until with a sudden clatter all the pigeons burst from the cotes, and flew here and there through the dazzle like glorious butterflies, until they found their senses and fled away into the darkness behind. Then it did not need the one word that rose on every lip to tell us the house was on fire!

Up spake the Roman, first as usual: "Louis, your villa burns, and your poor slaves are bound for Hades before their time! Quick man, into the house and warn the women. I will get ladders, and water if there is any to be had, and rescue some of these sleek serfs of yours; their death would touch me very closely." And away he went, while I ran into the house in haste, to warn my mother and the others. But they already knew only too well—the upper corridors were full of stinging yellow smoke, and every open bedroom door showed fair ladies, newly risen, making such hasty toilets as, God wot! they never made before. I ran to my mother's room, and found that dear lady, with her mouth full of hairpins, doing up her grey hair, while she prayed for all our safety with all the fervour those pins would let her. " Mother," I cried, " down to the hall, and never mind the hair to-night: you will be safe there, and I will send the others to you. Where is Miss Smith?"

" Go and find her, Louis, for heaven's sake—she may still be sleeping!" I did not need twice bidding, but went off like the wind; and there by a door, in a long, hooded overcloak we all knew well since she sometimes wore it in the garden of an evening, stood Miss Smith. She had turned on the electric lights in her passage, and was going from door to door, rousing those within, and, though as pale as the soft linen which peeped from her half-buttoned coverture, was sweet and collected as ever.

" Down to the hall!" I cried, " dear Miss Smith. There you will be safe——"

" Oh, but I am in no danger here as it is. Surely it is the servants who are in danger! Do go to them."

" Very well, then; Lepidus has gone there, and I will go too if you will come down." I thought she winced a little at the Roman name, but she merely said, "Yes, yes, but go to them, Louis; the fire is there, and it is for them I fear." So away I went, for it was no time for parley, and on the main staircase nearly ran into the arms of Mullens, who was coming up hot and breathless.

"Allanby," he shouted, "your Roman friend burst in the doors of the yard to look for ladders, and the ladders were not there—every one has been taken for the rick-making a mile away!"

"And the fire hose won't work," cried Smythers, who had come in at his heels; "the pond has shrunk to nothing, and black mud gurgled out of the nozzle before we had been at the wheel a minute! Lepidus broke in the garden door of the servants' wing, and three times rushed within, and three times came out with all his clothes smoking; it is burning there like a furnace, and the staircase has gone down. Ah! here he comes himself!" And as the speaker stopped, in rushed the Centurion, black and scorched, with the axe with which he had been cleaving down doors still clutched in his hand, and looking pale, I thought, for the once.

"Louis!" he cried, spying me, "surely there is some back way through this ant-heap of a house of yours to the slaves' quarters—by Pluto's self I never meant to get these poor thralls of yours into such a hell. Show me the way, or better still tell me where it lies and run round yourself to the courtyard. There is still water in that husky old pump of yours, if one could but get it up fast enough, and black sludge in that horse-mire you have saved for this occasion. Hold the flames down for all you are worth, cousin, while I cut a way through here to these roasting servitors."

As he finished speaking, Priscilla came down, and, as she knew even more of the house than I did, I hastily handed him over to her; while I myself ran out of the hall and round to where the courtyards were all aglow, and the walnuts now shone in coppery splendour with a rolling canopy of smoke above them, as though they were growing over the mouth of Tophet.

The fire had broken out just where the secondary buildings branched off from the main block, and had the wind continued to blow as it had done all day nothing could have saved the Manor. Fortunately it had turned; before it the flames ran all down the range of store-rooms and much-timbered larders, above which the domestics slept, cutting them off with singular completeness from the courtyard below. There were no ladders available, no water; while the foolish, frantic women could be seen, through the haze of smoke hiding their windows, running to and fro in wild dismay. Down in the yard an ever-growing crowd of men and women from the outside cottages were shouting and working with feverish energy at those pumps that gurgled and choked with the mud which was all they could draw from the ponds. And all my mother's prize chickens were cackling madly; all the pigs in the sties over the wall wailing and grunting, though in no real danger, as if the throes of dissolution were already upon them; and our coachman's grey parrot, lately bought of a wandering sailor, had broken loose, and was sitting on the roof ridge swearing horribly.

It was as wild a scene as one could hope to see; and as I stood staring at the flames, while a score of futile expedients to rescue the unhappy men and women chased each other through my mind, a sudden shout rose from the crowd, and above the crackling of the timbers and bursting of overheated window-panes there came a sound of hammering, fierce tumultuous hammering, until, in a minute or so, a little forgotten trap-door in the roof of the Manor, sometimes used to let workmen up for repair to the roof, splintered, and flew from its hinges, and out through the broken frame-work jumped Lepidus! He sprang down the red tiles as nimbly as a cat, crossed the low coping, the only thing there separating the level roofs, at a bound, and came running along the leads above us as though he had lived all his life upon roofs. When they saw him all the crowd sent up a yell of welcome which, for a time, hushed even the screaming women inside.

He came nearly opposite to where I was standing, a burnished figure in the strong glare against the black sky, and set to work upon the roof with his axe in a way wonderful to behold. He scattered those tiles about him like dead leaves, cut through the tie-pieces, and, taking a longer grip of the axe, lopped lath and plaster underneath till the white dust rose in a volcano; and in an extraordinarily short space of time there was a hole through the roof big enough for one man at a time to crawl from. Inside meanwhile they had been aware of what he was doing—had got a table under the coming hole, so that when the Centurion threw away his weapon and shouted down the chasm half a dozen hands rose instantly in response.

Helped by those inside, he drew them out like chickens from a bag. The groom and the butler; Janet, the pretty light-haired pantrymaid; the dairy girls; the scullery maids; the cook—they came out of that smoky abyss one after another in comic haste. Lepidus would stand no thanks or emotion. He sent them scuttling up the leads, over the tiles, and up to the trapdoor, where Mullens and another gripped and dragged them in without ceremony or decorum. The stout cook failed in the escalade of the tiles, and had to be hauled in on her back, like a sack of flour; the equally portly butler, who would not be helped, three times essayed the same slippery climb, and three times rolled back "like a gigantic white beetle struggling out of a sand pit," as the irreverent Smythers said. It would have been comical to see those poor people come out of one hole and, dodging across the smoking roofs, drop into another, if it had not been so pathetic.

I was still watching them when another shout was raised behind, "The stables! the stables are on fire." And, alas! a burning flake had blown in at an open loft door, had fallen on a great stock of straw and hay, and filled all the upper part of the stables with flame in less time almost than it takes to write it. This, however, mattered comparatively little. There were no lives in danger; while, the fire being overhead, all we had to do was to loosen the doors, lead out the frightened horses, and leave the rest in the hands of Providence and our insurance office.

I therefore turned my back on the rescued domestics, and, running over to where the horses were already neighing loudly as they smelt the danger, had their doors thrown open. By the light of a score of lanterns in the hands of ready helpers, we rushed in to the rescue, and the first thing that met my eye was "Satan" ready saddled and bridled, with a flat cloth strapped behind the saddle pillion fashion, and that accessory to all wickedness the boy Binks at his head. I can only wonder now that I was not more surprised to find the great horse thus ready for travel at such an hour; but in the excitement of the moment, surrounded by shouting grooms and angry steeds, who flung and jerked at their headstalls and struck sparks from the flint paving as they plunged about, and kicked over lanterns and buckets in their wild eagerness to be outside—amidst the shouting and hubbub it was impossible to ask questions. "Out with him, Binks," I cried, "hold on to him like fury: take him round to the front, where he will not see the flames;" and it seemed to me that imp of darkness smiled as he answered:

"That's where I am a-taking him, sir." Then I busied myself with the other poor brutes, thinking no more of it for the time. And now comes the point of the evening.

I had emptied the stables, and, as the Manor itself was practically safe, the fire burning itself out at its own sweet pleasure, I was naturally anxious to know how my mother was taking matters; and, after a few hurried instructions to the most capable men in the crowd, ran out of the yard and crossed the lawn towards the house itself. Stopping a moment on the edge of the shadows to get breath and straighten my tumbled raiment, I could see the garden front of the place before me clear in the tranquil moonlight, the empty windows ashine with the lights within (for the people were watching the blaze from the rearward passages), the hall doors and casements all wide open; and then as I looked, to my amazement, a tall man strode out across the verandah lights, half leading, half dragging a muffled woman with him. For a moment they stood there, clear black figures against the brightness within; and then another shadow came up to them from outside, that of the black horse and the boy who led him. Even more quickly than I can write it, the man sprang into the saddle, and bending low spoke to the girl. For a moment she seemed to hesitate, and then gave him her hand as it seemed in blind obedience, and the next minute was seated behind him. I heard the thud of the horse's hoofs coming towards me, and that exulting rattle of bit and bridle which "Satan" always gave when he shook his great head, and stretched himself down to a gallop: they passed so close by me

I could almost have touched them unseen. The man was Lepidus—no one else in the world rode as he did; and the woman who clung to him so closely, with arms round his neck and head hidden on his broad shoulders, was Priscilla Smith!

Was it she? Yes, for certain it must have been. I had not seen her face; but the long, all-covering cloak was Priscilla's beyond a doubt. I could scarcely believe my senses: the ground seemed rising and falling beneath my feet. I staggered back into the house, where the people were just coming back into the hall, and meeting my mother, "Mother," I cried passionately, "where is Priscilla?"

"Where is Miss Smith?" answered my parent cheerfully, "why here, safe and well; such a good girl she has been, so brave, so helpful, so——"

"I don't believe she is here!" I cried in my anger. "Let me see her."

"Why, certainly, my dear. Priscilla, Priscilla! here is Louis ravenous to see you in the flesh, and to assure himself you are unhurt," called out my mother.

The moment or two of intense suspense that followed seemed like an age to me; and then the guests parted, and up from the rear came Priscilla herself, now in her ordinary every-day dress, and, smiling, gracious, and charming, swept up to me and laid that all-assuring hand on my arm.

CHAPTER XVIII

THE LAST RESORT

NOW I had the great discretion in that moment of surprise not to make any rash inquiries; a mystery there obviously was, a keen and startling mystery, but it was not one to be improved by general discussion. So strange was it that if Lepidus had not actually been absent from the company, if the skirts of that woman, whoever she was—so like to Pris, and yet as certainly not Pris—if her skirts had not actually brushed me in the dark, I should have been tempted to think the excitement of the evening had turned my head for the moment. But I held my peace, and then about half an hour afterwards, my mother mustered the whole household, servants included, and had a roll-call of us. Every one was present except the Centurion—and Janet the pantrymaid!

"Good gracious!" exclaimed my parent, "I hope nothing has happened to poor Janet; she was always a wayward girl, and a night like this would have quite upset her."

THE LAST RESORT

"No," said Miss Smith, "Janet is all right. She was one of the first Mr. Lepidus drew up through the hole he had made in the servants' roof; and, as the poor girl was in a thin nightdress, and quite dazed, I brought her down here and wrapped her in my long cloak, and myself pulled the hood over her head, that she might dry her tears at leisure. Janet, I am sure, is somewhere safe by this time."

"Yes," said a deep voice in the doorway behind us, "I am glad to be able to relieve your anxieties to that extent: I myself have just seen her into the safe keeping for the night of the woman at your gate lodge." And, turning, there was Marcus Lepidus himself, looking very strange in face, and splashed with mud from top to toe.

Then all on a sudden the truth flashed upon me, and, weak and undecided as I had grown, my hands clenched angrily at my side, and a bitter anger rose uncontrollably in my heart. I saw it all. That reckless being, half man, half spirit, I was harbouring had planned it all—had set the house on fire himself (so I thought in the first rush of my wrath) in order that in the confusion he might have a chance of carrying Priscilla off; and how nearly he had succeeded was patent. It was but a guess then, born of my jealousy; but it was right nevertheless. Long afterwards Janet told Priscilla, and she me in turn, how in the smoke and confusion of the hall the Roman had suddenly strode up to her as she sat shrouded in Priscilla's cloak, and, saying the dazed girl hardly knew what, had at last half persuaded, half commanded her to mount with him the horse waiting outside. He had galloped away with her into the country, how far she knew not, and it was only when he had to stop to tighten her pillion-strap that he took her in his arms and lavishing fierce endearment on her, had thrown back the hood that screened, as he thought, " Prisca Quintilia," and had found instead plain Janet Page! First he raged, and then he laughed, said the girl afterwards; and well I could imagine it. Then, after a time, gentle even in his lawlessness, he had dried the poor, misguided, bare-footed serving maid's tears, had mounted again, and finally left her safe and unharmed at our lodge gates.

This I did not know at the time; and all the next day, spent mostly with my mother, planning new buildings amongst the blackened ruins of the servant's wing, my animosity and anger grew against him. Late in the evening we met by chance, alone, in the hall, and there I accused him of what he had done, and the worse he had hoped to do against me and mine. Lepidus, who had been all day as surly as one of those boars he used to hunt in the British woodlands long ago, and had drunk deep at dinner of our oldest bins—was not the man to stand that in any mood. Briefly, he dared me to come outside and settle the matter as, he said, these things were settled before the world grew so polite. I doubt if we had ever come to the ridiculous pass of a duel had the claret at dinner that night been newer, or our feelings less strained by recent events. For my part I have the highest appreciation of personal honour, but the greatest contempt for the vindication of it by deadly combat. The mere fact that the just man is as likely to get pinked by the villain's rapier or perforated by his bullet as the wrong effectually damns it in my mind. In the old days our Viking ancestors argued out all such disputes before the *Thing,* the assembly whose decision represented that public opinion which, until the gods interfere more directly in our affairs, is the best tribunal, provided it is truly ascertained, we can hope for. This was the duel legitimate. When it passed into personal combat it was beneath contempt, since nothing was so certain then as that the fight would go, without consideration of the question at issue, to the man whose muscles were the more tough; whose heart was more callous to the import of the moment, and whose stomach was better in order.

I had always felt this, and envied Lepidus the joyous whole-heartedness with which, when we had decided to "have it out," he turned to look for weapons. Everything that terrible man did gave him the fierce pleasure of an absorbing interest. I, on the other hand, was cursed with an infernal habit of thinking—a miserable, cankering capacity for seeing things in their true aspect, which sapped the foundations of happiness and watered down the very wine of life itself.

"Come on, sir," said the Roman in a low voice, leading me eagerly into the hall, where the lights were burning dimly, most of the guests having gone to bed. "What is it to be? What weapons have you? For, by the mortals, from the nails of your heroine Deliah to the flails out in the barn yonder, all are the same to me."

"There are some rapiers there on the trophy— an equal pair," I answered sullenly, indicating the place whence on that first evening of his coming—oh, so long ago—he had taken down a boar spear and half killed our butler. Little did we think then when we should next need weapons from those hooks! We went across the floor, and the Roman took down one of the two Spanish blades. They were long, fine, keen-pointed, basket-hilted, gold-embossed—the very things to have prided the heart of a truculent Castilian peer two hundred years ago; and my guest twirled his blade round to get the feel of it, and glanced up and down the figured steel for a minute or two, half in admiration, half in scorn of a thing so slender. Then he struck a swordsman's attitude before a high leather-backed chair, whirled the blade again, and with a sudden lunge drove it through the armorial chair-back up to the hilt. He drew it out, and putting his finger into the puncture: " Jove! " he cried, " What a little hole for a man's soul to creep out of! And yet I suppose they knew their business who made these pretty toys—well to your liking I dare say, cousin, but not quite the articles we from the Tiber have hacked a bloody way to empire with. Nevertheless they will suffice to-night. Pick up your toasting-iron, friend Louis, and come on; there's a lovely moon shining, and all as still as all will be for one of us to-morrow."

Outside, flushed and excited, he led the way over the smaller lawn toward the rhododendron shrubbery, humming as he went a Tuscan verse under his breath, and making a lunge now and then at a rose leaf or tall poppy-head in the flower beds we passed. And I followed behind him, chin on chest, now, as always, dominated by his strong will—feeling myself a coward, and knowing myself a fool;

noting the petty incidents of the evening as a silly sheep on the way to the shambles stops a moment to nibble the grass by the roadside; noting the splendid purple of the sky low down upon the horizon, and how it paled to tenderest silver-grey where the great moon, playing with a silver web of clouds, rode in silent state overhead; noting the happy murmur of the river singing itself to sleep in the dark glen, and the sharp voices of the bats picking their way through the golden star fields in the east; hearing the kine lowing on the crofts a mile away; and the crickets calling to each other in the dewy field; seeing the silver night-beads twinkle on the grass, and the white tears glittering in the blue eyes of the gentians—hearing and seeing these things as though they mattered a scrap to me, and so absorbed that I started guiltily when the wicket gate swung to behind us.

And now in the open meadow the waif of royal Rome suddenly turned, and said, " How, sir, does this place please you ? A fair sward; no 'vantage for either in wind or weather, save the moonlight, and that we will share between. Will it do? "

" Oh, yes," was my answer, " as well as any other."

" Come on, then," said the Roman, sticking his rapier point into the dewy turf while he turned up his cuffs, and then trying his blade again—bending it between his hands until the supple steel described an arc. " Faugh, what a withy wand to put into a man's hand! How my old comrades of the XXth Legion would have laughed to see me handle such an over-grown bee-sting, such a pigeon spit! And yet perhaps it is suitable for the work in hand; come on, sir! " And, whirling round the blade, *he struck me with the flat of it* across the cheek.

Honestly I doubt if he meant to; the light betrayed, the length deceived him. But that blow stung my sleeping manhood. The words had been rude before it; but the blow, keen and cold across my face, ran into my veins, and with a start and shudder I drew myself together, and tossed the point of my own rapier up to my adversary's breast—a man again in a moment. And Lepidus, seeing me stiffen, came gleefully on—as, to do him justice, he never failed to when danger lay ahead. He engaged me in a second, and quicker than it takes to write, we were at it gaily.

Now, I for my part was a very fair fencer, and in the old college days had covered the leather fencing jerkin of more than one excellent swordsman with chalky " points " ; all that old knowledge coming back to me in an instant was my salvation. Also I had this advantage, that the Centurion fought with a weapon strange to him, both by theory and practice, a thing as unlike the heavy, chopping Roman sword he had always used in the past as could be. So much for my advantage. His was greater strength and activity, a reckless courage, and a fiery zeal which nerved his arm and filled his brain and gave him, as doubtless it had often done before, the dreadful force of a dozen colder men. In brief, there was little to choose between us; and, my blood once up, we went at it for two or three minutes with ever increasing eagerness. Then the Roman drew first blood, making a furious lunge at me, which I half guarded; his rapier point flashed off my hilt, and going through the top of my shoulder lifted a little strip of flesh, which gave way as he recovered, and bled out of all proportion to the wound.

Henceforward I noticed with the strange indifferent interest one often attaches to such things in emergency, that only the lower half of his sword shone when he whirled it in the moonlight, the rest was red. Two minutes afterward I parried another thrust, and in the recovery cut the Tuscan across the wrist—not badly, but enough to glove his fighting hand with crimson, and set those strong white teeth of his, and bring the real fighting look into the handsome face that shone upon me in all the fascination of its contending passions as now and then

I got the moonlight on it. There was no one to cry a welcome halt, no one to separate us, and the Roman, fired by the smart of that cut, pressed me with redoubled fury, raining cuts and lunges that rattled on my guards like winter hail, environing me with a glimmer of steel, scorning my science, and beating me ever backwards by the sheer fury of his onset. Quicker and quicker came my breathing, and more and more giddily the stars swung round and round us—it was reduced to a sheer matter of endurance; and how could I hope to contend with those iron muscles, and the furious courage that had won in a hundred fights against far longer odds?

Round and round we went, stamping the meadow grass down in a blackened circle, cutting, parrying, and lunging, with a heart-wholeness that took light reckoning of any science. The moon went in and out between the clouds, and the bats circled squeaking round our heads; sooner or later some luckless plunge, some sudden 'vantage to one or the other, must have turned that grim folly into black tragedy; but just when the crisis was at hand, and I at least could not have kept the game going for many minutes more, a tall, white figure stepped swiftly between us in the full shine of the moon, and, making no more of our weapons than if they had been willow wands, held up two white hands, and exclaimed in a voice that stayed our ardour in an instant, " Stop, stop, I command you! "

It was Miss Smith; and, what between fatigue and loss of blood from my hurt, I could scarcely make up my mind for a moment, as I fell panting back, whether she was there in flesh or spirit.

Seldom has a mortal lady, lately come from iced coffee and music in a modern drawing-room, looked more bewitching. Priscilla had gone to her room some little time before we left the house, and, partly disrobing, had opened her window for a space to look out on the night. Now it happened that her casement faced the very lawn and thicket beyond which we were acting like silly boys in defence of our manhood, and thus it happened that the lady, turning her pretty eyes upon the splendid peacefulness of the evening, was presently aware of a most inharmonious sound. Surely she must have thought, no workmen could be hammering away like that so late afield, no mowers were whetting their scythes at such an untimely hour? that steely rattle never came from the river, no bird or beast ever made such a sound! Then, as she listened, all on a sudden the meaning of it flashed upon her quick woman's mind; and, snatching a shawl from a chair-back, she rushed from her room and down the stairs.

There she was before us, slippered, short kirtled,

bare shouldered, her wrists still braceleted, the great string of pearls she had worn at dinner rising and falling tumultuously on that white bosom the thin wrap covered so scantily; her half-loosed hair breaking from its ribbons, the moonlight bringing her up like a silver statue against the black backing of the shadows beyond, splendidly regardless of convention in her frightened beauty. Well might we gaze on her, and wonder to which world she belonged!

It was she that spoke first: "Oh, how horrible and wicked of you both; oh, how silly and stupid to maim and cut each other like rioters outside a tavern! Give me your sword, Mr. Lepidus, and yours, Mr. Allanby."

Very sulkily and foolishly we obeyed, my rival saying as he handed his over:

"The cause, lady, must be our excuse for the folly."

"And if I was the cause, let me be the remedy, too," said the charming lady, turning her eyes first to one and then the other. "Oh, promise me you will never try this silly thing again! Think how sorry either of you would have been had the other been hurt, and think how to-morrow I should have hated him that gave the hurt——"

"That were a consideration like to damp the keenest anger."

bare shouldered, her wrists still braceleted, the great string of pearls she had worn at dinner rising and falling tumultuously on that white bosom the thin wrap covered so scantily; her half-loosed hair breaking from its ribbons, the moonlight bringing her up like a silver statue against the black backing of the shadows beyond, splendidly regardless of convention in her frightened beauty. Well might we gaze on her, and wonder to which world she belonged!

It was she that spoke first: "Oh, how horrible and wicked of you both; oh, how silly and stupid to maim and cut each other like rioters outside a tavern! Give me your sword, Mr. Lepidus, and yours, Mr. Allanby."

Very sulkily and foolishly we obeyed, my rival saying as he handed his over:

"The cause, lady, must be our excuse for the folly."

"And if I was the cause, let me be the remedy, too," said the charming lady, turning her eyes first to one and then the other. "Oh, promise me you will never try this silly thing again! Think how sorry either of you would have been had the other been hurt, and think how to-morrow I should have hated him that gave the hurt——"

"That were a consideration like to damp the keenest anger."

"Why, then, promise me that this ends here," she said, looking at me, while at the same time she laid a finger of entreaty on the Roman's hand, so that we shared between us glance and gesture. What could we do but assent, with that sweet apparition standing peacemaker between us? Now that the hot blood was running cool again the naked stupidity of the affair became tenfold obvious to my mind, and an unromantic thankfulness possessed me that nothing worse had happened. For suppose something *had* happened, and I, a creditable country squire and justice of the peace, had been left standing in the moonlight over the slaughtered body of my guest! Suppose—but, there! the matter would not bear suppositions, and I gave my word to Miss Smith with a heartiness that, perhaps, spoke more eloquently of my discretion than of my valour. Lepidus accepted the situation too, with brief good humour; and so Priscilla led us presently back in triumph towards the house.

Where the shrubbery path ended upon the lawn she stopped, and turning said again, "Remember, you have promised no more of to-night's foolishness, and not a word to anyone. Think, dear Mr. Lepidus, how they would laugh if it were talked of!"

The Centurion promised in the name of both of us there should be no more swordsmanship; and we passed indoors, and at the stair-foot said good-night to our sweet peacemaker, apparently reconciled.

But no sooner had the hem of her skirt disappeared in the upper passages than the Roman, with set face, turned to me and said: "It is a pity to let this thing cool down, cousin Allanby, when we have wrought ourselves to a white-heat to settle it. The smiths say good metal like yours and mine, white-heated, too often never pays for forging in the end. Believe me, there is no way with the difficulty we are in but a sudden way. Next week, if we let ourselves cool down, the matter will still be just as pressing, the way out just as difficult. Therefore, good cousin, while we still be molten, let us put it through—if not by sword, why then by something subtler. My uncle Marius——"

"Curse thy uncle Marius!"

"Oh, with all my heart. He was a tough rogue that uncle Marius, and was so well cursed alive he is not like to mind a little dead. I was only going to say he knew, and taught me, many cunning ways, whereby an imprisoned soul, restless for one reason or another, could very easily and comfortably shake off this heavy encumbrance called a body, and wing its way elsewhere. Now, cousin, I would suggest that you should let me mix a potion—not much, or nasty to the taste—but just such as he would have prescribed for this malady we suffer from, limpid, brief, and certain; and that with this divine elixir ready mixed we both go boldly in to the lady of our troubles, tell her like soldiers how it stands between us, that we both covet her, and that the round world is no longer big enough for both. Let her choose between us, and let him whom the lady will not have, have the cup instead."

"Are you serious, Lepidus?"

"Yes, quite."

"Then let it be as you say," I answered. "There is no way else I know of, and this at least is quick and painless. To-morrow, then, we settle it—here's my hand, old fellow. I never meant it to come to this, but I see no other way."

"Right well and manly spoken, cousin," said the great Roman, "here's my hand in turn: Jove! that uncle Marius were here! 'Tis just the issue to our trouble that would have delighted him above all else."

CHAPTER XIX

"SPOILS TO THE VICTOR; DEATH TO THE VAN-
QUISHED"

SO it had come to this, and I cannot say I was greatly grieved! I had been so wrought on lately, it seemed so impossible that either I or Lepidus could win final favour with that sweet arbiter of our fates, and the other survive, that after the first shock the Roman's barbarian scheme appeared the only reasonable way out of the difficulty. I have seen two schoolboys, with all the world young and golden at their feet, plan just such a deadly cast for a trivial cause; and there are, I am certain, frames of mind in which death is robbed of all its meaning, and becomes a cheerful alternative only. So it was with me when the Centurion had expounded his plan for "taking Fate into our councils," as he airily called it. I went up to my room late that evening, locked myself in, and throwing back the top of my great roll-desk set myself to make things as straight as might be for my executors, should chance call their services into being.

Yet how much there was to do at such a moment! I sat amazed at the complexities of life as I stood face to face with the chance of losing it. Again and again I started up, from no spirit of cowardice, but from sheer awe of the array of the virtuous things I had left undone, and the bad ones I had vowed to amend; and as often as I got to my door on the way to tell Lepidus I could not go yet, the thing must be postponed, so often I shrank from the thought of what he might think of me, and came back to my seat. And there I sat all night, destroying, sorting, and apologising, making such amends as one can in an hour or two for a lifetime of neglected opportunities—till my room was a white sea of torn papers, and the lights grew dim to my tired eyes as the dawn came trickling in behind the curtains. Then I got up, and taking my candle, went down the passage to my room. I had to pass the Centurion's on the way, and noticed he had put his boots out to be cleaned, while from within, as I stopped a moment to listen, there came the regular and undisturbed sound of his child-like sleeping. Happy fellow, ideal mortal, who could sit so light to the to-come, who had no executors and no unpaid obligations, no great expectancies ahead and no sorrows behind, to whom all life centred in the ardour of the moment—no wonder he could sleep like that!

As for me, do what I might, I could not rest; for an hour or two I tossed on my bed watching the day slowly wake, and it was only when the first sunlight was overlaying the morning with gold that I dropped off into uneasy slumbers, and dreamt that Lepidus and I were mixing sherbet for all my social creditors in the village schoolroom, the which refreshing draught my mother and Pris were taking round the circle, and administering to each expectant individual in turn by means of our best silver soup ladle, and from a bucket marked with ominous distinctness—" Poison."

At breakfast time I was red-eyed and sullen, and to me it seemed that all looks were turned my way with reproach and suspicion; even the Roman was less elated than usual, while the Bishop's muffled tones at the far end of the table sounded in my ears like a funeral oration.

At last it was over, and then Lepidus brightened up. He came to me as soon as the guests had drifted away, and, catching my arm with something of the old friendship, whispered in my ear, " The little anteroom by the conservatory—be there in half an hour! I have told Miss Smith there is something of interest on hand for her, and she has promised to come into the drawing-room a little later; so, dear cousin Louis, we will put this thing through very conveniently. By the way," he added cheerily, after a moment's hesitation, and giving as he spoke a glance at a little phial containing some greenish crystals in his breast pocket, " can you lend me a pestle and mortar for a few minutes? Not that one you use for mashing the young jackdaws' food—so unhealthy afterwards for the jackdaws—but any other would do." When I told him I had not one, " Oh, never mind," he laughed, " Binks will lend me a hammer—very insoluble stuff, you know—but once mixed certain as Jove's own thunderbolt." And, nodding to me as though he went but to brew a dose for a distempered ferret, the Centurion strode away with that easy, confident stride of his to look for Binks, and the hammer.

Lepidus broke up that wicked stuff, whatever it was, in the gun-room—I could hear him pounding away all that miserable half-hour; and when it was over I met him in the ante-room, as he had suggested. He brought " the mixture " with him, and had an air of obvious triumph on his handsome countenance.

"Look!" he said, showing me the pale green powder, " the surest medicine in the world for cases like ours. I remember seeing my mother mix some once for a slave of hers, and I was so fascinated I hid in a cupboard and saw the man unwittingly drink it—saw him start and reel as the fire ran into his veins; half turn about and go headlong down, and lie there squirming and clawing at the cloths, while the death-yellow came into his face, and his chattering teeth set hard in a smother of blood and foam——"

"Ay," I answered, forgetting everything just then but the long forgotten as I rested my hand upon the shoulder of my Roman self, and leant with him over the green dust that was in a few moments to set one of our twin souls travelling into space.

"I remember! 'twas because he had stolen nectar from my mother's store—he had a thirsty throat, and was always trying to embellish the slave's black bread and water. Do you recollect how another time he mixed and drank the lees from all the tankards on a feast table, and was fuddled for two days afterwards?"

"The mother fuddled him that last time," said the Centurion, with a laugh, "mixed him a draught that cured him of thirst for ever, and sent his soul to serve in hell! And now to business. May I ring for a tumbler?"

When the maid came, Lepidus, unabashed to the

end, smiled splendidly on her, and ordered a glass and some wine, spending the interval until they came striding up and down the room, the while he talked of strange long-dead scenes and people, every sentence calling a flitting picture to my mind. And so swift and life-like those things were that it seemed the whole of that ancient page of ours flashed out in those few minutes in a whirl before me, full, vivid, and crowded; but so intangible that as fast as one scene came upon the heels of another I forgot its foregoer.

Then while the gay pantomime was still unwinding before my half-shut eyes, there came a tap upon the door, and in came the maid with a neatly napkined tray, and on it a cut-glass beaker, wine, and cake upon a silver dish. The Roman laughed lightly at that refreshment. "Thanks, damsel," he said; "for the drink; Mr. Louis here and I have got a thirst between us not to be lightly quenched; but we are not hungry, I do not know when we shall be hungry again—eh, cousin?" I shook my head, marvelling how he could speak so gaily; and just as the door was closing on the maid he called her back. "Here, you pretty sprig of virginity: go to Miss Priscilla Smith, give her Mr. Allanby's compliments, and say he wants to bask in the sunshine of her eyes for a few minutes; or, more simply, say Mr. Allanby would be grateful to her for all the rest of the life that may be left to him if she would come into the drawing-room. You understand?"

"Yes, sir," answered the girl, who, poor thing, had a very tender spot for the Centurion deep down in her simple heart; and as she closed the door the Roman drew the tray over to him, poured the powder into the glass, covered it with wine, shook it up, and then, taking a coin from his pocket, turned to me. "Quick," he said, "there is no time to be lost. We go in to her *together,* mind; and he who wins this toss I will now make puts his case first to her, with all heaven in front and hell behind him! She shall hear us *both;* then choose. And he who loses comes here and *drinks*—you understand?"

"Yes," I answered, feeling as though I were living on the dregs of life, as I always did when the Roman was excited; a horrible cowardice in my blood, and my stupid mind so clouded I could find nothing better to think of than what my mother would say when she found out there was a hole in the damask napkin with which I was playing.

"Cry, then," said the Roman in a voice which rang with the pride of those lordly ancestors of his, and tossing the coin into the air. "Cry, you dweller on the moss-hags; heads or ships, which is it, you barbarian?"

And mechanically I called out "Heads!" as the coin fell; and heads it was! Then Lepidus, throwing the gold upon the tray for the maid, gave me his hand (which never again did I touch in life); and so we stood for a space, hand-fast, eye to eye, while a ray of sunshine came in at the window and played tenderly about the potion on the table, the elixir of life for one of us, and of death for the other, filling it full of quaint, eddying forms and lovely opal tints. And then the drawing-room door beyond the curtained archway opened softly, closed again; and we heard a woman's easy footfall go over to the window.

If I were to try for twenty years I could not tell you exactly what took place in the next twenty minutes. Never in my life had I come to an emergency less fit. My very soul quaked within me, not with actual fear, but with an overpowering sense of all I felt I had lost—for the battle seemed certain defeat even before it had commenced. I was not myself, the Roman had been draining my vitality from me all these days and weeks; and now at the very crisis of my life I was sick with an absolute bodily sickness, as well as unnerved in spirit.

How I even began that momentous interview is a mystery to me; but begun it had to be, and with a desperate effort I went up to the girl we had come to woo so strangely, and while Lepidus stood in the background, arms folded and head bent, all his molten passions sealed up for the time in the silence of a statue, I went over to Miss Smith, and with a horrible sense of insufficiency blurted out my errand. I know she started, glancing uneasily at my pallid face and the other man in the shadows—wondering the while, no doubt, why I had brought such a listener with me; but it was no time for delicacy, and, feeling a little better when the first words were spoken, I plunged desperately forward, reminding her of her troth and my love, of the fidelity she had sworn before the other came upon us, of the rivalry between us, palpable to her as to everyone, and of the impossibility of either living his life to its end without her. I conjured up the old affection and my steadfastness, imploring her again for the love she had once given so freely, saying I was unworthy—I felt it, I knew it in every fibre—but that that very consciousness spoke of my affection. It was a poor speech for the occasion, it sounded hollow and commonplace even to me—a hireling advocate in a hurry for his lunch would have done better for an uninteresting scoundrel at the judgment seat. Its insufficiency was the last bitter drop in the cup of my humiliation; but I could do no more; and when it was over with hands across my face I stepped back into the shadow.

Then Lepidus sprang forward. In the stress of my own emotions I had all but forgotten him, and it was not till I had said my very last word, and was standing like a culprit waiting doom, that the Roman took his turn. Without waiting for even a sign from the pale girl—breathlessly marvelling at the ordeal we were putting her to—he sprang to the onset with the same vigour that had doubtless carried him victorious up the bloody glacis of many an old-world fort, and almost before I knew he was moving he was before Priscilla, he had got her hand, saluting it with soldier gallantry upon one knee; and then the next minute, up on foot again, was pressing the fair enemy back as it were from her defences by the sheer weight of his determination and eloquence.

Lord, what a soldier he must have been! What a fellow to meet in a sally-port! How the British bucklers must have cracked, and palisades and spear-shafts splintered where he led an onset! How could any mortal girl stand up against such wooing, now tender and deep, now splendidly imperious—claiming her love as a right, now offering the wealth of his affection in the present, and then throwing over her hesitation, by covert reminders, the glamour of the past, of that ancient love that was rooted in the innermost recesses of her soul. I myself was dazed by the irresistible torrent of his pleading, the magnetism of his love. Had it been for me to decide, I do believe I should have decided then and there for him. As it was, I say again, I stood agape, marvelling, spell-bound, like one who watches a great actor come upon the scene on the heels of some limping mummer, and feels himself swept away without power of resistance.

Minute after minute the Roman went on, while the colour came and went on the fair face he watched so keenly; and then, with a last appeal that would surely have melted the heart of a marble nymph, his voice softened, he let the hand he had been holding drop, and bending his head in fine humility folded his arms and stood in turn waiting his doom.

And the lady? she, when the stream of that fiery eloquence stopped, turned away from us for a space; and I can guess, though I have never dared to ask, what the struggle was of those few silent moments. They were an age to me, but an age of numb indifference; the Roman had all my life in him, as certainly as though he had all my blood in his veins. I was but the bystander, the one waiting to be outcast, a cypher of indifference even to myself; until as I watched, hoping nothing, and not fearing much, Priscilla roused herself, *and went over and took the Centurion's hand!*

" Oh, Mr. Lepidus," she began, looking perfectly lovely in her anxiety, " I am so sorry for this that is between you two. I never meant it, and should be sorry till I died if I thought I had in any way led to it. For the love you say you have had for me I am grateful, grateful as any girl must be for such a splendid gift. And I will not deny that there has been something in you, which as yet I do not understand, that has stirred a strange response within me. But, oh, Mr. Lepidus, I have struggled against it, fearing, I knew not why. That struggle was my duty, duty as sacred to me as my love itself; and you, if you feel towards me as you say, will be glad that duty has won. I am grateful to you, more grateful than I can tell; but I have given my troth to Mr. Allanby here, and I cannot, I will not, I do not wish to withdraw it."

* * * *

" You are certain of this, lady," said Marcus Lepidus quietly, after a pause.

" Quite certain of it, and may God forgive me if by any carelessness I have laid you open to pain."

Then the strong man, as gravely and gently as

though she were but a sister who had come to some wise decision, took both her hands in his, kissing them and her forehead; then, turning, led her to me. He put her hands in mine, and, laying his hands on our shoulders, said, " May the felicities of the Infinite, and the friendships of Those who Endure be with you always, my dear comrades of a day!" and, without more ado, turned and left us.

For me, I was so overwhelmed that I think it was Pris who led me, rather than I her, to a sofa. I scarcely realised I had won; I was in a state of torpor, and not even the delightful nearness of that beautiful girl, who had just given me such an unexpected proof of her affection, was sufficient to rouse me. I sat numb like that until on the vacancy of my mind there fell a little tinkle of glass upon metal, a thin musical sound, like the falling of rain-drops upon the surface of a well. At the moment I thought nothing of the sound but I remembered it afterwards!

Almost at the same instant a shiver passed through me, and an indescribable sense of returning strength came upon me; my head cleared, my heart beat anew, life reasserted its interest, and all of a sudden the glory of my victory, the immeasurable extent of my happiness rushed into actuality. With a deep sense of relief, coming from some source I knew not of, I turned to the charming girl at my side, and gave her thanks for what was indeed beyond thanks. And she was as blushful and sweet as you could wish; she nestled in to me almost for the first time, like a country girl whose lips have just given away to her lover the open secret of her eyes. Now, as I look back, I perceive that at that moment the page was turned, a clean new chapter of our lives begun under the mysterious design of Providence; *then* I did but know we were wholly absorbed in each other, there was no need for words—how should there be, for each knew all the other could say more than well.

We had sat like that, hand-fast, in supreme happiness, for some little time, when Priscilla, breaking the silence, looked away to the window with something like tears in her eyes, and murmured almost to herself, "Poor, poor Mr. Lepidus! I wonder how he will take it!"

Poor Lepidus indeed! The generosity of him who has won the game filled my heart at the mention of his name. How, indeed, would he take it? How? And, then with a cry and a start, I recalled *for the first time* our compact! It was impossible he would carry it out, I cried to myself; it was surely but a grim jest of his. To me, the winner, it seemed life might well be full of happiness yet for him, the loser! Where was he? Surely he would never put that cruel jest of his into execution, and presently again I should hear the cheery voice of the gallant Roman bantering me on my success.

I sprang to my feet, now forgetting Priscilla in turn, and flew to the curtained portal. I tore the hanging aside, and glanced within. Everything was exactly as we had left it—the chairs, the table, the tray, the trivial cake and biscuits, the wine-decanter; but Lepidus was not there! I rushed to the tray, and snatched up the glass that had held the deadly decoction. It was empty—*drained to the last dregs!*

Then, as I replaced it slowly with trembling hand, the meaning of that tinkling sound I had heard dawned upon me. The Centurion had come straight in here, and, faithful to his word, as he always was, had carried out our agreement with proud simplicity. It was his setting down of the glass on the tray I had heard; and as the death draught loosened the brave life in him I had felt it at the same instant fly back to my own veins!

Where was he? Where had he gone? I flew out into the passages, and from room to room with fierce eagerness, but nowhere was he to be seen. It was only afterwards, on the evening of that memorable day, when the actual truth was like lead upon my heart, that I gathered from one servitor, and another, a partial knowledge of the way he had taken when he left that fatal room. Janet had watched him cross the hall, and he had smiled graciously as ever to her. A footman had seen him stumble and clutch at the pillars as he went out into the grounds by the side-door through which he had first entered the Manor. A gardener, sweeping dead leaves, had noticed him tear a hasty rose or two from a bush, and throw them in at Priscilla's open window above the portico, then round to the stables he had passed for a minute, his agony increasing at every step.

"Binks, Binks!" the Roman had shouted; but there was no answer, until a stableman came forward and, touching his cap, said with a smile, for everyone loved Lepidus:

"Binks is away, sir,—gone down to the village on an errand of the missus."

"Oh, very well," gasped the Centurion, steadying himself by the gate-post, "'tis not much, but I owe him fourpence ha'penny for gunpowder to put in the housekeeper's candlesticks. See, here is a shilling. Let him give me the change when we meet again. And tell him—tell him that Marcus Lepidus, neither here nor hereafter, forgets debts, great or small." And with a friendly nod to the man, the great Roman reeled away.

"He went away," said the fellow to his friends in the hall that night, " swaying to and fro just like one of them tall poplars in the wind. Every moment I thought he'd be down, but I hadn't the power of a bean-stalk in my whole body to go after and help him. I saw something was amiss, but I was just glued in that gateway, for I had seen his face before he turned, and there was something there that went straight through me and out the other side, and left me, not scared, but clean bereft of my senses. Lord, how handsome he did look! He'd got a face when 'twas all right with him that would set all other men cursing their images in the glass, but with the pain on him—there! It's no good asking me about it, I darst no more have put him a question or followed him than I darst have followed the devil himself."

These things I learned in the evening. I myself had searched the house out, and the gardens, in the first moments of our loss; and then, guided by instinct, had gone off as fast as feet could carry me to the pine-covered knoll where first I had found him. There, surely, if anywhere he would go when the game he had played so manfully was lost, and there, after him, I hurried. Up the well-remembered path I went, breathlessly, peering on every side for a trace of the Roman, thinking he spoke in every sigh of the branches overhead, and so won the top at last. All was silent and deserted; the squirrels were still playing round the bole of a neighbouring tree, as they had done on that great afternoon long ago; a blue pigeon was hunting amongst the pine-needles on the russet carpet of the ground. And in my fear I called aloud, "Lepidus! Lepidus! friend, comrade, my better self, where are you?"

Surely he would hear; he was never deaf yet to the voice of friend or foe; and as I listened, out of the thick arcades of the low, black branches there came a responding whisper, "Where are you?"

"Lepidus," I cried, "poor, poor Lepidus!" And again the echo answered softly, "Poor, poor Lepidus!" Then, knowing the hill was but sharing in my sorrow, over to the crypt I hurried, and saw without surprise that the covering slab had been newly lifted and thrown back!

After a few moments' hesitation, I ran to the dark little entrance, and, calling "Lepidus!" again, without waiting for the answer, sprang down into the cell. Groping eagerly forward, until my eyes became accustomed to the gloom, I found the stony bier, and there—there upon it, laid out straight and calm, his feet crossed like an old crusader, and his strong hands nerveless by his sides, was he whom I sought!

All the rivalry and jealousy of those days was

forgotten in that moment of pity, and only the love and wonder, born of our strange friendship, remained. I threw myself upon him, as I had done when my breath called him to life, caressing and calling to him, lavishing on him almost a woman's tenderness. And to my eyes presently the crypt grew strangely light, though I did not marvel at it at the moment, with just such a brightness as he used to tell me came when spirits were about, and by that light I saw that he was dead—dead beyond recall; and even as I held him there upon my shoulder, in that strange, soft radiance, the last semblance of life went out of that comely face, as the shine goes out of the western sky at nightfall. For many minutes I held him tight to my breast, till the last spark had gone, and it was but a cold, empty husk I held, then gently replacing him on the bier of his own choosing, I placed my own head in turn on his shoulder, and wept without shame or stint.

* * * *

It was nearly two years afterwards that we, my dear wife and I, came back to the Manor House from long travel abroad. And with us there came—to delight the heart of my excellent mother, and throw the household into helpless confusion—the newest of new babes.

Those two women, obedient to their unalterable destiny, were wholly absorbed in that pink fragment of humanity, that swaddled nonentity with the mild blue eyes and uneasy digestion! But *I* was not a bringer forth of guessers at the great riddle; I, alas for myself, was one of those who guess and guess, spoiling all this life by speculation on another, and Lepidus haunted me in those familiar rooms and corridors. I had grown very tender to him of late —how could it be otherwise? I had been the winner in that brief contest that had brought us face to face for a time. It was I who, against all likelihood, had won from him that prize for which he had waited a thousand years, and had come back to this life again. It was by *my* side she slept at night, and it was my little one over whom she bent, while the warm April tears of her delighted motherhood fell like gracious rain upon its face.

How could I bear him malice? I had thought of him times without number during those wanderings. I had thought of him in Picardy, as I watched the dusty oxen hauling their ploughs through soil that tradition said was still ruddy with Gaulish and Roman blood. I had turned my back sternly on the modern, and pictured him into life again amongst the ruins of the Forum, there in his own Imperial city. I had lain out amongst the tangled vines on

Sicilian hillsides, and pretended to myself that that white-sailed oil felucca slipping over the blue plain below was *his* galley. I had thought of him in the footsteps of Antony, and by the broken stony dais of his great kinsman, and far away into places where even the Imperial eagle never penetrated.

But, somehow, he never came to me so strongly as here, where I had known and loved him and his great heart, cramped and confined as it was by petty modern surroundings. Every room was full of him, every passage-way resounded to my inner ears with the sound of his swift, confident steps. His cheery, bright voice, with more expression in the bare sound of it than in the full speech of most of us, was on the stairs; I could hear him laughing in the hall, as unfeignedly as a thrush sings when spring sunshine unwinds the grey winter vapours from the spruce stems. He was in the courtyard, graciously happy amongst the servitors; and in the drawing-room amongst our guests, dispensing his Imperial condescension without a touch of arrogance. He was in the gun-room, pointing out to astonished listeners why balista slings were better than Joe Mantons for general sport; and in the billiard-room, behind the blue smoke wreaths, telling me with vague half-hesitation of shadowy marvels, whereof even to this minute I know not the truth or value.

Wandering round and round, with his name on my lips, I grew so haunted, that it was almost as though the Centurion were calling me to come to him there on his mound; and directly after breakfast, on the second day following our arrival, I started for the pine wood. There was another and a plainer reason drawing me there, for I was eager to see how our sculptor guest had carried out a commission given him, to set up a more than life-size statue of Lepidus on the knoll. If he had failed to get the spirit of the place by a hair's-breadth I should hate his labour; and how well he might have failed!

It was a beautiful morning in early summer: the leaves out, the lawns glossy with dew; a dead calm on the lake, and the far landscape tinged with a soft light with the faintest touch of rosiness in it. A cock starling on the tall chimney-stack was warbling to his mate under the tiles, the pointed feathers on his under-throat erect, and glittering with his emotion, like steel points in the sunshine; the pigeons were cooing in their cote; a chiff-chaff was chattering in the low rhododendrons. And there, in my path, was my wife, all in white; the light of the morning on her pleasant cheeks, contentment with the ways of Providence in her eyes, and her babe in her arms!

I had intended to go alone, and now meeting

her, after the first kiss, I hesitated. And she saw my project, as she sees most things, and looking me full in the eyes, while a shade of gravity came over her sweet countenance, she said, simply, " I am coming, too."

So we three went together: through the well-remembered gate, over the crisp meadow track, and up the twining path between the red pine stems. Halfway up we stopped a moment to gather breath. Then on again, until the shadows thinned, and twenty yards further that well-remembered little amphitheatre amongst the crowning pines burst upon us, and what we saw held us spell-bound for a moment.

The lovely little amphitheatre, locked in by the green arms of the pines,—surely as sweet a spot as ever Nature dedicated to peace and repose,—was again just as I had always known it. The brooding shadows all about it; the low feathery branches that lifted now and then, as though unseen draperies brushed them; the speckled sunshine making tender mosaics on the turf; the crimson foxgloves standing pensive in the arbours, and overhead the pigeons softly crooning lullabies—everything was the same. But what fixed our eyes at once was that there, right in the centre, between sunshine and shadow, stood the memorial I had ordered; and the first delighted glance told me it was well done—past all my expectations. It might have been so poor, and it was full of splendid life; it might have but marred the spot, yet, instead, it filled it with that presence we knew and loved—filled it with the inspiration of reality, as only genius working lovingly can do,—and it did not need the confirming pressure of my dear wife's hand to make me feel that Lepidus was somehow present in that green bronze effigy!

The cunning artist had sent his thoughts back to that day when the Roman, to please us, rode our great black horse over the stable gates, and round the park; and finally, you will remember, pulled that mighty beast, that no one else could sit, back on his haunches by our doorway. It was the very incident again in adamant! There, on a low, unrailed platform of the native stone lying all about, and already welded together by kindly time and green mosses, reared the bronze horse, pressed back by the strong hand upon the reins, his full veins standing like knotted cordage from his arching neck, his skin glossy with the sweat of his humbled pride, his mane and tail still all a-sweep with the suddenness of his checking; and astride of him, sitting with gallant ease, the Roman rider, broad shoulders back, hands down, and keen, brave face half turned towards us. It was Lepidus himself!—the same bold eyes that never flinched shining from his face, the same smile about his mouth, linking in a golden bond a fiery spirit and a gentle heart—the Roman, down to those heels so tightly pressed against the sweating stallion's sides. And as I looked in admiration and delight, the dear lady by me, moved by the same feeling, stepped swiftly forward.

"Oh, Lepidus," she said, "dear Lepidus! may those who rule our fates, and time our goings and comings, give you all the joy and consolation we could wish you!" And then, stirred as it were by a sudden inspiration, she uncovered the face of the little one there, where it lay close to her bosom, and stepping to the Roman's knee, with a half blush and a moment's hesitation, laid that youngling, that handful of pink flesh and dainty lace, in the rider's arms.

Perhaps it was only my heated fancy, or the shifting shadows of a branch above, but it seemed to me for one moment—for just so long as the dry husk the squirrel discarded in the nearest fir tree took to flutter to the ground—that the great bronze head was bent a little to that tender babe, and to the wistful mother by it; and for a fleeting second or two, over the comely face, and about the corners of those Imperial lips, there flickered a smile of new meaning—of pleasure, of approval, and of contentment, lasting and real!

LOST RACE AND ADULT FANTASY FICTION

An Arno Press Collection

Ames, Joseph Bushnell. **The Bladed Barrier.** 1929

Anderson, Olof W. **The Treasure Vault of Atlantis.** 1925

Arnold, Edwin Lester. **Lepidus the Centurion.** 1901

[Atkins, Frank]. Frank Aubrey, pseud. **The Devil-Tree of El Dorado.** 1897

[Atkins, Frank]. Frank Aubrey, pseud. **King of the Dead: A Weird Romance.** 1903

Bennet, Robert Ames. **Thyra: A Romance of the Polar Pit.** 1901

[Bennett, Gertrude Barrows]. Francis Stevens, pseud. **The Heads of Cerberus.** 1952

Blackwood, Algernon. **The Fruit Stoners.** 1935

[Boëx, Joseph-Henri]. J.-H. Rosny aîné, pseud. **The Xipehuz** *and* **The Death of the Earth.** Translated from the original 1888 and 1912 French editions by George Edgar Slusser. 1978

Bruce, Muriel. **Mukara.** 1930

[Burton, Alice Elizabeth]. Susan Alice Kerby, pseud. **Miss Carter and the Ifrit.** [1945]

Carew, Henry. **The Vampires of the Andes.** 1925

Chambers, Robert. **The Slayer of Souls.** 1920

Channing, Mark. **White Python:** Adventure and Mystery in Tibet. 1934

Chester, George Randolph. **The Jingo.** 1912

Clock, Herbert and Eric Boetzel. **The Light in the Sky.** 1929

Coblentz, Stanton A[rthur]. **When the Birds Fly South.** 1945

Constantine, Murray, pseud. **The Devil, Poor Devil!** 1934

Cook, William Wallace. **Cast Away at the Pole.** 1904

Cowan, Frank. **Revi-Lona:** A Romance of Love in a Marvelous Land. [c. 1890]

Day, Bradford M., compiler and editor. **Bibliography of Adventure:** Mundy, Burroughs, Rohmer, Haggard. Revised edition. 1978

de Comeau, Alexander. **Monk's Magic.** 1931

[de Grainville, Jean Baptiste François Xavier Cousin]. **The Last Man, Or, Omegarus and Syderia.** Two vols. in one. 1806/1806

Dunn, J. Allan. **The Flower of Fate.** 1928

Eddison, E[ric] R[ucker]. **Styrbiorn the Strong.** 1926

Fleckenstein, Alfred C. **The Prince of Gravas.** 1898

Fyne, Neal, pseud. **The Land of the Living Dead.** [1897]

Gillmore, Inez Haynes. **Angel Island.** 1914

[Gompertz, Martin Louis Alan]. "Ganpat," pseud. **Adventures in Sakaeland Comprising Harilek** *and* **Wrexham's Romance.** Two vols. in one. 1923/1935

Green, Fitzhugh. **Z R Wins.** 1924

[Gregory, Jackson]. Quién Sabe, pseud. **Daughter of the Sun.** 1921

Griffith [-Jones], George [Chetwynd]. **The Romance of Golden Star....** 1897

[Guthrie, Thomas Anstey]. F. Anstey, pseud. **Humour & Fantasy.** 1931

Haggard, H[enry] Rider. **The Mahatma and the Hare.** 1911

Haggard, H[enry] Rider. **Wisdom's Daughter.** 1923

Haldane, Charlotte. **Melusine or Devil Take Her!** [1936]

[Harris-Burland, John Burland]. Harris Burland, pseud. **The Princess Thora.** 1904

Hartmann, Franz. **Among the Gnomes.** 1895

Hodder, William Reginald. **Daughter of the Dawn.** 1903

Knowles, Vernon. **Sapphires: Here and Otherwhere** *and* **Silver Nutmegs.** Two vols. in one. 1926/1927

Kummer, Frederic Arnold. **Shades of Hades: Ladies in Hades** *and* **Gentlemen in Hades.** Two vols. in one. 1930/1930

Large, E. C. **Asleep in the Afternoon.** 1939

Le Queux, William [Tufnell]. **The Eye of Istar.** 1897

Leroux, Gaston. **The Bride of the Sun.** 1915

Lindsay, David. **Devil's Tor.** 1932

Linklater, Eric. **A Spell For Old Bones.** 1950

London, Jack. **Hearts of Three.** 1920

[Lunn, Hugh Kingsmill]. Hugh Kingsmill, pseud. **The Return of William Shakespeare.** 1929

Marshall, Sidney J. **The King of Kor;** Or, She's Promise Kept. 1903

McHugh, Vincent. **I Am Thinking of My Darling.** 1943

Menville, Douglas and R. Reginald, editors. **Dreamers of Dreams:** An Anthology of Fantasy. 1978

Menville, Douglas and R. Reginald, editors. **Worlds of Never:** Three Fantastic Novels. 1978

Merritt, A[braham]. **The Fox Woman and Other Stories.** 1949

Morris, Kenneth. **Book of the Three Dragons.** 1930

Murray, G. G. A. **Gobi or Shamo.** 1889

Owen, Frank. **The Purple Sea.** 1930

Potter, Margaret Horton. **Istar of Babylon.** 1902

Reginald, R. and Douglas Menville, editors. **King Solomon's Children:** Some Parodies of H. Rider Haggard. 1978

Reginald, R. and Douglas Menville, editors. **They:** Three Parodies of H. Rider Haggard's *She.* With an Introduction by R. Reginald. 1978

Rolfe, Frederick [William] and [Charles Harry Clinton Pirie-Gordon]. Prospero and Caliban, pseuds. **Hubert's Arthur.** 1935

Savile, Frank. **Beyond the Great South Wall.** 1901

Scott, G. Firth. **The Last Lemurian.** 1898

Sheldon-Williams, Miles. **The Power of Ula.** 1906

Sinclair, Upton. **Prince Hagen.** 1903

[Smith, Ernest Bramah]. Ernest Bramah, pseud. **Kai Lung Beneath the Mulberry-Tree.** 1940

Todd, Ruthven. **Over the Mountain.** 1939

Vivian, E[velyn] Charles. **Aia: Fields of Sleep** *and* **People of the Darkness.** Two vols. in one. [1925]/1924

Vivian, E[velyn] Charles. **A King There Was--.** [1926]

Wells, H[erbert] G[eorge]. **The Wonderful Visit.** 1895